UELINE GRIMA has been writing since she was very young,
irst experience of rejection when she submitted a short story
her namesake *Jackie* magazine in her teens. In 2015, after
ciding to take her writing more seriously, Jacqueline embarked
n a Creative Writing MA at Manchester Metropolitan University,
graduating with a distinction as well as the 2018 Janet Beer prize
for outstanding contribution. Her work has since appeared in
a variety of publications, both in print and online. Jacqueline
writes in the living room of the home she shares with her three
grown-up sons and an even more grown-up black Labrador called
Taz. She spends a lot of time dreaming of having her own office.

T0049907

The Weekend Alone

JACQUELINE GRIMA

ONE PLACE. MANY STORIES

This novel is entirely a work of fiction. The names, characters
and incidents portrayed in it are the work of the author's
imagination. Any resemblance to actual persons, living or
dead, events or localities is entirely coincidental.

HQ
An imprint of HarperCollins*Publishers* Ltd
1 London Bridge Street
London SE1 9GF

www.harpercollins.co.uk

HarperCollins*Publishers*
Macken House, 39/40 Mayor Street Upper,
Dublin 1 D01 C9W8

This paperback edition 2023

1
First published in Great Britain by
HQ, an imprint of HarperCollins*Publishers* Ltd 2023

Copyright © Jacqueline Grima 2023

Jacqueline Grima asserts the moral right to be
identified as the author of this work.
A catalogue record for this book is
available from the British Library.

ISBN: 9780008581299

This book is produced from independently certified FSC™ paper
to ensure responsible forest management.

For more information visit: www.harpercollins.co.uk/green

Printed and bound in the UK using 100% renewable electricity
at CPI Group (UK) Ltd

All rights reserved. No part of this publication may be reproduced,
stored in a retrieval system, or transmitted, in any form or by any means,
electronic, mechanical, photocopying, recording or otherwise,
without the prior permission of the publishers.

This book is sold subject to the condition that it shall not, by way of trade
or otherwise, be lent, re-sold, hired out or otherwise circulated without
the publisher's prior consent in any form of binding or cover other than
that in which it is published and without a similar condition including this
condition being imposed on the subsequent purchaser.

*For my mum, who introduced me to books,
but who didn't get to read this one.*

Bella now

Bella listens to her mobile phone connect, her husband's voice sounding distant as he invites her to leave a message. She's always been fascinated by the way even her closest loved ones sound odd and alien-like when they're recorded, Jack's tone more nasal, his way of speaking more upbeat than it is in real life, as if every statement ends in a question mark.

She takes a deep breath and tries to focus, her mouth not quite working in time with her brain, words lagging behind after thoughts have already crossed the finishing line. She doesn't think she's ever felt so tired. 'Hi, Jack, it's me …' A slight echo of her own voice comes back to her, as if it's bouncing around the black hole of Jack's messaging service. 'I was hoping you'd answer. I presume you're busy.'

She closes her eyes, picturing Jack as he briefly kissed her goodbye before he went to work this morning. He's always loved his job, his position as one of the youngest senior sales managers in his firm's history meaning they've always been able to pay their bills on time, have nice holidays. She remembers, just for a second, wanting to call him back, suggest he take the day off and spend some time with her. Instead, she let him go.

She swallows heavily, worried she's going to run out of time, having little idea of how long she's got before the messaging service cuts her off. She moves her mouth closer to the phone. She needs to concentrate. 'I know I shouldn't tell you this over voicemail, that I should speak to you in person, but ...' She hesitates again, clearing her throat. The fogginess in her head is making it difficult to string a sentence together. 'I need to say this now or I might not have the courage to say it at all. Don't come home this weekend, Jack.'

Suddenly she wants to spit the words out, eject them from her body as if they're diseased. 'I know this might be a bit of a shock, but I've been thinking about it a lot. After everything that's happened recently, everything we've been through over the past few weeks, that *I've* been through, I think we might need some time apart. It's not permanent, Jack. I'm sure we'll move on, like we always do. It's just that I feel like I need some space. And with the kids away ...'

She suddenly wishes, more than anything she's ever wished for before, she thinks, that Freddy and Paige were here. That this was a normal Friday, all of them looking forward to some family time this evening, when they might enjoy fish and chips, or pizza on their laps in front of the television. A cosy crime drama or one of the mind-numbing comedies that Freddy enjoys so much but that nobody else particularly likes. No doubt, if her children were here, she wouldn't be having to make this phone call. Wouldn't be telling her husband she needs some time alone.

She takes a breath again. 'With the kids away, I thought it was an ideal opportunity to take some time out. Have a think about where we go from here. I thought ...' She feels a tear spring to her eye. 'I thought maybe you could go to that Premier Inn where we ...?'

She stops herself. Jack's an adult. Not far off turning forty. Quite capable of deciding where to stay when his wife asks him not to come home because she's feeling as if their marriage needs reassessing. Her husband has always been competent. Not the kind who relies on her to get him up in the morning, or who expects

2

her to find him a clean tie each day, like some of her friends' partners seem to do. When he goes on his frequent business trips, his organisational skills are almost military, an overnight bag always kept in the boot of his car in case of unforeseen events. Events exactly like this. 'Anyway, I'll leave that up to you.'

She thinks, just for a second, shifting her head slightly, her neck stiff as she contemplates her next few words. It's time to end the call. 'Don't call me back, Jack. I probably won't answer. I'll see you in a couple of days, and we'll take it from there, shall we? Okay, bye.'

She closes her eyes again. For the few brief seconds that the phone is still against her ear, the short time left on the messaging service waiting expectantly, in case she hasn't finished, Bella feels an overwhelming urge to say something else, to shout down the line to her husband and tell him she didn't mean any of what she said. To cry and scream and tell him they can work this out. That they can get past this hurdle, recover, be stronger …

As the cold tip of the knife touches her throat, Bella knows there's no point. She hears the end-of-message beep as the man standing above her moves the phone away from her ear.

Six weeks earlier

Bella pulled the fridge open, peering inside to see what she could quickly whip up for Paige for her breakfast. Her daughter often refused to eat in the mornings, preferring instead to munch on chocolate bars during her break, no matter how many healthy options Bella tried to entice her with before she left. She frowned as she looked at the shelf that ran along the inside of the fridge door.

'Freddy? Did you drink all the milk?'

Freddy was sitting at the breakfast bar, stuffing toast and jam into his mouth as if someone were going to take it away any second. Eating in the morning, or at any time, was no problem for her growing son, it seemed.

He shook his head. 'Nope.' The word was muffled as he stuffed another slice into his mouth.

'Well, someone has. The shopping only came yesterday and there doesn't seem to be any left. That's quick, even for this house.'

Bella peered into the fridge again, thinking that perhaps, if she looked hard enough, the milk she was sure she'd bought might magically appear, and also knowing that if Jack came into the kitchen now, he would tell her off for standing with the door open, wasting electricity. She shrugged as she banged it shut. 'Maybe it was Paige who drank it then. In that case, she'll have to have a stale croissant for her breakfast instead of cereal.'

She walked over to the bread bin, pulled out one of last week's uneaten croissants and put it on a plate. She looked up as her daughter breezed into the kitchen, her school bag already hanging from her shoulder, long hair pulled into a tight pony-tail. Whenever Bella looked at Paige lately, she was struck by how much she'd flourished. She was a young woman now, her fourteen-year-old face having lost the softness it once had, her cheekbones more defined. Her eyes were so like Jack's – nut-brown with a hint of just-turned autumn leaves – they sometimes took Bella's breath away.

Paige eyed the croissant as she grabbed a textbook from the table. 'No time to eat, sorry.'

'I'll wrap it in foil for you.'

'Sorry, gotta go.'

'Don't forget it's clarinet practice tonight.'

The front door slammed, Paige gone as quickly as she appeared, the fruity scent of her favourite body spray the only sign she'd ever been in the kitchen in the first place.

Sighing, Bella picked up the croissant and dropped it into the bin. Parenting failure number one of the day. And it was barely even eight o'clock. She turned to Freddy. At least her little boy still listened to her. For now, anyway, she thought, wondering if his coming thirteenth birthday, in the summer holidays, might be the start of a different story. 'Come on.' She waved her hands to entice him off the stool, as if she were waving away a fly. 'You've eaten enough toast to feed a football team. Time to get a move on.'

Freddy grimaced. 'Do I have to? It's so nearly the holidays. You wouldn't believe how many people skip the last few weeks of term. Greg Harper has gone to Spain already. He won't be back until September.'

'And just think of all the drum lessons he's going to miss while he's gone, which means you, my lovely son, will be way ahead of him when it comes to this term's grading.' Bella guided him towards the door.

'Yeah, right.'

Bella stopped for a second, suddenly remembering something she had to tell him. 'Oh, by the way, before you go, Grandma rang yesterday. She wants to know if you're still up for spending a week or so in the Lakes with them this year. She says it won't be the same if Grandpa's fishing buddy doesn't come and visit them.'

Freddy seemed to think for a few seconds. 'Is there still absolutely *no* mobile signal at Grandma and Grandpa's?'

'Probably, but if you decide not to go simply because you can't text your friends, I can always tell Grandma to bake her homemade double chocolate fudge cake for someone else …'

Freddy's eyes widened. 'No, no, that's okay. I'm sure I can fit a week with Grandma and Grandpa into my busy summer schedule for one more year. As long as you let me go to that gaming convention with my mates in August.'

'Ask me again when you've passed your drum exam with flying colours.'

'Aw, I'll totally be the odd one out if you don't let me. Imagine the PTSD I'd suffer in the future, especially as you're letting Paige go to *France.*'

'That's different. She's going with her friend, and her friend's *parents—*'

'Whatever …' Leaning past her, Freddy grabbed another piece of toast from the plate on the counter before heading out of the room, almost colliding with Jack as they both reached the doorway at the same time. The two of them did a dance, each moving to the same side in tandem, before bursting out laughing.

Jack moved to let his son through. 'Work hard.'

'Can't promise.' Freddy waved over his shoulder as he grabbed his bag from the bottom of the stairs and headed out of the front door. He and Jack had the same routine every morning, the same words said to each other every school day since Freddy was a little boy. As if the two of them were performers on a stage.

Bella leant against the counter with her arms folded. 'He gets more like you every day.'

'Lucky him.' Coming into the kitchen, Jack kissed her forehead before grabbing a piece of toast that Freddy had left. He took a couple of quick bites before putting it back on the plate. 'You were up early.'

Bella began to wash the dishes in the sink. The kitchen always looked like a bomb had hit it in the morning, no matter how spotless she left it the night before. 'I've got a lot to do, that's all.'

'On your day off?'

'I'm meeting Rosie. I need to get tidied up so I'm not coming back to a pigsty.'

Jack slipped his arms around her waist, resting his chin on her shoulder. His skin smelled of the shea butter soap she always left in the bathroom. 'You'll be complaining you're tired later. Don't think I didn't notice you slipping out of bed last night. What was it this time? Browsing holiday homes in Barbados? Or internet shopping?'

Bella turned, her face level with his chest. She had always noticed how she and Jack seemed to fit together, as if they were two pieces of the same puzzle, her most comfortable place in all the world in his arms. 'Just a bit of shopping. I didn't order much. It seemed a better option than disturbing you with my tossing and turning …'

'Hmm …' Jack rolled his eyes. 'I'll look forward to seeing your face when you have no idea what's in the ten parcels that arrive one after the other over the next few days.'

Bella batted him away. 'Speaking of which, did you drink the milk? I'm sure it came with the shopping delivery yesterday, but now there doesn't seem to be any.'

'Are you sure you put it on the order?' Jack moved away from her, straightening his tie.

'I can't see why I wouldn't. I don't usually forget anything …'

'Probably the kids then. You know what they're like. They think it's Christmas whenever we stock up.'

Bella pictured Freddy, shaking his head as he fed toast into his mouth. Would it be the first time her son had cleared out the cupboards or the fridge and then denied it? She sighed. 'Not to worry. I'll pick some up after I've seen Rosie.'

Jack kissed the tip of her nose. 'Have a good day. Say hi to your sister.'

'I will.'

As Bella watched Jack fold his jacket over his arm and head towards the front door, she tried to recall the online shopping list she'd put together on her phone a few days before: bread, cheese, fruit and salad. A few things for the freezer. Had she forgotten the milk? She couldn't remember.

Shaking her head, she crossed the room towards the basement door, pushing the handle down to make sure it was locked before gathering her own things together.

Bella now

Bella looks up at the man in front of her as he moves the phone away, ending the call before slipping the phone into the chest pocket of his shirt with one hand. The other is still holding the knife to her neck. At least she's still alive, she assures herself. Still breathing. For now.

'Well done, beautiful Bella. I never knew you were such a good actress. You almost had even me convinced. An angry wife, wanting some much-needed alone time, away from the husband she's not sure she loves anymore.'

Bella feels a tear slip down her cheek. She tries to move her hands, the reams of silver workman's tape that bind her wrists to the wooden chair she's sitting on meaning she can barely shift them half a millimetre. Her head is still foggy, her eyelids feeling as if they have weights on them. 'Please ...' She looks up at him again, the light from the old yellow bulb on the ceiling behind him haloing his dark hair. 'I did exactly what you asked. I didn't say anything apart from what you told me to. Please, can you at least move the knife away?'

'Of course.' He moves the blade gently across the skin of her throat before pulling it away with a flourish. Bending his knees, he crouches in front of her, their eyes almost level. He puts a hand to her cheek and gently moves his thumb back and forth.

'Please, don't cry, Bella. You did great. I'm very proud of you.'

Bella looks at his face, the long scar that decorates his left cheek, the skin around it puckered and mottled. Part of her wants to spit at him; another, larger part, aware that she shouldn't make him angry. 'No one will believe the message. We've been married for over fifteen years. I've never said not to come home before. It will be obvious to anyone who knows me that something isn't right ...'

In a split second, the knife is back at her throat. Despite her whole body wanting to submit to a bout of violent shivering, Bella tries to keep her head perfectly still. If she moves, even a fraction, he could end her life here and now, the children having to spend the rest of their days without their mother, her family living their remaining years in permanent grief. 'Please ...' She closes her eyes. 'I'm sorry ...'

'So you should be.'

Bella breathes a shaky sigh of relief as he moves the knife away. Opening her eyes again, she watches as he straightens, the steep wooden stairs of the basement rising up behind him. She vividly remembers the last time she was here. The space beneath her family home is not somewhere she has visited for a long time, Jack usually the only member of the household who ever ventures down, shouting up to the kitchen to ask if she needs anything: a screwdriver or a can of WD-40. Or one of the many expensive power tools they've bought over the years that rarely get used, the easier option being to simply get someone in.

She tries to shift her body again as she looks around the room, the same tape as tight around her ankles, and the chair legs, as it is around her wrists. Bella's lip quivers, tears threatening to spill down her cheeks again. She doesn't want to cry, aware that drawing attention to herself, making herself even more vulnerable than she already is, could put her in more danger.

Trying to keep her gaze steady, she looks at the knife in his hand, the weak reflection of the ceiling light glinting from its long blade as he leans towards her again. Fresh fear floods her body. 'Please don't hurt me.'

He shakes his head, as if reassuring a child. 'Don't worry, Bella, I've got no intention of hurting you.' He smiles. 'Not right at this minute, anyway. Not when you're behaving yourself so well, doing exactly as I say.'

'The knife …'

'I know. It's scary, isn't it?' He looks at the blade for a few seconds, as if he's admiring his own reflection, before slipping it back into the sheath attached to a belt at his waist. He looks at her again. 'I'm afraid there is something I have to do before I go though, Bella.'

She frowns. 'What do you mean?'

He shrugs. 'Well, we can't have you making too much noise while you're down here on your own, can we now?'

Reaching into the back pocket of his jeans, he pulls something loose, turquoise material, dotted with yellow, unfurling from his hand. Bella recognises it: the thick, cotton scarf her husband bought her a couple of Christmases ago. She's never liked it much, she can't seem to help thinking. The least favourite of her scarf collection.

'No, please …' Bella tries to speak as he brings the scarf towards her, wrapping it around her face and knotting it around the back of her head. As he catches her hair, the sting of her scalp brings fresh tears to her eyes.

'Sorry, Bella, but I need to keep you quiet. I can't take any chances.' He looks almost sad as he pulls the makeshift gag tight, stuffing the material between her teeth.

Bella feels herself going into shock, bile rising in her throat as a paralysing numbness spreads through her limbs. As she watches him walk away from her, glancing briefly over his shoulder as he heads back up the stairs to the basement door, she can't believe this is happening. Can't believe that this man has abducted her and strapped her to a chair from her own kitchen. That he is threatening her with a knife he'll no doubt keep with him at all times. That he's tied one of her own scarves around her mouth, to stop her from screaming.

She can't believe she's being held against her will in her own basement.

Not for the first time.

But for the second time in her life.

Six weeks earlier

Bella was glad to see Rosie. It had been a month or more since they'd last got together for coffee, both of them caught up with kids and busy lives. Both of their husbands worked long hours and were often away from home for days at a time, meaning any social engagements often had to take second place to parental responsibilities. With Rosie's twins barely into toddlerhood, it was even more difficult for her sister to get away from the house than it was for Bella herself.

She approached the corner table where Rosie was sitting, pulling off her denim jacket and hanging it over the back of a chair. The weather outside was typical of a British summer, slightly damp with bursts of intermittent sunshine that didn't last very long, an extra layer needed for those chillier periods when the clouds overhead thickened. She puffed out air as she sat down. 'Sorry I'm a bit late. Sometimes I wonder if a hurricane passed through my house in the night and I didn't notice. I swear it's like Groundhog Day. Starting again with the exact same routine every morning.'

'Tell me about it.' Rosie smiled. 'This morning, the twins decided they'd both had enough of toilet training and that peeing all over the bathroom floor was the funniest idea ever. Cameron did it twice, can you imagine? I don't know how he manages to store so much liquid. I swear that child was a camel in a former life.'

Bella laughed. 'I can just picture it. The way he dissolves into fits of laughter at his own antics gets me every time. Where are they today?'

'Martin's mum's. Let her clean up after them for a couple of hours. Then maybe she won't brag to her friends so much about how angelic her little cherubs are when they're with her.' She pushes back her chair. 'I'll get us some coffee. If I don't get a caffeine fix soon, I might curl up into a ball and start crying.'

'Didn't you buy last time?' Bella began to root inside her bag. 'Shit, I think I left my purse in the car.'

'That's not like you.'

'I think I'm just tired. Didn't sleep too well …'

Rosie waved her away. 'Don't worry about it. Call it my way of paying you back in advance for all the whinging I'm about to do about motherhood and marriage. Latte?'

'With an extra shot, please.'

Bella looked around, the coffee shop quiet, only a small handful of shoppers filling the tables and soft sofas, trailing wooden stirrers through the thick foam of their frothy coffees. In a few weeks, she guessed, the atmosphere would change completely, the town's shops and restaurants packed as schools let out for the summer.

As she did in every place that wasn't her own home, she scanned the faces of the other customers – an older lady in a far corner who seemed to be on her own; a young couple holding hands across the table; a tired-looking man in work overalls, probably on his break – just in case. Scrutinising her surroundings was a habit she'd found difficult to break over the years, the therapist she used to speak to every week telling her she'd get over it eventually, Jack constantly telling her to relax whenever they were out together. As much as she'd have liked to do both, she'd never quite managed either.

She watched Rosie order their drinks, thinking how her sister's frame was very much like Paige's, a short torso and sturdy legs, how different she herself was from the both of them. Her daughter seemed to have inherited traits from everyone in the family – Jack's eyes, her aunt's stature, her grandmother's stubbornness – but apparently lacked the genes of her own mother. She knew Freddy was more like her, the same gangliness and long arms and legs she herself had hated when she was younger. The same tendency towards worry.

She smiled as Rosie came back to the table, moving one of the tall mugs across the wood towards her. 'Thank you. I can't remember the last time I just sat and enjoyed a coffee without leaving half of it to go cold. Between Paige's end-of-year exams and both of their music lessons, there hardly seems to be a minute. And here was me thinking I might be able to work full-time again when the kids got older.' She poured two packs of sugar into her drink, the granules sitting on top of the foam for a few seconds before disappearing. 'Jack says I'm silly to even want to. He says I do enough already.'

'He's right.' Rosie stirred her own coffee before taking a sip. 'You don't have to feel guilty about not working full-time, Bell. It's not like you need the money. You don't have a mortgage and I have no doubt that Jack's wages are plenty enough to cover the rest of the bills.'

Bella nodded, feeling a little embarrassed, as she often did, at the lack of challenges in her financial situation. She and Jack were luckier than most couples, her parents having gifted her the former farmhouse she and Rosie had grown up in, the one her mother had inherited from her own parents, when they retired early and decided to downsize to the Lake District, Rosie receiving a cash lump sum instead. Life seemed to be so much more difficult for a lot of their friends, who spent so much time working, they hardly saw their children. 'I suppose you're right.'

'Why don't you give it a few more years? Paige will be off to uni before you know it, Freddy will be more independent, then you'll have the freedom to do what you want.'

'I guess so ...' Like her sister was doing now, Bella had stayed at home for a while after the children were born, but had soon realised that, in order to be the best mum she could be to Freddy and Paige, she needed the company of other adults. Part of her had been nervous about entering the workplace again, especially after what she'd been through before she had the kids. But getting her job as an events coordinator at her local hospice had been one of her proudest achievements. After all, it was what she'd struggled to finish her degree for.

She remembered what Jack had said when she'd told him she wanted to work again. *You don't have to do this, you know. Not if staying at home would make you feel safer.* She was grateful for his words, and Rosie was right, Jack's salary was more than enough to keep them going until the kids were older, but Bella knew it wouldn't suit her to stay at home forever. To hide away from the world that had put her through so much.

She steered the conversation away from herself. 'So, what about you? Are you going to go back to work?'

Rosie moved her head from side to side, weighing up her answer. 'I think so. Probably within the next year if we can afford the childcare. The partnership told me they'd keep my position open so I guess it would be silly not to. And I do miss the animals, much as I feel like I'm living in a zoo in my own house at the minute.'

'It certainly seems a shame to waste five years of vet school. You'll know when the time is right. And I'd be happy to help out with the twins if I can.'

'Thanks. I appreciate it.' Rosie was quiet for a few seconds, seeming to be watching Bella over the rim of her mug. She put it down. 'So, are we going to talk about it?'

Bella sipped her own coffee. 'About what?'

'You know what. I know you, don't forget. Probably even

better than Jack does. You might be able to fool him by saying you're fine, but I can see what's going on behind your eyes. You're worried.'

Bella sighed. 'I can't help it. I feel as if I've gone right back to square one. Travelled back in time by nineteen years ...'

'How long has he been out?'

'Not long. A few days.' It had actually been just over a week since the Victim Contact Scheme had telephoned Bella and told her the news she'd been dreading for a long time. That Lawrence Knox, the man who had kidnapped her, held her hostage in the basement of her own home almost two decades before, had been released from prison. She'd spent most nights since unable to sleep, usually getting up quietly to prowl the house and check all the doors and windows were locked before booting up the laptop to try and keep her mind occupied. 'The board didn't hesitate in approving his release apparently. They're completely convinced he's a reformed character.'

'And you're not?'

'How can I be? After everything he put me through?' She blinked away the tears that were threatening to fall. She hadn't cried for a long time – not since she'd found out about the guilty verdict all those years ago when a dam had burst somewhere inside her – although, even now, she often felt like it. Even when Lawrence was locked away, she'd never felt quite safe. Never felt she had the same freedom her friends and family enjoyed. Now, she wondered if she ever would again.

'Do you know where he is?'

Bella pursed her lips. 'I can only presume he's in Leeds. It's where he grew up, his home town, but they won't tell me any more than that. What I do know is that he can't come here. It's one of the conditions of his release, alongside not contacting me in any way. If he so much as steps inside Warrington, he's in big trouble.'

'Well, that's something at least.' Rosie reached across the table and covered Bella's hand with hers. 'It's understandable that you're worried though. We were there, Bell. Me and Mum and Dad. We saw what he did to you. How he changed you. Our lovely girl …'

Bella nodded. She couldn't speak.

'Have you spoken to them about it? Mum and Dad?'

'Only briefly.' Bella glanced at the door as more customers entered the shop. Even talking about the past had spooked her. 'I spoke to Mum on the phone yesterday, but I couldn't bring myself to discuss the details with her. You know what she's like …'

'What about the kids?'

'Jack thinks we should sit them down at the weekend and talk to them. Tell them the whole story.'

'How do you feel about that?'

Bella shrugged. Part of her wondered if they should have already told Paige and Freddy about what had happened to their mother years ago, been open with them when they were young, but she knew they wouldn't have understood, wouldn't have been able to comprehend the enormity of what she'd been through. Freddy's sensitive nature meant he would have worried about her. 'I don't think we have a choice, to be honest. If they hear anything at school, or overhear Jack and me talking, all they have to do is a quick Google search and they'll find out everything.'

'Good job kids don't usually have much of a desire to google their parents.' Rosie chuckled. 'I think they're grown-up enough to handle it now.'

'I just want them to know to keep themselves safe. Just in case.' Bella picked up her coffee. How many times had she said those words to herself over the past week? When her need to double and triple check doors at home, keep track of the kids, look around in coffee shops, seemed worse than ever?

'They'll be fine.' Rosie smiled. 'You all will. I'm sure of it.'

*

18

Bella picked up a thin parcel from the doormat, remembering, as she put it on the hall table, the guitar strings she'd ordered for Paige a few nights before. The house was quiet, the stillness of the daytime often seeming surreal compared to the chaos of later on when everyone was home. In just a couple of hours, Freddy would walk through the front door demanding snacks, closely followed by Paige and, no doubt, one or two of her friends. The commotion that ensued when her children were around often reminded Bella of when she and Rosie had lived here with their parents, their friends often choosing their house to hang out in due to the constant supply of homemade goodies her mother insisted on providing.

She took off her jacket and hung it up before heading for the kitchen, averting her eyes from the basement door as she dumped her bag on the table as she always did. Setting the two bottles of milk she'd bought on a chair, she thought about her day. As jittery as she'd been recently, she'd enjoyed having a few hours off, the relief of sharing with her sister how she'd been feeling over the past week making her feel just slightly more relaxed than she had that morning.

Rosie was right. The fact that Lawrence's release conditions meant he wasn't allowed in Warrington was something she should be grateful for. She needed to get on with her life, take comfort from the knowledge that he had to stay miles away from her. If not for herself, then for Jack and the kids. Her anxiety and tendency to panic wasn't always easy to live with, she imagined.

She glanced up at the clock. Just enough time to make some cakes before Freddy came home, a treat for him after a long day and something Paige could share with any friends she brought home from school. She reached into the top cupboard and pulled out flour and sugar, searching at the back for the small cake cases she usually kept a supply of. She laid them all out on the counter before heading towards the fridge for eggs and butter, grabbing the milk from the chair where she'd left it, to put it away.

As she pulled open the fridge door, Bella gasped, the small light illuminating the inside, the shelves full after yesterday's delivery. For a few seconds, she thought she was imagining things, her mind scrabbling around for memories of that morning, the conversation she'd had with Freddy, as if it were a computer search engine trying to retrieve the correct information. *Maybe it was Paige who drank it then,* she remembered herself saying, Jack confirming her suspicions when he'd talked about the kids going overboard after the shopping arrived. She'd felt angry, frustrated, as she often did, at how her family went through so much food and drink so quickly.

She blinked. In the nook on the inside of the fridge door, three large bottles of semi-skimmed milk stood like soldiers.

Bella now

She's uncomfortable, her back and legs beginning to stiffen in the couple of hours or so since he left her alone, the occasional blink of the old light above her giving her a headache. The chair she's being forced to sit on, that she's strapped to, isn't designed for long-term comfort, the seat not cushioned in the way a desk or work chair might be. Her feet tingle with pins and needles. The gag in her mouth is making her want to retch.

She shakes her head to try and clear it, her mind a little less foggy now as she thinks back to earlier in the day, trying to put what has happened to her in some kind of order. To create a timeline of the second abduction of her life. She remembers saying goodbye to Jack, his last words to her before he left for work a little less loving than they might have been a few weeks ago, the atmosphere between them frosty as her husband asked if she'd be okay on her own. She'd tried to reassure him, fully aware that her recent behaviour, her constant anxiety, had been worrying her family. She wanted to stress to Jack that she was coping, that she just needed some time to work through what was happening to her, to make some decisions on how to move forward. He'd simply looked at her before heading out the door.

She closes her eyes, the idea that she's ended up here, in the basement again, making her want to cry and laugh hysterically at the same time. It's like the plot of a bad melodrama, she thinks. Something she and Jack might watch on TV together after the kids have gone upstairs. She tries to calm herself, focusing her mind on what happened next this morning. The kids. Where are they? she wonders, remembering how fervently she wished they were here as she was forced to make the phone call to Jack's voicemail a short while ago.

Her thoughts slowly clear again. It's the summer and Paige has already left for her holiday in Nice, Louise's parents having picked her up in their 4x4 three days ago, her smile wide as she waved goodbye from the back window. Bella smiles as she remembers her daughter's excitement. Looking forward to her first holiday with her best friend's family, the idea of luxury camping a novelty after the hotels Jack and Bella always book when they go away as a family.

Satisfied that Paige is safe, she shifts her mind to her son. Of course, just this morning, it was Freddy's turn to go away, her parents coming to pick him up and take him back to their cottage in the Lake District twenty minutes or so after Jack left, her son his usual anxious self as he fussed over his luggage, worrying that he didn't have everything he needed. Bella remembers talking to her mother in the kitchen as her dad helped Freddy get himself ready. Mum was concerned, worried about Bella and whether they should have come to stay with her for a few days instead. *Are you sure you don't need us? You know I'll never be able to forget what happened before. Never stop worrying ...* Her brow creased as she spoke.

Well, guess what, Mum? Bella thinks now. Here I am again. Abducted and tied up in exactly the same place as last time almost as soon as you turned your back. If the situation weren't so serious, it could almost be funny.

Thinking more clearly now than she was earlier, Bella is glad that Freddy and Paige aren't at home. That the two of them are out of harm's way, hopefully enjoying their summer, unaware of what's happening to their mother. She hopes they'll never know. That she'll get out of here soon and her kids will be none the wiser as to what she's been through. She did it last time, she thinks, pressing her lips together. Escaped from her abductor and lived to tell the tale. To have an *almost* normal life. Make memories with her own family in the house she's loved since she was a little girl. Why shouldn't she do the same again? She shifts her position in the chair, trying to sit up straighter and motivate both her mind and body. She is strong, she tells herself. She saved herself before. She can do it again.

She remembers how she felt immediately after Freddy left, the house quiet and suddenly too big, as if every noise she made as she pottered around the kitchen, quickly tidying away the breakfast dishes, was echoing back towards her. On her own, she'd felt exactly as she told Jack she wouldn't, twitchy and anxious, her eyes constantly straying to the basement door, the opposite side to the one she can see at the top of the stairs now. She remembers doing her best to dismiss her feelings of paranoia, of being watched, humming to herself as she slipped on her trainers, readying herself for her morning run, a routine she'd missed since being signed off sick from work a couple of weeks or so earlier. Trying to act normal, she'd stuffed her phone and keys into her bumbag, checked her safety whistle was at her neck, and pulled the front door shut behind her.

She grimaces to herself, remembering how ridiculous she felt for being so paranoid, despite everything that had happened. Except it wasn't paranoia, was it? She knows that now.

Because it was after she returned from that run that everything changed, the sharp sting of a needle in her neck leading her to where she is now.

Frightened and alone, with no one to help her.

Six weeks earlier

Freddy and Paige looked worried as they both sat down on the living room sofa. It was unusual for the four of them to be in together on a Saturday. Bella usually dropped Freddy off at the house of one of his mates after his weekend drumming lesson and Paige often begged for an advance on her allowance before heading into town. A few months before, Jack had told his daughter that, at fourteen, she was old enough to get a paper round to top up the small amount of money they gave her. It would prepare her for the real world, he'd said. Bella wouldn't hear of it. It was far too dangerous.

'What's going on?' Freddy's face was pale.

'Nothing to worry about.' Bella sat on one of the armchairs next to the hearth, Jack on the opposite side. 'We just want to talk to you about something.'

'Please don't tell us you're pregnant.' Paige's lip curled into a sneer. 'Because that would be just … ew …' She put a hand up, palm out.

Bella rolled her eyes. 'Of course I'm not.' There was a time when she'd wanted a third child, she and Jack having briefly looked into the cost of adding another room to the house, extending into the garden or converting the attic. In the end, they'd decided two children was enough for them.

'Are you getting divorced?'

'No, Fred.' This time it was Jack who answered, shaking his head.

'Because Liam Langan's parents got divorced and he never saw his dad again.'

Bella held out a hand. She'd known Freddy would be anxious as soon as she and Jack had told him they wanted them both home for a family meeting after their weekend activities had finished. *Can't you just tell me what's up now?* he'd said that morning as he and Bella had climbed into the car to head for the music studio. *Get it over with?*

Bella had refused to elaborate. *Let's just wait until we're all together.*

She looked at her son now, her heart aching at the thought of him worrying. Ever since Freddy was little, any tiny change of routine, every obstacle life threw at him, had caused him to panic. Like herself, he would often think too far ahead, inventing worst-case scenarios and worrying about them before they'd even happened. If there was one thing she would change about her adorable son, it would be the worry gene he'd inherited.

'Freddy—' she kept her voice calm '—we're not getting divorced. Your dad and I are fine.' She looked at Jack and smiled. How could Freddy even think that was what they were going to tell him?

'Then what is it? Is Grandpa ill? Or Grandma?'

Jack held out a hand. 'Fred, just calm down; it's nothing like that. Listen for a sec and we'll tell you.'

The room quietened before Jack gestured towards Bella, as if to say: *Go ahead, this is your story to tell.*

She cleared her throat. 'A long time ago, when I wasn't much older than you guys, something happened to me.'

'Something like what?' Paige's eyes widened.

'Just listen to your mum, Paige.' Jack's voice was sombre.

'It was when I was at university, in Leeds. I met a boy. His name was Lawrence. He was a student who started at the same time as me, doing an art degree.'

'Oh my God, you fell pregnant. I knew it. You have a secret child.' Another melodramatic Paige sneer.

'No, no, that's not it, Paige. It wasn't serious. Not on my part anyway. We only went out on two or three dates before I decided that Lawrence really wasn't for me. He was ... How can I put it? Intense. He had some issues he needed to work through before he could commit to a serious relationship. So I told him I didn't want to see him anymore. I broke up with him.'

'So, why are you telling us this now?' Paige obviously hadn't heeded the instruction from her dad to just listen.

Bella paused, wondering how to tell her children – her gorgeous, innocent children – what had happened to her next. She looked at them across the room, suddenly seeing the lounge as it had been then, just over nineteen years ago, she herself sitting where Freddy and Paige were now, the sofa different, the soft florals of her mother's conservative taste. Opposite her, around about where Jack was sitting all this time later, a woman police officer had sat with her hands together on her lap, gently asking questions. All Bella had wanted was for everyone to leave her alone, so she could curl up in a corner somewhere and cry. Now, she looked to her husband for help.

Jack took up the story. 'Lawrence wasn't happy that your mum broke up with him. Apparently, his feelings for her had developed into something quite serious and he was angry that they weren't being reciprocated. So, he began to follow her. Turning up whenever she was out with her friends, joining the same clubs as she did, attending the same events, even taking up the violin so he could attend lessons with the same teacher ...'

'*You* played the violin?' Paige again.

Bella smiled. 'You know Aunt Rosie and I were musical growing up. We practised most days, just like you both do. I think I was always a bit more enthusiastic about it than my sister was, but I'm not sure I was ever quite the prodigy Grandma was hoping I'd be. Not as talented as you two are, that's for sure.'

'Anyway,' Jack continued, 'the situation got so bad that Mum had to eventually involve the university, and the police. Lawrence turned up at her student flat one day and refused to leave. Another time, he broke in when your mum wasn't there. He was given a warning on both of those occasions.'

'What happened next?'

Bella looked at Freddy. How clever her son was. Obviously, she and Jack wouldn't be telling their children this story if the situation hadn't got worse. Much worse. Did she really have to tell them the rest? 'Well, Lawrence didn't listen, not even to the uni authorities or the police, and when it got to the point where he seemed to be waiting for me around every corner, I decided to come home for a little while. The university gave me some time off from classes. They thought if I wasn't around, it would discourage him, help him get over me.'

'Only that didn't happen.' Jack interrupted. 'It turned out that Lawrence had a friend who worked in the admissions department at the uni, and he persuaded that person to give him your mum's home address.'

'What?' Paige half rose from the sofa. 'They told him where you lived? How could that happen?'

Bella held out a hand. 'Security wasn't quite as tight in schools and unis then as it is now. But believe me, the person responsible didn't work there for very much longer after that.' She closed her eyes briefly, trying to block out the memory of her shock when Lawrence turned up at her home, the place where she thought she was safe, where he'd never find her.

'Please tell me he didn't turn up here.' Paige, warrior, protector of the vulnerable since she was very young, was indignant.

Bella nodded. 'Unfortunately, he did. He watched the house for some time without me knowing – weeks – fully aware that the more time passed without me seeing him, the more I'd relax and think it was over. Then, when I insisted your grandparents and Aunt Rosie went on a little holiday they'd had planned for ages, he made his move ...'

'Move?' Freddy looked as if he was about to cry.

Jack nodded. 'He drugged your mum and tied her up, downstairs in the basement.' He looked across at Bella. 'Who knows what would have happened if she hadn't been clever enough to escape. I guess none of us would be here now.'

Freddy moved across the room and squeezed himself onto the chair next to Bella. He put his arms around her. 'Is that why none of us are allowed to ever go down into the basement, Mum?'

She sighed. 'It is.'

'You said it was because you were scared we'd fall down the stairs and hurt ourselves.'

'I know I did, Freddy.'

'I'm so glad you got away.'

Bella kissed her son's hair. She was glad Jack hadn't said how long Lawrence had kept her in the basement, his version of the story making it sound as if she escaped in mere minutes as opposed to almost a week. She'd lost five whole days of her life in that room.

'So, what happened?' Paige was keen to hear the end of the story. 'Did the police come? Did they catch him?'

Jack nodded. 'They did. And after he was eventually tried, following almost a year spent on remand, he served eighteen years in prison. Not a single day less than he deserved.'

'Thank God for that.' Paige looked relieved. She seemed to think for a few seconds before speaking again. 'Wait. You said *served*. What does that mean? Where is he now?'

Bella looked at her daughter. She pulled Freddy closer to her. 'That's exactly what we wanted to talk to you about today.'

She looked at Jack. Now for the difficult bit, she thought. Having to tell her children that the world wasn't quite the safe place they thought it was.

*

'Do you think they took it seriously?'

'Absolutely … Coffee?' Jack put a pod in the machine and switched it on.

She nodded. 'I'm just not sure they would really do what I asked and dial 999 if they saw something suspicious. They might freeze, or think they're overreacting.' Bella sat down at the table, remembering how she and Rosie used to sit in the exact same place and draw at weekends while their mother cooked. The room was very different then, she and Jack having done a lot to make the house their own. Her parents' kitchen had been much less modern, the cupboards oak-brown, the tiles a muddy combination of chocolate and orange. She supposed it must have been up-to-date compared to her grandparents' décor a generation earlier.

'Believe me, they know we're serious.' Jack set out two mugs. 'Did you see Freddy's face? I think he was envisioning his life suddenly becoming like a scene from an action film. He'll probably call the police if someone so much as glances at him.'

Bella sighed. 'I hate the thought of him worrying. I'd do anything to turn the clock back, I really would. I can't bear that Lawrence still has this control over me, over all of us, after all this time. Making us frightened. Is this ever going to end?'

Jack came over to the table, sitting down on the chair opposite before taking her hand in his. 'Bell, we're fine. This is all just precaution. The board approved Lawrence's release because they believe he's changed, and we have to trust them in that decision. Chances are he won't be stupid enough to risk doing anything that might send him back to prison and you, me and the kids can carry on with our lives as normal.' He smiled. 'I won't let anything happen to you, Bell. We're safe, trust me.'

Bella hesitated. Was Jack right? Would they really be able to go about their lives as though Lawrence Knox didn't exist? Not look over their shoulders forever? Eventually, she nodded. 'Okay, I hope you're right.'

'Of course I am.'

'Although you'll never know how much you terrified me when you made that milk suddenly appear in the fridge yesterday. I thought for a minute I'd completely imagined the shelf being empty.' Bella smiled, rolling her eyes.

Jack chuckled. 'Sorry, I did mean to send you a text to say I'd nipped home with it at lunchtime, but it totally left my head.' He got up again, heading back to the counter.

'Now we've gone from having none to having an excess.'

'True, but part of me thought you might forget, after chatting with your sister.'

'I wrote it on my hand.' She shook her head. 'Not to worry, I've no doubt the kids will drink it.'

Although she was keeping her tone light, Bella had got a fright when she'd seen the bottles in the fridge door, struggling to settle even after she'd called Jack at the office and he'd explained he'd bought the milk himself. She still wasn't sure how she could have missed such an essential item off her shopping list in the first place. As she watched her husband make the coffee, she tried to push the thought away, knowing her recent overly anxious state and inability to sleep was making her focus on silly things, things that didn't matter.

What she should be doing now is enjoying her husband's company, taking pleasure in the fact that his management role meant he was home most weekends these days, even if he often had to be away for a few days during the week. Saturday and Sunday felt like family time, time that they could really enjoy being together. 'Thanks for thinking of it anyway.'

Jack went to the fridge and pulled the door open. 'Well, I wouldn't be able to enjoy my coffee without it. Besides, I've told you a thousand times, the house isn't just your responsibility. We're a partnership, aren't we?' He looked at her, an eyebrow raised.

'Of course we are.'

Even as she smiled, Bella wondered if she should even be drinking the coffee her husband was making, imagining herself trying not to disturb him during what was no doubt going to be another sleepless night ahead. She pictured herself, roaming the house again, trying to keep her thoughts at bay, the prospect of another bout of insomnia, another morning tomorrow feeling drowsy and not quite awake, something she wasn't especially looking forward to.

Taking the mug Jack put on the table, she blew across the top before taking a small sip. Perhaps she should try and fit in a nap if she had time.

Jack now

Jack is tired, large grey shadows flitting across his eyes as he stares at the computer screen. He rubs them, trying to clear his vision. It's been one of the busiest days he's had for a while and it's barely even lunchtime. Already he's had to leave the office twice to run errands, not unusual when his calendar is full but some days more wearing than others. His stomach rumbles loudly. He was running late this morning and didn't have time to pack his usual sandwiches. He needs to get himself some lunch soon.

At least it's Friday, he thinks to himself. One positive after a really shitty week, a weekend of beer and feeling sorry for himself beckoning. He looks down at his phone on the desk, staring at it for a few seconds before touching the screen to wake it up. He's saved the voicemail from Bella, not wanting to let it disappear after he listened to it the first time. He dials his messaging service and listens again.

He puffs out air as he hears his wife's voice at the other end of the line, a little high-pitched, her breathing irregular, as if she's having trouble controlling her emotions. She's stressed, he thinks, knowing the signs. That's how she gets, so worked up that she can't quite function properly, her mind and body going into overdrive. He hopes she's okay, not heading for the kind of breakdown she's been close to once or twice in the past. The last few weeks have been tough on her, he knows that, the decision to release Lawrence Knox tipping the ground from beneath her. Her worst nightmare come true.

He thinks back to when they first met, Bella a shy and nervous twenty-two-year-old, in her final year at uni, trailing behind her peers after what had happened to her. Reluctantly attending a party hosted by a mutual friend, Jack had spotted his future wife almost as soon as he got there, immediately drawn to her waves of dark hair, the timid way she surveyed the room from beneath long lashes, seeming to be constantly on her guard. It was a while before she let him get close, the two of them going for drinks with groups of friends a number of times before she agreed to meet him for a proper date, making sure beforehand that her friends knew exactly where she was at all times. Jack hadn't pushed. Somehow, he'd known. Known that Bella carried a shadow with her, a past that was constantly whispering in her ear, that wouldn't let her go.

It was six months before she told him. By then they were spending all their spare time together, Bella staying over at Jack's tiny flat most nights, waiting for him when he got home from the sales job he hadn't long started. She seemed to feel safest there, even when he was out. The night she began talking, telling him what had happened to her not long after she started uni, he'd listened without interrupting, topping up their glasses with cheap red wine, only stopping her flow to order them some Chinese food over the phone. Afterwards, when he knew everything, he'd held her. She was safe now, he told her. He would look after her. They'd married just a few months later.

Of course, there had been ups and downs. Times when Bella had fallen back into periods of utter desolation. Withdrawing into herself for weeks, even months, at a time. When Paige was born, his wife was convinced that something was going to happen to their daughter. That someone was going to hurt her in the same way she herself had been hurt. It was inevitable, she'd said, as if she attracted pain, trauma following her no matter how hard she tried to run from it. Jack did his best to help her through the difficult times, the two of them usually coming out the other side stronger, closer.

He ends the call and pushes his chair back, making his way out of the small office. He needs to eat, to get away from the team just for an hour or so. To think. His sales have been good this month, the most expensive kitchen the firm has ever sold now on his team's impeccable record. No one will begrudge him a long lunch once in a while.

He approaches his PA, sitting at her own desk in the reception area. 'Jazz, I'm popping out for a while. I need a break …'

'Good for you. I've told you, you've been massively overdoing it lately, especially with everything you've had going on at home. You're going to end up burnt out. Look what happened to Graham. Proper total breakdown and off work for almost a year.'

'I'm not going to end up like Graham.'

'You never know.' Jazz raises a perfect eyebrow. 'Can happen to any of us when the slave drivers here expect us to completely give up our lives for the sake of work. Present company excepted of course.' She smiles.

'I'll be fine. I just need some food and some fresh air. It's been a busy morning. Hell, a busy few weeks.'

'I know. I don't envy you with everything you've had on your plate. How is Bella?'

Jack purses his lips. He isn't usually the type of person to share details of his private life at work, to be consistently vocal about what's going on at home, like some of his colleagues are, but he and Jazz have known each other quite a long time now. She's the only person he ever considers confiding in if he's worried about something. Eventually, he shrugs. 'Actually, she's not so great at the minute. She left me a voicemail earlier.'

'Everything okay?'

He shakes his head. 'Not really. She's had a tough time lately, as you know. Things have got on top of her.' He hesitates. 'She wants us to spend some time apart. Over the weekend.'

'Oh my God …' Jazz's mouth drops open. 'She told you this by *voicemail*? That she wants to split up?'

Jack waves his hand. In the message, Bella cited specifically that all she wants is some breathing space. Not for them to separate. Didn't she? 'Not split up, no. At least I don't think that's what she wants. Jeez, I'm useless at reading people. Even my own wife half the time.' He clicks on his phone screen, chewing on his bottom lip as he thinks for a few seconds. Would it seem weird if he asked his PA her opinion about something so personal? He thinks about the way she always seems willing to listen, how she seems to quite enjoy being consulted about matters other than work. Making a decision, he holds the phone out to her. There's no doubt he needs a second opinion on this. 'Do you think you could have a listen? Women are so much better at this stuff than we are.'

Jazz takes the phone and holds it to her ear, her frown increasing as she listens to the message, her eyes on Jack. When she's finished, she hands the phone back. 'She sounds upset. Poor Bella. I worry for her, I really do. Have you tried calling her?'

'A bunch of times …' Jack clicks on his screen again, looking at the list of the day's outgoing calls. 'She's not answering. It's just going straight to voicemail.'

'Sounds like she means business.'

'Indeed.' Bringing up Bella's name, he presses his thumb to it before holding the phone to his ear. 'I'll try her again now.'

'Good idea.'

Jack walks a little way from the desk, hovering by the entrance to the main office as he waits for the line to connect. He shakes his head as he hears his wife's voice, telling him to leave a message in the same chirpy way she has every other time he's called her: *Talk after the beep and I'll get back to you. Eventually …* 'Voicemail again.' He looks back at his PA.

Jazz shrugs, mouthing at him. 'Maybe leave her a message?'

He nods, turning back towards the doorway as he listens for the tone at the other end. 'Hey, Bell, it's just me. Hope you're okay. I know you said you don't want to talk, but I just wanted to say, if you change your mind about being on your own, I'm here. I can come home anytime. Neither of us have been quite ourselves lately, have we, with everything that's happened? But I hope we can come out the other side eventually. I love you. Speak soon.' Ending the call, he walks back to Jazz's desk. 'I guess I'd better book a hotel ...'

Jazz immediately picks up the phone on her desk and presses a key. 'You go get your lunch and I'll sort it. Don't worry. I'm sure, after the weekend, Bella will feel much more equipped to talk things through. And I agree, she doesn't want to split up. She just needs some thinking time. All women do every so often. She'll come round eventually.'

Jack smiles. 'Thanks, Jazz. I knew you'd be better at this stuff than me.'

He slips his phone into his pocket, sighing heavily as he heads back towards his office to get his jacket. Just one weekend, he thinks to himself as he pushes open the door. One weekend to get through and, hopefully, his life will return to some kind of normality.

Bella now

Her thoughts are clearer than they were a couple of hours ago, her mind functioning on more of a normal level. As much as it can in such circumstances. She knows now that, like the last time she was abducted and brought down here, she was drugged, the sting at her neck this morning, when she returned from her run, a vague memory, as if she'd been caught by a wasp in her sleep. She recognises the signs: the sleepiness, the foggy head. Remembers feeling the same nineteen years ago as the drug slowly left her system. For the second time in her life, she was injected with something that rendered her almost unconscious. Perhaps still able to move but unable to make decisions. Unable to save herself.

She thinks back to last time, her mind reluctant to dredge up the memories she's been trying to suppress for so long. Tuck away, like a divorced person might do with their wedding album. That time, her parents and sister had offered over and over again to forgo their trip and stay with her. They could have just as nice a holiday at home, they'd said, despite the money they'd forked out, the clothes and toiletries they'd bought especially, when they didn't know Bella would be returning before the end of term in need of their support. Part of her had wanted them to stay, the nervousness caused by her experience of being stalked still with her, but she was miles away from Lawrence now, she told herself sternly. There was no need to worry. She was safe in her family home, preparing herself to eventually go back to uni and finish her degree, determined that Lawrence wouldn't upend her life completely. Surely staying at home, without her parents and Rosie, was the first step to getting her independence back?

Or that's what she'd thought.

It was only a matter of hours after they'd left when Lawrence had made his move. Her skin bristles now, despite the stuffiness of the warm basement, as she remembers the moment she woke to find she wasn't alone. She'd gone to bed with a book, making doubly sure, as her parents had drummed into her before they left, that the front and back doors were both locked and bolted, the windows firmly closed. It was a futile exercise as it turned out, the police telling her later that Lawrence had been hiding in the basement for days, possibly even weeks, disappearing from uni not long after she herself had left to return home. He'd thrown the bedroom door open sometime after she'd turned off the light, taking advantage of her disorientated, sleepy state to drug her and carry her downstairs. When she'd woken up, she'd been sitting almost exactly where she is now, the chair beneath her then a little more old-fashioned than her own, taken from her parents' kitchen.

She feels bile rise in her throat again, the thick scarf at her mouth almost choking her as she tries to push away the memories, glad now that her younger, terrified self had no idea she would be in the exact same situation almost two decades later. If she had, she's sure she would have simply given up, the idea of going through the same experience twice simply too big to comprehend. The nausea builds until she's trying to stop herself from retching, her stomach spasming painfully as she hopes it's too empty to bring anything up. She can't remember the last time she ate. Last night with Jack and the kids? Or did she sit that one out, her family dynamics a little awkward lately, her husband and

38

children seeming to be spending more time as a three, herself on the periphery? She knows she didn't eat this morning, the granola and coffee she'd planned to have after her run violently interrupted by her abductor.

She jumps as the door at the top of the stairs opens, the muscles in her arms and legs objecting at being restrained by the strong tape. She watches as he descends the stairs, her heart thudding in her chest.

A smirk slowly forms on his face as he approaches her, as if he's finding this whole thing one big joke. He pulls the gag to her chin. 'How are we doing, beautiful Bella? Missed me?'

She takes deep breaths, the air around her stale. 'Don't flatter yourself.'

'That's a shame.' He pulls a sad face, the scar on his cheek wrenched downwards as he moves his mouth. 'Well, I can always stay upstairs if I'm not wanted. Leave you to your own devices down here for—' he shrugs '—I don't know, how about for ever?'

Bella's heart lurches. She sits up as straight as she can, determined not to show him how much the idea of being down in the basement indefinitely terrifies her. 'Fine by me.'

'Be careful what you wish for, Bella.' He waggles a finger at her. In his other hand, he's carrying a tray with what looks like a plate of food and a glass of water. 'Now, how about some lunch? I've made you a nice healthy salad with some chicken I found in the fridge. You must be hungry ...'

Despite her growling stomach, Bella purses her lips. 'No, thank you. I'd rather starve than take anything from you.'

He looks at her for a few seconds before shrugging again. 'Please yourself. Don't say I didn't offer.' He walks back towards the stairs, sits on the bottom step and begins to scoop up chicken and lettuce with his fingers. He talks with his mouth full. 'By the way, you've had a few missed calls.'

Bella looks up, a thud hitting her chest as she watches him rise slightly, pulling her phone from his back pocket. Could someone be calling to let her know they're on their way to see her? Worried about her? 'Who?'

He holds the phone in the air, swallowing food as he clicks on the screen with his thumb. 'Ah, your darling hubby, calling numerous times … Ooh, and it looks like you got a voicemail.'

The tinny sound of Jack's voice fills the air: *Hey, Bell, it's just me … I know you said you don't want to talk but … if you change your mind about being on your own … I can come home anytime … I love you. Speak soon.*

He grins. 'You just couldn't wish for a better hubby, could you, beautiful Bella? Doing exactly what you asked, giving you *space*, letting you know it's you who's in control. Maybe you'd better send him a quick text, just to let him know you're okay.' Another laugh as his thumb moves over the screen. 'And, of course, let's not forget to add the kisses you seem to like so much.' He smacks his lips together, making a kissing sound as he finishes typing.

Frustration coursing through her, Bella grunts loudly as she fights with the binding at her wrists, pulling her hands in as many directions as she can to try and loosen it.

He chuckles. 'You know there's no point in trying to free yourself, Bella. That tape is extra strong. Even the strongest man in the world wouldn't be able to shift it.' He puts the phone away and carries on eating, his chewing loud in the quiet room.

Bella's shoulders sag as she stops struggling, her empty stomach grumbling again. She lifts her chin, thinking. Now that the gag is out of her mouth, she could scream. As loudly as possible. Surely someone will hear her? A dog walker? Or a passing jogger making their way down the lane? She looks at him, seeing that he's watching her, his eyes narrowed.

'Don't think I don't know what you're thinking, Bella.' Standing up, he puts the tray on the step, slowly making his way across the small space between them. He stands in front of her, his left hand moving to the knife at his waist. 'What you're thinking is, now that your mouth is uncovered, while I'm distracted eating my delicious and healthy chicken salad lunch, you'll scream. As loud and as long as you want to. And then, before you know it, some handsome prince will come running to your rescue. Am I right?'

Bella clamps her mouth shut. How could he tell what was going through her mind? Was it so obvious?

'Come on, Bella, you can tell me the truth. Who would blame you? I'm sure I'd try the same thing in your position. Although …' he puts a finger to his chin, as if he's thinking '… didn't you try that last time you were stuck down here? Screaming at the top of your lungs? And did anyone come running to your rescue then, Bella?'

Bella pictures her younger self, doing exactly what he said she did, screaming as loudly as she could the first time the gag was removed from her mouth on the first day. It was one of her mother's scarves that time, bright purple polyester, uncomfortable and scratchy, her abductor holding her head and wrestling it back on before her sudden shrill sound could reach anywhere beyond the walls around them. In her mind, she sees the outside of the house, the large garden in the quiet lane. It's just as remote now as it was then, surrounded by the farmland her grandparents used to work with their own hands before they sold it off, keeping only the property they lived in. The nearest neighbours haven't long moved in, a young couple with decent jobs in the city, renovating one of the old cottages that has been empty for a year or two. They're at least half a mile away, the nearest house in the opposite direction probably even further away from where she is now, hidden, deep under the ground.

'Of course no one came …' He keeps his eyes on her, stroking the handle of the knife at his side. 'You could give it a go though. Go on, Bella. I dare you …'

Bella looks at the floor, shaking her head as she tries not to cry again. She doesn't stand a chance, she thinks, his reflexes no doubt so quick, she could be dead before any sound has even left her throat. There's no more likelihood of her being heard than there was last time.

He chuckles. 'Never mind. It was worth a thought.' He reaches towards her. 'Now, if you're so determined you don't want to eat what I've generously offered you, I'll just have to cover your mouth again.'

His hands are rough against her skin as he pulls the scarf back into place.

Five and a half weeks earlier

Bella stood outside the house, stretching her hamstrings. She was looking forward to her run, her body feeling sluggish and her mind struggling to focus as the effects of too little sleep, of staring at the laptop screen instead of recharging the way she should have been, began to take their toll. Recommended by her therapist many years before, running was an activity that had always helped clear her head. To free her of the many thoughts she found so difficult to block out, not to mention the internal conversation she constantly seemed to be having with her anxious self. She especially needed it this week.

At first, she'd found rigorous exercise difficult, her early attempts at a slow jog awkward and short, her cheeks red with embarrassment, her gangly body not seeming to be built for coordination. Bella persevered and, within six months or so, was managing four or five kilometres at each outing, a habit she'd tried hard to maintain after she returned to uni. Now, she ran three times a week if she could, the hour after the kids left for school and before she headed into work probably her most relaxed time of the whole day.

She stepped out into the lane, checking the whistle at her neck before looking right and left and setting off, its presence helping calm her as her feet hit the pavement, her body soon finding its natural rhythm. The morning was bright, the type of late June day that made a person feel as if the world was full of possibilities, the fields that surrounded her golden with their crops, the trees lush and green. Bella focused on her breathing, trying to empty her mind and push away the thoughts that had plagued her the past few days. Thoughts of milk she could have sworn she'd bought and abductors who were now free to do what they liked.

The area surrounding her house was quiet as usual, just one lone dog walker with a huge golden Labrador disappearing around the curve in the distance. Bella always ran in the daylight, the thought of the total isolation of running at night, as so many runners did, too overwhelming for her. A few years before, with Jack's encouragement, she'd joined a running club, the idea of exercising en masse, as opposed to by herself, appealing to her. She'd left after just one session, the group's habit of running after dark, torches strapped to their foreheads, leaving her anxious, her muscles responding by tensing up and cramping, the opposite of what they needed. She couldn't do it. Not when she couldn't see what was ahead. *Who* was ahead.

She neared the end of the lane, her arms and legs beginning to work together as she remembered the self-defence classes she'd taken as a fresher, just a week or two into her first term at university. What a joke, she thought now. Lessons in how to twist an attacker's wrist so that they'd lose their grip, or how to manipulate someone's arm behind their back so they had no choice but to drop to the floor. Not a word included in the sessions about what a person should do if they were jumped and drugged in their own bedroom in the middle of the night. If the chance to escape was made up of milliseconds in which your disorientated mind could barely form a coherent thought. Bella had had no chance against Lawrence Knox, she accepted that now, her acceptance part of the healing process, or so her therapist had told her. The healing process she'd never quite managed to complete, even with all the support she'd had.

She entered the main road, turning left to jog alongside the traffic heading towards the next town. Her chest tightening with the fumes, she exhaled and persevered, preferring to be in plain sight once she was away from the house, despite the many cars she knew wouldn't do her health any good. She puffed out air again, her mind straying to the chat she and Jack had subjected the kids to at the weekend, attempting to make them aware of the potential dangers that might lie in wait for their family. It was just a precaution, Jack had insisted as they brought the meeting to a close, let the kids get on with their day. It was highly likely there was really nothing to worry about. She hoped so, she thought now, trying not to think about how anxious she'd been feeling. She really did.

She ran on, crossing the busy road at the top end and running along the other side before crossing again and doubling back, the same routine, until she felt herself beginning to tire. She slowed as she saw the left turn up ahead, the opening to the lane, the opposite end to where she and Jack lived, hidden by overhanging trees. As she adjusted her direction to turn, her ears picked up what sounded like hurried footsteps behind her. Another runner, the pounding rhythm of rubber hitting the pavement matching her own, almost as if someone was deliberately running in sync with her. Bella never wore earphones while she exercised. She couldn't understand how other runners could deliberately make themselves so vulnerable.

She turned her head slightly, her knees jolting as the ground beneath her changed from flat to rugged, the few isolated cottages at this end of the lane speeding past her in a blur. In her peripheral vision, she could just about catch sight of a blue sports shirt, a faded baseball cap. Bella's heart skipped a beat as she looked at the countryside that surrounded her, the large farmhouse in the distance, the driveway seeming impossibly long. She reached up and touched the whistle. Still there, its string secure around her neck.

Bella stared at the lane ahead of her, the long expanse of rough road that, as it often was, seemed to be devoid of life. She swallowed heavily, her breathing becoming laboured as she looked over her shoulder again, noticing that the runner's baseball cap was pulled low, shadowing his face. Lawrence had always worn a cap, usually coupling it with some kind of logoed sports shirt, once following her home from her violin class with the hat pulled so low it almost hid his face completely. She'd been walking home alone, not unusual for students in an overcrowded city, even at night, her stalking experience not so intense then that she feared for her safety. She was confident, relaxed, Lawrence more of a nuisance at that stage than a threat.

It had been a few minutes that time before she'd realised he was following her, taking the same turns she was, his footsteps stopping when hers did, continuing every time she started walking again. As she began to feel more and more uncomfortable, Bella's thoughts had slowly begun to turn towards the awkward young man she'd tried to be a friend to but whose intense manner had left her not wanting to be in his company. Trying to ascertain the best way out of the situation, she'd followed a piece of advice she'd been given in her self-defence classes and had gone into a crowded pub, watching at the window as Lawrence glanced inside before quickening his pace and walking past. His eyes had briefly met hers as he looked away, the baseball cap that shadowed them a faded red colour with blue lettering. That was when Bella first began to suspect she might have a problem on her hands.

Now, as she began to run faster, bile rose in her throat as she contemplated the idea that the person running so closely behind her might indeed be Lawrence once again, jogging through the streets he was supposed to be banned from, seemingly without a care in the world. Was she being paranoid? Her mind playing tricks on her after the worry of the past week? It wasn't often she saw another runner in the lane at this time of day but, of course, that didn't mean there were none. Perfectly innocent joggers who were simply taking the same route she was. Although, even if the man behind her was innocent, she told herself, surely any decent human being would know that running directly behind a lone woman, even in broad daylight, was a bad idea?

Still too far from the house to simply sprint home, Bella looked around, her pace slowing just a fraction as she spotted the small garden centre and café she and Jack often popped into for a Saturday coffee, a popular venue for school mums and ladies-who-lunched on weekdays. Pursing her lips, she made her decision, running as swiftly as she could through the car park and the stacks of various plants for sale, towards the entrance. Coming to a sudden halt outside the door, she tried to catch her breath, her calf muscles cramping as she turned and surveyed the lane she'd just left, the fingers of her right hand firmly holding on to her whistle, ready to blow.

The man who was running behind her glanced in her direction, his eyes, beneath the baseball cap, briefly meeting hers before he continued his slog down the lane, the scene an echo of the one in Leeds so many years ago. But unlike Lawrence Knox, this man was muscular, Bella noted, his build different from her stalker's, his powerful gait suggesting he was quite a few years younger than Lawrence would be now. Watching him disappear behind a copse of trees, she exhaled in relief. The man wasn't following her. He was simply running, following a route, the same as she was, albeit a little close to her heels. She let go of the whistle at her neck.

Jack was probably right, she thought, allowing herself a little chuckle at her paranoia. Over the past week or so, her husband had seemed convinced that they didn't have anything to worry about, despite the upset Lawrence had caused earlier in her life. Pushing open the door of the garden centre, Bella headed towards the café to buy a bottle of water, her throat dry as it often was when she was anxious. As she stood in the queue, wiping sweat from her forehead, she fished her phone out of her bumbag and connected it to the free Wi-Fi. Clicking on WhatsApp, she typed out a message to her sister:

Very nearly deafened a complete stranger with my running whistle. Talk about paranoid ...

As she pressed the arrow to send, her phone pinged with the notifications that had built up while she'd been disconnected. One in particular caught her eye as it loaded, and she stopped scrolling. The notification was from Facebook, and Bella gasped as she read it. She began to shiver as the sweat on her skin dried beneath the café's air conditioning.

Larry Knox has sent you a friend request.

Bella now

She studies the room around her, trying to remember the last time she ventured down to the basement without feeling completely terrified. A long time ago, she thinks, long before the days when Lawrence Knox came into her life and turned it upside down. Before all the places that once made her feel safe and secure became places to be feared.

Despite her current circumstances, she can't help but smile to herself, the wadded scarf chafing at the corners of her lips, as she remembers when her grandparents used to live in the house. The space beneath was used for storage then, rows of aluminium shelves stacked full of the vast array of fruits and vegetables picked from the farm: tomatoes, courgettes and gooseberries in the summer, green cooking apples and pears in the autumn months.

As the fruit ripened in the dark space, it would eventually be replaced by the numerous chutneys and jams her grandma used to create on the old Aga, the whole family often heading out to the nearby fairs and markets and setting up a stall full of the covered and sealed jars. Some of Bella's earliest memories involved herself and Rosie, sitting in the kitchen at the top of the basement stairs, waiting patiently for a taste of Grandma's latest concoction. The way she ceremoniously presented it to each of them on a dry cracker, warning them each time not to burn their tongues, was something Bella would never forget.

As she looks around her now, her mouth gagged, her hands and ankles bound, it seems difficult for Bella to believe the basement was once a source of pleasure, a place she and her sister both enjoyed using as a playground, the shadowy corners ideal for hours-long games of hide-and-seek. Comforted by the images of the past that flit through her mind, she imagines herself curled up beneath the stairs, or trying to make herself as thin as she could behind a shelving unit, waiting for Rosie to find her.

When they were little, they'd spent most weekends here, their mother leaving them with their grandparents while she had a break from her domestic duties, shopping or meeting friends for lunch, the whole family experiencing mixed feelings when the house became their permanent home. When their grandmother had died just three short years after their grandfather, they were all delighted to be moving to somewhere that was so special to them, their mother's childhood home, but sad at the reasons behind the uprooting.

She tries to breathe around the scarf, swallowing down the constant saliva in her mouth as she wonders if her own children would have played hide-and-seek here if she'd allowed them to. Freddy and Paige have never been down to the basement; Bella always makes sure the door is firmly locked, one key on the set in her handbag, the other on Jack's keyring. She remembers Freddy asking her once if he and his friends could go down and explore, her son showing off a little in front of a boy who'd just joined his class. *Just this once,* he said. *It'll be fun.* There was no way Bella would have ever said yes, the idea of her children being in the place that was now the source of so many nightmares for her simply inconceivable.

Screwing up her eyes and peering into a dark corner, she suddenly wonders if the violin she used to play is somewhere among the old suitcases and boxes of children's books her parents left behind when they moved. When she was younger, Bella had often come down to the basement to practise, venturing beneath the house the best way to avoid annoying her father whose tolerance for his daughters' musical aspirations wasn't always apparent. What Bella had told Paige, when she and Jack had spoken to the kids about Lawrence, was only part of the story, she realises now, as she pictures her sister and herself, carefully negotiating the wooden steps with their instrument cases.

It was true, she herself was always more enthusiastic than Rosie about the music lessons their mother wanted them to take, her sister often dragging her feet, and her own violin, on a Saturday afternoon when they both made their way to the little cottage their mum's music teacher friend lived in. What Bella hadn't told her daughter was how much she'd shone in those lessons, how talented her teacher often said she was, her interest only waning when she was at uni and Lawrence had insisted on turning up at the lessons she'd tried to continue with there. Part of her would always bear a grudge against him for dousing her passion. Among other things.

She remembers how she and Rosie had occasionally argued about their different attitudes towards music, her sister sometimes belligerent towards her, mocking Bella for the way she apparently *sucked up* to their teacher. She'd grown out of it eventually, finding interests of her own as she became a teenager: sciences and computer skills, the after-school physics club where Rosie was the only girl among ten or so boys. The two of them had never been especially competitive since.

Bella shifts her position on the chair, looking at the cobweb-covered brown brick around her, the dense grey ceiling above, as she wonders what might have happened if she'd screamed when she threatened to, the sound no doubt bouncing off the damp walls, echoing back towards her ears. Would she have been wrestled into submission, the gag wrenched back over her mouth, like she was last time? Goose bumps prick at her skin as she pictures her abductor's face as he laughed at her earlier.

He was right in what he said, she thinks. Screaming didn't help her last time; her throat had simply ended up hoarse after she'd let out what seemed like the loudest, longest scream possible in just a few seconds, no one coming to help. What would be the point if no one can hear her, any cries for help she attempts to make in the brief moments when the scarf is removed from her mouth simply echoing around her, mocking her, reminding her that no one is listening?

Reminding her that she's completely alone.

She shakes her head. Thoughts of the past, of her and Rosie's adventures in the basement, have been comforting, but now she needs to focus on the present. On finding a way out of this blasted situation. Forget the screaming, she thinks. About anyone coming to her aid. She has to focus on how she alone is going to escape.

Because she will, she tells herself. She'll get out of here soon. Hopefully sooner than she did the last time she was held in this godforsaken place. And she'll make sure her captor never gets a chance to put her through this nightmare ever again.

She pushes the scarf with her tongue to try to stop it from choking her.

Five and a half weeks earlier

Reaching the front of the queue, Bella ordered coffee in a disposable cup, the bottle of water she intended to buy forgotten. Wanting to take a few minutes to look at her phone again before she headed home, she scanned around the room for an empty table. The café was busy for a weekday, an offer of two-for-one drinks apparently bringing the customers forward in droves. As Bella tried to cross the room, aware of how much her sweat-dampened running clothes stood out against the tailored trousers and blouses, the men's buttoned-up shirts, she had to suddenly step sideways, a waiter swearing under his breath as he bumped her elbow with a large tray.

She squeezed herself into a corner between the stacks of dirty dishes on a tall rack and the women's toilets. As she clicked on her phone screen again to wake it up, her heart thudded in her chest, her other hand swiping at the beads of sweat still sitting on her top lip. Despite her body having cooled by now, the effects of her run wearing off, she felt clammy, her skin prickling as she opened her Facebook app again. Did she really just see what she thought she had?

Waiting for the intermittent Wi-Fi to load the app, Bella sipped her coffee, scanning the crowded room again, wishing Jack were with her. They'd been to the garden centre together many times, the two of them often walking up the lane on sunny spring days, holding hands like they used to when they first met. Usually, they'd buy a few bedding plants for the garden and, afterwards, come into the café for coffee and cake. Days like that were her favourite kind, both of them relaxed, enjoying some down time. Despite the frustration her husband must sometimes have felt when she was at her most anxious, she knew if Jack were here, he would instantly be able to calm her down. To at least attempt to give her a rational explanation for what suddenly seemed to be happening to her: her world tilting on its axis once again.

She screwed up her eyes as she looked back at her phone, the reading glasses that made her feel old at home on the kitchen counter. Clicking on her recent Facebook friend requests, Bella studied the list that contained three names before the most recent one: a client from work wanting to connect with her the week before so they could more easily exchange messages, and a couple of old school friends who'd looked her up a few months ago. After carefully checking they were genuine, as she always did, she'd accepted the other requests.

At the top of the list, the shortened version of Lawrence Knox's name glared at her, the words *confirm* and *dismiss* underneath seeming to goad her, daring her to make a decision. To see what would happen if she decided to be friends with this man. Staring at the phone screen, Bella wondered, despite the blue and white words right in front of her, if she was imagining what she was seeing. If her brain was somehow tricking her into thinking the past was catching up with her when, in reality, her phone was actually saying something else. She shook her head. No, despite her recent distrust of the world and the people around her, the mistake she made thinking someone was following her as she ran along the lane a few minutes before, she knew she wasn't going crazy. Lawrence Knox, *Larry*, the man who had almost destroyed her life when she was barely an adult, who had caused her to live in fear ever since, wanted to connect with her on social media. Was asking if she would consider being his friend.

Feeling slightly nauseous, the spot she was standing in almost as crowded and claustrophobic as the rest of the café, she clicked on Lawrence's name, the link buffering a little as she waited for it to take her to his profile page. Bella held her breath as the images slowly cleared, tears blurring her eyes as she braced herself for seeing a picture of the man who had caused her so much pain. Would he look the same? Older, maybe a little greyer, but still Lawrence? Would she be able to bear looking into his eyes after all these years? She swallowed as the page loaded, her skin prickling as she suddenly saw that the page's profile picture was not a picture of Lawrence at all, but a generic image, no doubt taken from Google: a cartoon of a stereotypical criminal in a suit decorated with arrows, a swag bag over his shoulder. His head was thrown back, as if he was laughing loudly.

Bella felt anger rise through her. Did Lawrence think this whole thing was funny? To be upending her life again after everything he'd put her through before? Did he think the whole experience – abducting her, drugging her, holding her at knifepoint for five whole days, not to mention scaring the life out of her again now – was some kind of joke? If so, Lawrence Knox was an even sicker individual than she thought, and he deserved to be locked up forever.

She scrolled down the page, a lot of the information on it protected by Lawrence's privacy settings, the few posts she could see merely generic: copied and pasted, cheesy quotes or childish memes shared from other pages. There were no photographs, nothing personal. Nothing, apart from the shortened name, that connected the creator of the page to the man who had abducted her. Negotiating the menu at the top of the screen, Bella clicked to see Larry's *About* info. Again, nothing. No relationship status, no workplaces to show. Nothing that could tell her if this person was really who she thought he was. Who he *must* be.

Bella felt her chest tightening in the same way it had during her run, when she'd thought the jogger behind was a threat. As she looked around the busy café again, she suddenly felt suffocated, as if all the air had been sucked out of the enclosed space, the customers – the young boy refusing to hold his mother's hand as they made their way to the toilets; the crying little girl; the waitress arguing with a group of six about a missing meal – all too close to her.

She tried to take a breath, almost dropping her phone as it suddenly vibrated in her hand. Her sister replying to her WhatsApp message about the jogger behind her:

OMG, he would have got a bit of a shock!

Rosie had added a row of laughing-face emojis.

Bella put her coffee cup on a nearby shelf, trying to stop her hands from shaking as she typed out a new message:

It's not that funny, Rosie. Anyway, forget that, I need to talk to you about something else. You'll never believe what I've just seen. Call you in a min when I'm home xx

She made sure the message had sent before shoving her phone back in her bumbag and picking up her coffee.

She needed to go home.

Jack now

The hotel Jazz booked for him is beige and corporate. Not the Premier Inn that Bella suggested in her phone message but somewhere his firm has often used for events and team-building days. It isn't cheap but isn't the most expensive in the area, the room rates often reduced at weekends to encourage tourists in and make up for the lack of business travellers. He wonders briefly if he can get away with claiming it on expenses before deciding it's not worth the hassle.

He closes the room door and pulls off his jacket, throwing it onto the bed along with the overnight bag he keeps in the car. His stomach is growling, the small amount of lunch he eventually ate barely filling him. He's always had a good appetite, he and Bella eating well, especially at weekends, but recently he's not been so hungry. Too much on his plate, so to speak, worrying about his wife. The past few weeks have been a rollercoaster ride for all of them. At least the kids are safely out of the way. He hopes they're both enjoying their holidays, feeling a little more secure in their respective changes of scenery. They deserve it, after everything they've been through.

He sits on the bed, picking up the room service menu and scanning it, the beef ribeye catching his eye before he casts it aside again. He can't decide how he feels. Hungry, not hungry.

Glad of some time alone, yet fully aware of the silence of the hotel room compared to the constant activity of the house. His moods are all over the place. Is it any wonder? Just this morning, he was at home, heading off to work while Bella helped Freddy pack some last-minute things for his trip. Now look at him. On his own in a hotel room, wondering how his wife is coping after he's seemingly abandoned her.

He picks up his discarded jacket and roots in the pocket for his phone, sitting for a few seconds, staring at the last text that came through from Bella's phone just short of an hour ago:

Got your voicemail. Sorry I didn't answer, but I'm just not ready to talk yet. I'm okay though, don't worry. Hope you haven't raided the minibar already! xxx

He reads the words twice over, wondering if he should call her number again. He remembers what Jazz said at the office earlier: *She just needs some thinking time. All women do every so often.* What would other husbands do in this situation? he wonders. What would he himself have done if this had happened before the events of the last few weeks? Before they began to be so distant from one another?

In the end, he texts back, his thumbs not as quick over the screen as his daughter's are when she's messaging her friends:

Glad you're okay. Totally get how you're feeling, but just text if you need me. Anytime, day or night. Keep in touch, Bell. Love you always xxx

He presses *send*, the phone suddenly making him jump as it begins to vibrate in his hand. His mother-in-law's name fills the screen.

'Gail, hi. Everything okay?'

'Fine, Jack. I'm just ringing while we're stopped at the services.

We'll be home before long and will no doubt lose mobile signal again and I just wanted to tell you the journey has passed with no issues. I know how you both worry. I tried Bella but she isn't answering. I didn't bother leaving a message …'

Jack's always been fond of Gail, remembering how, when he and Bella first got together, his future mother-in-law welcomed him into her family as if she'd known him forever. His first trip to the house he and his wife now lived in was an occasion he'd be unlikely to ever forget. An only child who'd been distant from his mother before she died and who'd barely known his father, Jack was immediately taken aback by how close Bella was to her parents and sister, their home a constant hive of activity. He doesn't want to worry her too much. 'She's probably enjoying a soak in the bath. How's Freddy?'

'He's fine. He's just nipped into the shop with Brian. He's in good spirits, considering …'

Jack feels a lurch in his stomach. Poor Freddy. He's had to put up with so much recently. So much pain. 'I'm glad …'

'I just hope the break does him good.'

'Me too.' Jack understands Gail's concerns. After what happened to Bella when she was young, she and Brian still worry enormously about the whole family.

He remembers once how, during an early visit to the house where he himself would eventually live, Bella's mum had taken him to one side while the rest of the family were playing board games in the living room. *You have to know,* she said, keeping her voice low, *that Bella is fragile. She tries to act like she's over what happened to her, but believe me, Jack, it's all a front. A brave face. She'll probably never get over it. That's why you'll always have to look after her. If you're as serious about her as you say you are, you need to know what you're taking on.*

Jack assured Gail that he was, indeed, very serious about her daughter. He promised her there and then that he would do everything in his power to take care of Bella. And he can see now that Gail was right. *Fragile* was an apt word to have used to describe his wife, especially after what he's witnessed over the last few weeks.

'Are you still there, Jack?'

He clears his throat. 'I'm here.'

'I hate to see Bella struggling. She looked so pale when we saw her this morning. And thin. I sometimes wonder if moving away was the right thing to do, but it's reassuring to know that you're there looking after her. I know we don't say it often enough, Jack, but Brian and I are so grateful for everything you've done for her. The way you've looked after her all these years.'

'Hmm, yes ...'

'What? Is everything okay?'

Jack looks around at the drab walls of the hotel room, weighing up the pros and cons of lying to Gail. Of telling her that everything is fine and that she should simply go and enjoy her time with her grandson, compared with telling her some harsh truths. 'Actually, Gail, Bella has asked for some time on her own this weekend. I'm sure there's no need for either of us to panic, but she's asked me to stay in a hotel for a couple of days. I just thought it might be better to tell you now, then it won't come as a shock to you if ...'

'If what, Jack? You split up? Surely things aren't that bad? Bella would never want that. She loves you.'

'I thought so too, but, lately, I'm honestly not sure what she wants. I don't think she knows herself. You've seen what she's been like, how unlike her normal self she's been. She's barely even getting along with her sister, and you know more than anyone, Gail, how close she and Rosie have always been. Maybe some time to herself is exactly what she needs. Maybe that's the only way we'll be able to move on from this.'

'Have you called her?'

'A few times, but like you, I'm just getting her voicemail. She has texted me though and she sounds bright enough. Says she just doesn't want to talk.' He shifts his phone from one ear to the other, hoping his words are reassuring to his mother-in-law. 'I don't think we need to worry, Gail, Bella is stronger than you think. Remember the last time, when Lawrence was first up for parole, and she disappeared to a spa for two days?'

'I do.'

'She turned her phone off completely that time, I didn't hear from her at all, but she came home eventually, and she was fine. She just needed some space to clear her head, which is clearly what she needs again now. And, at least, this time, she's not completely shutting me out.'

'You're probably right, Jack, I trust your judgement.' Muffled voices in the background interrupt Gail's words. 'Freddy's here. He wants a quick word before we set off again.'

Freddy's voice comes onto the line, high-pitched and excited. 'Hey, Dad, Grandpa just bought me the latest edition of that comic I've been collecting. He said it might keep me quiet for a while.'

Jack chuckles. He knows how much his son can talk when he's in a good mood. 'That's great. Make sure you say thank you.'

'I will. Is Mum okay?'

'She's fine, no need to worry.'

'No more *incidents* …?'

Jack sighs. 'No more incidents.'

'Okay, gotta go, bye, Dad.'

Gail's voice comes back on the line. 'We're on the landline if you need us, Jack, but otherwise we'll see you when we bring Freddy back next week.'

'Have fun.'

'Bye, Jack.'

'Bye.' He ends the call, his head dropping to his chest as he wonders what state his family will be in by the time he sees his mother-in-law again.

Five and a half weeks earlier

Bella put the takeaway coffee cup on the kitchen counter, the large latte she'd barely touched now unappetising and almost cold. Feeling like her body needed caffeine after the shock of seeing the Facebook notification on her phone, she'd requested the drink at the café counter and almost immediately regretted it. She turned on the tap and ran cold water into a glass, downing half of it before nausea gripped her stomach once again.

She headed over to the table, grabbing a clean hoodie from the nearby washing basket and slipping it on before she sat down. She suddenly felt cold, sweat from the run and her subsequent hurried walk home drying on her skin. As she stared at the basement door on the far side of the room, a sharp shiver ran through her. She'd obsessed about it over the years she and Jack had lived in the house, constantly asking him if the lock was secure, her days of playing down there as a child, later practising her music, long behind her. She knew it had frustrated her husband at times, the way she had to check the door herself last thing at night before she went to bed, in case one of the kids thought it would be funny to take the key from her bag, or from Jack's keyring, and turn it in the lock, replacing it quickly when they heard someone coming, forgetting to secure the door again behind them. It wasn't that she didn't trust Jack to check; it was simply that she couldn't settle, couldn't sleep, if she hadn't done it herself.

Nineteen years ago, Lawrence Knox had been down there, in that room below her house, and she hadn't had a clue. Who was to say the same thing couldn't happen again?

She slipped her bumbag from around her waist, unzipping it and pulling out her phone. After getting up from her chair, she went into the living room to find her laptop, bringing it back to the kitchen and resting it on the table in front of her. As she opened the lid, she picked up her phone again, scrolling through her contacts before clicking on her sister's name. She needed someone to talk to. Someone to help her make sense of what was happening.

Rosie answered after half a dozen rings or so.

'Did you see my message? I need to talk to you.'

'Well, hello to you too, Bella.'

'Sorry, I …' She tried to soften her tone. Snapping at her sister for no reason wasn't going to help anyone. 'I just need a friendly ear, that's all. If you're not too busy …'

'Of course, but you're going to have to give me a second. Katie's disappeared upstairs somewhere, and I've got Cameron propped against one hip with no undies on. If he decides to pee just at this very moment, then I'm in big trouble.'

'Okay.'

The line went quiet, Bella drumming her fingers on the table as Rosie's voice became muffled. Even in her distressed state, she couldn't help but admire how patient her sister was with the twins, the calm way in which she always seemed to speak to them, no matter what antics they presented their mother with, a stark contrast to the anxiety Bella often felt about her own family. Rosie had waited so long to be a mum, years of trying, of tests and expert opinions, taking their toll before Katie and Cameron, with their typical unpredictability, had arrived naturally. Rosie had taken to her role in their lives like a duck to water.

'Okay, sorted.' Rosie came back on the line, sounding out of breath. 'Believe it or not, Katie had undressed herself and got back into bed. I'll be so glad when they eventually start nursery. So, what were you saying?'

Bella inhaled, trying to calm herself down, the anxiety and claustrophobia she'd felt in the coffee shop coming back to her in waves. She wanted to talk rationally. Not to sound as if she were having trouble controlling her emotions. Yet, as she waited for her laptop to boot up in front of her, the old system much slower than her phone, she was sure that anyone in her position might feel shaken. She barely wanted to say the words out loud. Lawrence Knox, her stalker, had sent her an online friend request. 'I had a notification from Facebook this morning.'

'Is this anything to do with the jogger you thought was following you? Sorry, I know it's not funny, but I did giggle when I saw that first message. Poor bloke was lucky you didn't blow that blasted whistle right down his ear. Remember that time you rang the police when you thought ...'

Bella fought down the irritation that was building in her chest. Of course, she remembered the incident Rosie was talking about: the 999 operator getting cross with her when she'd thought a man in a red baseball cap and football supporter's shirt was following her around the supermarket, the suspect turning out to be an elderly gent who was simply wondering where she'd found the three tins of corned beef she'd stashed in her trolley. She was embarrassed to talk about it. Not to mention the fact that she had more urgent matters on her mind. 'Rosie, listen.' She almost hissed the words down the line.

Her sister was quiet for a couple of seconds. 'Okay, sorry. Again. What's up?'

'Someone calling himself *Larry* Knox has sent me a friend request and I'm pretty sure it's Lawrence.'

'What? You're kidding? Is he allowed to do that?'

'Of course he's not, not according to the licence conditions set up before his release, but they can't monitor every single thing he does, can they? They must have hundreds, maybe thousands, of ex-prisoners to monitor at any one time.' Leaning forward, Bella double-clicked on her internet browser, waiting for the window to open.

'I suppose. But it is out of line. What did you do? Immediately declined it, I hope.'

Bella hesitated. 'I haven't done anything yet. I just wanted to have a proper look at his profile first, to make sure I wasn't going crazy.'

'Bell, you don't have a choice. Never mind playing amateur detective, you need to decline the request straight away and report him. What did you find on his page? Please tell me he's not created some kind of shrine to you? That he's not still obsessing after all these years ...'

Bella closed her eyes for a second, part of her grateful there was no social media when Lawrence had been stalking her the first time around. It would have made it so much easier for him to find her, to track her movements, her friends, her interests. What she'd been through at his hands was already bad enough. She began to type Facebook's address into the search bar, waiting for the laptop to recognise it and take her to her own profile page. As she waited, she pictured Lawrence's cartoon profile picture, mocking her when she first saw it about half an hour ago, its cackling caricature face. 'I couldn't find anything very much, to be honest. It's all protected by privacy. No photos of Lawrence himself or of anyone else. I'm going to have a closer look on the laptop now. Sometimes you can see more than you can on your phone ...'

'Are you sure it was him? Did he ever use the name Larry?'

'I don't know if he did or not.' Bella shook her head. 'But of course it's him. Who else would it be, Rosie? Larry is short for Lawrence, isn't it?' On her Facebook page she searched for *Larry Knox*.

Rosie's voice became muffled again, as if she was holding her hand over the phone 'Cameron, please don't eat the Play-Doh ...' The line cleared. 'I suppose. But could it be a coincidence?'

Bella tried again to adjust her tone of voice, to not let her anger, her fear at what was happening to her, take over. This was her sister she was talking to. The person who, like Jack and her parents, had stuck by her side through everything. Who believed in her. 'A coincidence? Do you really think ...?' She frowned, searching through the list of Larry Knox profiles in front of her. Scrolling back to the top, she searched again. 'I don't believe it ...'

'What? What don't you believe?'

'It's disappeared.'

'What do you mean?'

'The page. Larry Knox's profile page, the one I was looking at earlier on my phone, it's gone.' Swallowing heavily, Bella clicked on her notifications at the top of the page. She felt a little sick again. 'And so has the friend request. It's been deleted.'

'Are you sure?'

'Of course I'm sure. It's not here. I saw it, Rosie. On my phone. I was standing in the queue at the café.'

Rosie sounded confused. 'Hold on. What café? I thought you said you'd been out for a run?'

Bella pursed her lips. She was still scrolling through the list of Larry Knox profiles, her phone now on speaker on the table so she could speak to her sister while using both hands. She tried typing in *Lawrence* Knox. Had he used his full name? No, the notification had definitely said *Larry*. Either way, she couldn't find the page. 'I went into the garden centre to get a drink. That was where I was when I messaged you and saw the notification on my phone.'

'And all this was just after you'd been scared by the other runner, the one you thought might be chasing you?'

Bella sat back against the kitchen chair. 'I know what I saw, Rosie.'

'Of course, of course you do. I just thought …'

'Thought what?'

'That maybe you were feeling anxious.'

'And that would make me see things? On my phone?'

'I don't know. Maybe …' Rosie's voice was muffled again as she spoke to one of the twins, Cameron giggling hysterically in the background before his mum came back on the line. 'No, of course not. I just think it's easy to …'

'To what?'

'You know, make a mistake.'

Bella sighed. What was the point of even continuing the conversation if the page she'd seen had now disappeared? If she could no longer access it? She looked through the list of Larry Knox profiles again. 'Could *you* look for him? Just to be sure? Maybe I'm missing something. Got an out-of-date version of Facebook on my laptop or some such …'

'Hmm. I could …' Rosie sounded doubtful. 'I'm not sure it would make much difference though. Are you really sure, Bell, that that's what you saw? It does seem a bit strange that it's disappeared between you going into the garden centre and getting home.'

Bella looked at her laptop, feeling her faith in herself seeping away, like water down a drain. She thought about Rosie's question. Was she really sure? She had been, but now she simply felt confused, losing confidence in what she'd seen as she was standing in the coffee shop queue, afterwards as she stood near the toilets. Her sister was right. She *had* been feeling anxious after her experience with the runner behind her, her mind racing, her surroundings busy and chaotic. Yet, surely, she hadn't imagined her stalker's name? 'Could you just check? See if you can see something I can't?'

'Let me get the iPad …'

Bella listened to the rustling on the other end of the line, as if her sister was rooting through a drawer or cupboard. As she waited for Rosie to come back, she opened Google, typing in Lawrence Knox's name. A few old articles came up, most of which she'd seen before, as well as a couple of newer ones she couldn't bring herself to look at. No social media presence, as far as she could see. At the bottom of the list, there was an art page. She opened it, seeing a few muted abstract paintings for sale. Few details about the artist apart from his name. Could it be *the* Lawrence? *Her* Lawrence, as she was reluctant to call him? She wasn't sure.

Rosie came back on the line, clearing her throat. 'I can't see anything so far ...'

'Probably because he's deleted everything.'

'Nope, definitely nothing. Lots of Larry Knox profiles but no one that seems to be *your* ...'

That phrase again. 'He's not *mine*. He had a picture of a criminal on his page.'

'A criminal?'

'Yes, like a cartoon. With arrows on his suit. I suppose he must have thought it was funny.'

'Honestly, there's nothing like that coming up here.' Rosie hesitated. 'I know this sounds a bit random, but do you remember Barry Knowles? From school? He just came into my head because I remember him sending me a friend request quite recently and I had to rack my brain to recall who he was. Could it have been him who sent you the request?'

Bella rolled her eyes. 'I know the difference between Barry and Larry.'

'Well, I'm just saying, because, you know, it's a very similar name and I think he's the type of person who sends requests to anyone he's ever met in real life, whether he's still in touch with them or not. You know, like *everybody*. Maybe he just thought better of it when he realised you probably wouldn't be interested.'

'It said *Larry*, Rosie ... I saw it.'

'But, if you were in a hurry? Or didn't have your reading glasses on? Remember that time I thought Keanu Reeves had tried to connect with me, and it turned out to be Kerry who I met on holiday?' Rosie chuckled.

Bella felt her cheeks flush with anger. Her sister was being flippant. Not taking her seriously. 'So, I receive a friend request from someone who appears to be the man who stalked me, imprisoned me in the basement of my home for five days, abused me, and you're talking about reading glasses and *Keanu Reeves*?'

'I was just kidding around, Bell—'

'And, as I said before, this isn't funny, Rosie. This is serious. If what I saw was right, Lawrence Knox was trying to connect with me online, doing exactly what he's not supposed to do, and all you can do is make stupid jokes!'

Rosie went quiet for a few seconds. When she spoke again, her tone was sombre. 'Now, hang on a minute, Bell. I think you've hit the nail on the head there, haven't you, when you say *if* what you saw was right? You were standing in a coffee shop, probably a whole load of people around you, the lighting not very good, no reading glasses with you, having just been frightened by someone you thought was following you. Now, you tell me they weren't perfect conditions for you imagining you'd seen something scary on your phone.'

'I didn't—'

'I get it, Bell. I really do. This is a very frightening time for you. The man who abused you is out of prison and you feel vulnerable all over again. I don't blame you for that, not one bit, but even you have to admit that this could all be some innocent mistake. Your imagination getting the better of you.'

Bella closed the lid of the laptop, feeling like a child who'd been chastised. Was Rosie right? Was it really possible that she'd misread the notification when she was in the garden centre? Seen Larry instead of Barry? How silly it sounded now. 'I'm sorry. I didn't mean to sound angry with you.'

'No, of course you didn't.'

'It's just … It's difficult, that's all. And I was so sure …'

'Of course you were. It could happen to anyone. I'm sure I'd be the same.'

'I doubt it somehow.'

'Look, Bell, I have to go, Cameron's now loading Play-Doh into the washing machine, but, if there's anything else, if you think there's someone lurking or you see anything else online, just call me, okay? And we can get to the bottom of it together.'

'I will.'

'I love you, Bell.'

'You too.'

Bella ended the call, her fingers shaking as she pressed them against the phone screen. She sat at the kitchen table for a few more minutes, staring again at the basement door across the room, picturing her younger self behind it, at the bottom of the stairs, bound to one of the kitchen chairs her mother had once thought so tasteful but then had felt compelled to replace after her daughter's abduction. Was she herself really so spooked by Lawrence's release that she'd imagined his online presence? She wasn't sure, but the fact that Lawrence Knox still had the power to make her feel so vulnerable, so fragile, that she would end up snapping at the sister she'd always been so close to, was something that made her immensely sad.

Her lip quivering, Bella got up from the table, quickly making sure the basement door was still locked before heading upstairs for a shower. She was already very late for work.

Bella now

She wonders what time it is, the phone she's so used to checking still in her abductor's hands. Along with her life. The windowless room around her makes it difficult to tell if it's day or night, the shadows that linger permanently in the corners, beneath the stairs and the stacks of shelves, crawling over various tarpaulins, shifting in front of her eyes, as if they're alive. She tries to think back to when he offered her lunch, a salad made from the ingredients she herself had bought when she last shopped, that she might have enjoyed if her usual routine hadn't been so violently disrupted. Her growling stomach tells her that must have been at least two, probably more like three, hours ago, what feels like the longest day ever now likely standing at mid to late afternoon.

She slumps back in her chair, the tape that binds her chest and abdomen to the wood making it increasingly difficult to sit comfortably, the pressure, as well as the gag at her mouth, making breathing difficult. Since he last disappeared up the stairs and into the kitchen, Bella has spent much of her time trying to wrestle herself free, attempting to work out the best way to loosen her bindings. Every time she moves, even slightly, the tape tears at her skin, ripping out the downy hair that covers her arms, bringing tears to her eyes. It's one of the strongest on the market, the same brand Jack bought once to keep an exploding Christmas tree, the branches virtually impossible to return to their previous arrangement, in the narrow box in which it had been delivered. As she looks down, she sees spots of blood on one of her wrists. It has literally ripped her skin away.

Gulping down sobs again, Bella feels as if her heart could break at how familiar the whole scenario feels: the bindings, the scarf, the uncomfortable chair. The constant throb of her bladder. Who could ever claim they've been kidnapped and restrained, in exactly the same way, in the same room, by the same super-strength workman's tape, twice in their life? It really is beyond belief. A stupid, stupid situation she's got herself into.

She closes her eyes, part of her wanting to fight the exhaustion that suddenly threatens to overwhelm her, a larger part wanting to give in, just for a few minutes. She hasn't slept properly for weeks and now all of her joints and muscles ache from her constant attempts to free herself. As she starts to doze, her mind drifts back to the first time she was brought down to the basement and tied up. The first time her freedom was violated in such a traumatic way that she wondered if she would ever get over it and had to have therapy for years after. The memories are vivid, even in her half-asleep state: Lawrence Knox suddenly, terrifyingly, appearing in her bedroom when her parents and sister were away, his plump lips pulled into a self-satisfied smirk as he grabbed her before she had chance to react.

It was only later, when she spoke to the police, that she found out about him hiding in the cellar, accessing the house through a loosely locked, ancient kitchen window her parents had been meaning to replace for years. Waiting patiently, he'd hidden down there until her parents and Rosie left. Until Bella was at her most vulnerable. Alone.

He'd kept her here for five days, Bella wincing now at the thought. She'd only found out how long it had been after she escaped, her sense of time barely functioning while she was captive, her tired and panicked brain constantly tricking her into thinking seconds were minutes and minutes were hours. Or sometimes, the other way around. When she finally got away, she felt as if she'd been down here for years.

She thinks about how she escaped that time, searching her sleepy mind for something that might help her now. It was more through luck than judgement then, her captor becoming tired as he tried to convince her, day and night, of his love for her, keeping an almost constant vigil by her side. If she would just agree to love him, he'd told her over and over again, to give him a chance, he would set her free and the two of them could be together forever. Bella fought him at first, her instinct, as it is now, to shout and scream that she hated him. That she could never love someone so disgusting. Someone who thought that the way to win a person's respect, their heart, was to treat them so badly.

In the end, she decided the only way to get free was to play him at his own game. To her surprise, Lawrence had fallen for it. Had agreed to unstrap her when she told him she was tired of fighting. That she just wanted someone to hold her close and take care of her. With the tape that held her to the chair gone, Bella had moved quickly, much more quickly than she'd expected from her tired and hungry body.

Perhaps if she uses those same strategies now, sooner rather than later this time, she might be able to free herself on the first day rather than the fifth.

She jerks awake as the door to the kitchen opens, a dull ray of natural light entering the room. Still daytime then. Perhaps late afternoon, as she'd predicted, by the way the light is yellowing, as if the sun is lowering beyond the unseen window. She tries to focus as she watches him descend the stairs, his footfall heavy.

'How are we doing, beautiful Bella?' He pulls the scarf away before moving back to lean against the creaky newel post, arms folded as if he's assessing her. 'Still awake?'

She stares at him. Despite her groggy state, Bella feels it's important to look as if she's alert, to not show the fear she's feeling inside. Perhaps it's a waste of time but she has to try. Try and show him that she's stronger this time. That she's prepared to fight. 'I'm fine. Better when I don't have to look at you ...'

'Ah, don't be mean. Don't you miss me when I'm not down here with you, Bella?'

'Like a hole in the head.' She turns her face away.

'I'm disappointed.' He pulls a sad face. 'What's the matter, Bella? Are you feeling low this afternoon? That's perfectly understandable. After what you've been through, I'm sure you'd be forgiven for feeling like giving up. For thinking that life really isn't worth living anymore. Who'd blame you? Kidnapped twice? Anyone would think you must only have yourself to blame ...'

Bella looks back at him, holding her chin high. 'This isn't my fault. So don't you dare try and make me think it is.'

He chuckles. 'Of course it isn't.'

Bella takes a breath, recalling her muddled thoughts of a few moments ago, when she'd been on the edge of sleep, almost falling into the abyss. Thoughts of escape. She tries to smile, not sure she can get her mouth to fully obey. She was younger the last time she was in this situation, more confident in her ability to convince someone she wasn't repulsed by him. That she found him attractive. 'Look, can we talk about this?'

He frowns. 'Talk? Sure we can, beautiful Bella. I could spend all day talking to you, you know that ...'

'I mean, talk about how we can resolve this?'

He lowers himself to the step at the bottom of the stairs, clasping his hands in front of him. 'What did you have in mind?'

Bella looks at him, her eyes following the scar on his face, the way it starts just below his left eye before curling to a stop, like the tail of a question mark, just above his mouth. 'That we can work something out. Work together to come up with a solution to this mess we're both in ...'

A slow smile forms on his face. 'I see.'

'You love me, don't you? You've told me enough times in the

past how much. Surely you don't actually want to see me tied up down here? Hurt? Frightened? If you untie me, we can talk.' She hesitates, feeling bile rise in her throat. 'Or do whatever you want ...'

His smile suddenly becomes a loud laugh. 'What is this, Bella? A lame attempt to seduce me? Or do you think you can prick my conscience, reach a soft spot I may have, and I'll let you go?'

Bella feels her cheeks flush. 'I just think we can find a solution that will suit both of us. If you just tell me what you want.'

He stands, taking a few steps towards her. 'What I *want*, Bella, is for you to shut up. This may have worked for you last time. This damsel-in-distress, I-just-want-to-make-you-happy act, but, believe me, it's not going to work this time. Do you really think I'm *that* stupid?'

'I ... I don't think you're stupid at all.'

'Good, because I can assure you, I'm not. *I'm* the one in charge here, Bella, and don't you forget it.' He points at himself and then at her.

Bella bites her lip, trying not to cry.

'Now—' he walks back towards the stairs '—if you're a very good girl and don't try anything stupid, I might just be nice enough to bring you an afternoon snack. And I strongly suggest you accept my generosity this time, or I might be tempted not to offer again. Ever. Do you understand me?'

She nods.

'Great, now we're getting somewhere. Wouldn't want you to waste away, would we? Not that your family seem to be particularly worried ...' He pulls out her phone again, dangling it in front of her, teasing her with its presence. 'Mummy dearest called, no message, mustn't be too worried about you then. Ah, and a text from darling hubby in reply to yours, *love you always* ... At least someone's thinking about you.'

Bella drops her chin to her chest, her eyes brimming. What she wouldn't do to be able to snatch her phone from his hand, the tape around her feeling more constricting than ever. All she wants is to get out of here. Get back to her family. How stupid she was to think she could persuade him to let her go. To think she can come up with an easy way to get out of here without help. It clearly isn't going to happen anytime soon.

Who would be lucky enough to escape this situation twice?

Five weeks earlier

It had been a busy few days. Freddy and Paige had both taken part in consecutive school trips and Freddy's drum exam, just a few weeks away now, meant he'd had to spend as much time practising as he could, both at the studios and at home, Bella often feeling grateful the neighbours weren't too near. She'd barely had time to think any more about the Facebook friend request that had disappeared and her subsequent conversation with her sister. Shortly after speaking to Rosie, she'd called the Victim Contact Scheme, the kind lady she spoke to assuring her that any online presence Lawrence Knox was allowed to have was being monitored very closely. Bella wasn't too sure. Even to her, it seemed pretty easy to create a Facebook account and then delete it, any evidence of its existence floating somewhere in cyberspace. If she *hadn't* been seeing things in the café and it really was Lawrence who had tried to contact her, all she could do was hope he'd made a silly mistake and that he wouldn't try anything like it again.

She climbed out of the car and headed into the hospice, waving to the receptionist as she headed towards the office. Work had also been busy the past few days, the event calendar, in the run-up to the summer holidays, full to bursting point. July and August were usually the best months for fundraising, the town centre busy with shoppers, not to mention all the outdoor markets and activity days going on in the surrounding areas. This past week alone, she'd organised a supermarket bag-pack, begun to collect toys and gifts for a summer tombola and started to coordinate a sponsored walk of a nearby park. She was glad to have three days off coming up, even if it meant listening to Freddy's endless drumming and Paige's constant whining that she had nothing to wear for her upcoming holiday to France. The girl still had over a month to shop.

Trish was sitting at her desk, always in early, an excuse to get away from the husband she seemed to enjoy pretending she hated. 'Morning, Bells.'

Bella winced at the way her colleague insisted on shortening everyone's name in her own way. 'Good morning. Here's hoping for a quiet one today.' She felt her eyes widen as she approached her own desk. 'Oh, are these for me?'

A large bouquet of flowers took up most of the room next to her computer, expensive-looking white and orange lilies, surrounded by wispy gypsophila. The arrangement was beautiful.

Trish smiled. 'Arrived first thing. There's a card. The only time Tony sends me flowers is when he's done something wrong. Jack got something to apologise for?'

'Not as far as I'm aware.'

Sitting down at her desk, Bella pulled a small white envelope out of the foliage. She slipped her thumb beneath the flap and prised it open, her frown increasing as she looked at the words written on the card inside:

For Bella, with love xxx

She smiled. It had been years since Jack sent her flowers, the two of them having little time for romantic gestures these days. Did her husband think she needed some reassurance after her recent worries about Lawrence? After her anxiety about telling the kids what had happened to her? She'd forgotten how thoughtful he could be at times. Bella struggled to imagine how she might have got through some of her darkest days without Jack by her side.

She pulled her phone out of her bag, aware that Trish was still watching her from across the room. Turning in her seat, she faced the wall as she clicked on Jack's name, attempting to keep their conversation as private as she could.

Jack answered straight away. 'Hey, missing me already?'

'I just wanted to hear your voice, tell you what a lovely husband you are …'

'Well, I didn't need you to tell me that. I'll have you know, I'm fully confident in my ability to carry out my husbandly duties.'

There was a dull thud at the other end of the line, Bella picturing Jack shutting his office door.

'And so you should be. I presume these gorgeous flowers are from you …' The line went quiet, Bella wondering for a few seconds if she'd lost her signal as sometimes happened in the depths of the building she worked in. 'Jack?'

'Is this where I say you're welcome and pretend I know exactly which flowers you're talking about so I can take the credit?'

Bella sat up straight. 'What do you mean?'

'I didn't send you any flowers, Bell. Did they come to the house?'

'No, they were waiting for me on my desk at work. You didn't send them?'

The line crackled. 'Again, I'd love to say yes. And now, of course, I feel immensely guilty for not having thought to buy you something nice with all the worry you've had over the past week or so, but, sorry … Obviously, my husband skills aren't as top-notch as I thought they were. Could they be from Rosie, maybe? Or your mum?'

'No. At least, I don't think so …'

'How about someone you've worked with? Or the relative of a hospice patient?'

Bella tried to think. 'I don't know. Maybe …' She had received little gifts before from visiting families. Usually chocolates or a nice box of biscuits she'd share with her colleagues.

'Was there a card?'

'Yes.'

'And?'

Bella suddenly went cold as she remembered a bunch of flowers arriving at her student halls many years before, the first of many. Lilies. White and yellow that time, as opposed to the orange in this bouquet. She dropped the little card she was still holding as if it were contaminated. 'I'll show it to you later.' Despite the message that was written on it being so generic, she couldn't bring herself to read it out loud over the phone, not with Trish earwigging. Not now she knew the bouquet hadn't come from her husband.

'Maybe my wife has a secret admirer.' Jack's voice was sing-songy before the line went quiet. 'Shit, Bell, that was a really stupid thing to say, sorry. You don't think ...?'

Bella felt the hairs on the back of her neck stand up. Was it just a coincidence? Her mind dragging up memories of the past while she was feeling so sensitive? 'I don't know.'

'Surely he wouldn't be stupid enough?'

'He was stupid enough to kidnap me in the first place, wasn't he? And then possibly send me a Facebook friend request just days after he got out of prison? Even if you and my sister did think I made a *mistake*.' Jack had been quick to agree with Rosie after Bella had told him about the notification she'd received. She glanced around the room, Trish seeming to be furiously typing, as if to make it clear she wasn't listening. Even if she was. 'I've got to go, Jack. I'll see you later.'

She ended the call before Jack could reassure her further. She had work to do, but, first, she had to get rid of these blasted flowers and text her children to make sure they were safe.

*

80

After clearing a backlog of emails, Bella called her sister.

'Do you fancy meeting for a coffee? During my lunch hour?'

'Er, you're not still cross with me? About suggesting you misread the Facebook thing?'

'I'm trying to put it behind me. Besides, you're my sister.'

'Okay. Well, I'd love to, but Martin's away and I'm not sure unleashing my two monsters onto the general public would really be very fair. You could come to me, if you like? As long as you're happy to drink your coffee whilst sitting at a table covered in dried-on, week-old mashed potato and bits of plasticine?'

Bella thought. Rosie's house wasn't far from the hospice, and, as much as she hadn't been entirely happy with her sister after the Facebook conversation, she needed someone to talk to. 'It's a date. I'll see you around twelve-thirty.'

Distracted, she attempted to finish her work, her thoughts constantly drifting back to the flowers and the mysteries – the milk she was sure she'd bought, the friend request – that had plagued her over the past week. Silly little things that might seem like nothing to other people but that seemed a lot bigger to her. Now, an expensive bouquet of flowers that was currently sitting in the wheelie bin at the back of her workplace, almost exactly the same as an arrangement Lawrence had once sent her, not long after they first met. Was she so stressed by his release from prison that she was sensing danger around every corner? Reading more into everyday occurrences than she usually would? She wasn't sure.

Eventually, she shut down her computer and grabbed her jacket from the back of the chair, calling out to Trish that she'd be back after lunch. The journey to her sister's house passed quickly, Bella barely registering her surroundings, driving automatically while her thoughts raced around her head.

Rosie was waiting for her on the doorstep, her house a modest middle terrace in the centre of the small village of Latchford. One of the twins was propped against her hip, the other hiding behind her legs. 'Hey, you sounded kind of upset on the phone. Everything okay? You haven't had more problems from Facebook, have you?'

Bella shook her head, following her sister into the house. She circled around a pile of brightly coloured plastic bricks that covered the hallway floor. 'Not as such, no. I just need someone to talk to.'

'Has something happened?'

'Let's go and sit down. I'm dying for a brew.'

They went into the kitchen, Rosie popping her daughter onto the floor before filling the kettle. She gently ushered the children into the hall. 'Go and play with your bricks, you two, while Auntie Bella and I have a grown-up chat. Stay where I can see you.' She grimaced at Bella. 'Otherwise, all hell could break loose.'

Bella smiled. She adored her nephew and niece, but, today, she felt she hadn't quite got the energy to give them the attention she usually might when she visited.

Rosie scrabbled around in the sink, rinsing out two mugs, one with a large chip on the rim. 'So, what's going on?'

Bella took a breath. Was she being paranoid, dashing to her sister's on a workday to talk about something that might seem completely mundane? Surely, receiving the gift of a lovely bouquet was something most people would be happy about? Then again, most people hadn't been through what she had. Hadn't lived the life she'd lived. 'Someone sent me a bouquet of flowers. To work. They were waiting for me on my desk when I got there this morning.'

Rosie pursed her lips. 'Jack?'

'No. He was the first person I called, and he swears he didn't send them.'

'Oh. The kids?'

Bella gave her sister a look.

'No, I guess that wouldn't be in the realms of possibility … Was there a card?'

'Yep.' Bella rooted around in her bag. She handed the small card to her sister.

Rosie read the message as she poured hot water into the mugs with her other hand. 'Well, it doesn't tell us very much, does it?' She pulled a carton of milk from the fridge. 'Could they be from a work colleague? Or a client?'

'That's what Jack said, but would they sign *with love*? And why wouldn't they just put their name?'

'I don't know. An oversight?' Rosie shook her head. 'I can see why this has bothered you though. It does seem a bit strange.'

'It does.'

Rosie stopped pouring the milk for a second, looking directly at Bella. 'Surely it can't be him, can it? After all this time?'

'I don't know!' Bella suddenly felt like crying. She glanced at the twins, playing in the hallway, aware she needed to lower her voice and keep herself calm. She'd have hated for the children to see her upset. 'But what I do know is that this bouquet, the lilies, is very similar to one he sent me years ago. The first one. Does that seem like a coincidence to you?'

Rosie put the mugs of coffee on the table and sat down. She stared at the card, still in her hand, as if she were expecting the message to tell her something more if she looked at it more closely. 'I don't know. I mean, does *love* mean *actual* love? It is something we say all the time, isn't it? In birthday cards and stuff? Without really thinking about it …'

'But we also say it when we *actually* love someone, don't we? And Lawrence thinks he loves me. Or at least, he did. This is scary, Rosie.'

'I know. Maybe someone has heard what's going on, with Lawrence being out of prison, and they want to reassure you?'

Bella shook her head. 'I can't think of anyone who would do that, apart from my immediate family. It's not a big enough story to have been all over the TV or the newspapers. And Mum never, ever, sends anything without calling to tell us it's on the way. You know how she doesn't trust the system.'

'I suppose …'

'There just seem to be too many weird things happening lately.'

'Like what? The friend request?'

'And, before that, the milk I was sure I'd added to the shopping delivery suddenly wasn't in the fridge.'

'What do you mean?'

'I went to get some out the next day, for Paige's breakfast, and it had gone.'

Rosie raised an eyebrow. 'That happens in our house all the time. Usually, Martin has drunk it and then he replaces it because he knows I'll go ballistic when there's none left for the twins' porridge.'

'Yes, but Jack swears he didn't drink it.'

'Then the kids …'

'Freddy said he hadn't either.'

Rosie shrugged. 'Then you must have forgotten to buy it.'

'But I was so sure … I'm usually so careful when I'm doing the shopping.'

Rosie looked at her. 'You left your purse in the car, didn't you, when we met for coffee? And you said yourself you haven't been sleeping well lately.'

'But—'

'Bell, I can see where you're going with this, but I really can't see Lawrence Knox breaking into your house and drinking your milk without you or Jack noticing, can you?'

Bella felt her cheeks flush. 'I know how ridiculous it sounds.'

'Think about it.'

'I know, I know.' Bella sighed. 'Do you think I should call the Victim Contact Scheme again? I already spoke to them about the Facebook thing, but perhaps I should mention the flowers? Ask them to look into it?'

Rosie put the card down on the table, taking a sip of her coffee. 'I'm not sure you should, to be honest. Not without concrete evidence. I mean, if the card had Lawrence's name on it, if you knew it was definitely him who'd sent the bouquet, then I'd say yes, but from what you've shown me, it really could have been anyone who sent it. They could simply have forgotten to add their name. And it's not as if the card contains a threatening message or anything.'

'I guess not.' Bella wrapped her hands around her own mug, feeling chilled despite the warm summer weather outside. 'I could end up looking like an idiot, couldn't I? Talking about flowers and missing milk. Not to mention the fact that they might stop taking me seriously if I pester them over what seem like silly things, with no proof.'

Rosie smiled. 'It's completely understandable that you're jittery. I'm sure anyone would be the same in your shoes.'

Bella was only half listening. 'I've just had a thought …'

'You have?'

'Pass me that card. The florist's name and number are on it, with the logo at the top. They might be able to tell me who ordered the flowers. Why the hell didn't I think of that before?'

Rosie frowned. 'Do you think they'd give out that sort of information? Could be a stab in the dark …'

'Worth a try though, don't you think?' Bella pulled her phone out of her bag, typing in the number on the card before holding it to her ear. As she waited for the line to connect, she examined the florist's details, the shop apparently based on the far edge of Warrington. If it did turn out to be Lawrence who'd sent the bouquet, she would definitely be able to complain he'd broken his conditions, that was for sure.

'Bloomin' Wonderful. Lizzie speaking. How can I help?'

'Oh, hello … I, er, I was hoping I could make an enquiry about a bouquet I received from you this morning?'

'Was there something wrong?'

'Oh, no, not at all. The flowers are beautiful.' Bella felt a twinge of guilt at having dumped them in the bin. She imagined the bouquet must have cost upwards of fifty or sixty pounds. 'It's just that I'm not sure who sent them, and I'd like to know so I can say thank you. If that's all right?'

'Oh, we usually include a message card. Was it missing?'

'No.' Bella watched Cameron bring a red plastic brick into the kitchen and give it to his mother, closely followed by Katie who wanted to join in the game. 'There was a card, with a message, but no name on it.'

'Okay …' There was a rustling at the other end of the line, as if the florist was perhaps working on another arrangement while she talked. 'Then I'm afraid I can't really help you. We only tend to take the recipient's details, rather than the sender's. We'd only have the payment details from them, which, of course, I can't share with you, and they might even have paid cash. The message on the card is usually exactly what the sender has asked us to write. If there's no name, then that must be what they wanted for whatever reason. Or they just forgot to say it. Sorry.'

'I see.' Bella rolled her eyes at Rosie, indicating her frustration. 'Is there any chance you'd be able to remember the sender coming into the shop?'

A heavy sigh. 'I'm really not sure, sorry. We're quite a big shop and we're very busy all year round. We get a lot of customers through the doors each day. Plus, it's not always me on shift. I have two assistants.'

'Please, if you could try? It's really important. The bouquet was for Bella Anderson, at St Paul's Hospice. They were sent to my workplace.'

The woman on the line hesitated for a few seconds before speaking again. 'Ah, as a matter of fact, I think that was me who took that order. It was just a couple of days ago.'

Bella closed her eyes, picturing in her mind, for just a few painful seconds, Lawrence Knox walking into a flower shop to arrange to send her a gift. Would he have tried to disguise himself? Perhaps pulled a baseball cap low over his face like he used to when he was following her? Maybe worn a wig, even in the heat of the summer? She tried to focus. 'Could you please tell me if you remember the man who made the order? Tell me what he looked like?'

The florist seemed to hesitate, the line buzzing slightly. 'I'm afraid I can't. It was a telephone order, you see, so I didn't actually meet the sender in real life.'

Bella felt her heart sink. 'Thanks for your time, anyway. Could I leave you my number in case you happen to remember anything else about the order? Anything at all?'

'I have it here on the caller display.'

'Great.'

'There is one thing I can tell you before you go though ...'

'Yes?'

There was more rustling in the background, as if the florist was perhaps beginning another task, readying herself to end the call. 'It definitely wasn't a man who sent you those flowers. It was a woman.'

Bella now

She surprised him, the last time. After Lawrence agreed to free her from the tape, it was obvious to Bella that he had naively been expecting her to jump into his arms. To admit that she loved him, that she had all along. That she'd been wrong to reject him after they'd been out together so few times and that she was willing now to get to know him. To give him a chance to prove to her what a loving partner he could be if only she'd let him. In reality, the scenario that took place on the day of her escape couldn't have been more different to what Lawrence Knox was hoping.

Bella pictures herself now, the images flitting through her mind's eye, as if she were watching a Friday night movie with Freddy and Paige. As Lawrence had removed her gag, pulled the last remnants of silver tape from her wrists, like a character in an action scene, Bella had made her move, the strength she still had in her muscles, after five days of little food and barely any movement, surprising even her. It was a hair grip that saved her. Something so simple, yet so useful, as it turned out. Her hair was longer then, so she'd used it the night she was abducted, taming a stray curl before she went to bed, forgetting the grip was there until a few days into her confinement. Lawrence didn't think to check her, sleepy and wearing only pyjamas, for any potential weapons. As she'd grabbed the grip from her head and aimed it at the delicate skin of his face, his eyes had widened almost comically. He really hadn't seen the attack coming.

As he'd clawed at his face, Bella ran up the stairs as fast as she could, praying her rubbery legs would hold beneath her, ignoring how the old wooden and splintered steps tore at the soles of her bare feet. Lawrence had left the door open, and Bella had fled through the kitchen and across the garden, remembering vividly now the shock she'd felt as she emerged into a late-May storm, the afternoon sky dark with thunderous clouds, flashes of lightning seeming so close they could singe her flesh. She'd put her arms over her head to protect herself. Within a few minutes, she was at a neighbour's house, begging the old lady who lived there then, her eyes wide, to call the police immediately as Lawrence's cries of frustration, echoing along the empty lane in between claps of thunder, reverberated in her ears.

She shifts her position on the chair, remembering the moment the police told her they'd found Lawrence Knox, that he'd been taken into custody. There were some moments of her confine-ment, the worst experience of her life, that she could barely bring herself to think about, feelings of humiliation, of absolute terror, blocked out in order to save what was left of her sanity. Other moments, like the one in which the kind female police officer told her Lawrence had been found hiding in a nearby abandoned farmhouse, she kept with her. It was the only way she had to remind herself that he was gone from her life. That she was safe now.

So much for that.

She swallows heavily as she feels a scream building inside her again. The thought of, once again, having to spend the whole night ahead in this claustrophobic, low-roofed room, the one that contains so many awful memories for her, fills her with horror. She's been here for hours already. Why has no one missed her? She was just a girl last time, she thinks, away from her friends at uni, her family on holiday, thinking she was probably out having fun, attempting to get back to normal after her stalking experience, when they tried, and failed, to reach her on the landline, oblivious to the real danger she was in.

This time, though, it's different, surely? She's an adult, an active member of her community. On the PTA, an important cog in the wheel of her workplace's fundraising team, supporting the kids in all their activities. She has a life. She is *visible*.

She shakes her head, remembering how she was recently signed off work by the doctor. Her parents are miles away, as are her children, her sister barely talking to her, after Bella hasn't been as nice to her as she could have been over the past few weeks. Of course she's not been missed, not in these few hours that have seemed so long to her but have likely passed in a flash for everyone in the outside world.

She tries to move again, shifting her behind on the seat of the chair, a sharp pain startling her as it passes through her pelvis. Her bladder is full to bursting, a subsequent deep ache telling her she will have to empty it soon, whether she wants to or not.

Taking a shallow breath, she attempts to shout, the damp scarf filling her mouth, the air that enters her nose musty, heavy with unseen grit. The noise that comes out is muffled, inaudible, even to her. 'Hey ...'

She stops and listens, wondering if she's imagining the muted laughter she thinks she can hear beyond the upstairs door. As she looks at the steps in front of her, she remembers again how she and Rosie used to come down here after school, the two of them always close, the best of friends, her sister only a year or so younger. For a few hours, they'd pretend they were practising their music, their mother no doubt listening upstairs, hoping her daughters' practice time, the money she'd invested in violins for them, would pay off one day. What was actually happening in the basement was more like Bella practising while her sister acted the fool, dancing around and talking about the latest boy who'd caught her attention at school. Bella smiles as she remembers how much Rosie used to make her laugh. The two of them had a lot of fun together growing up.

In a far corner, behind a heaped blue tarpaulin, she can just make out the neck of one of Paige's old guitars, the strings at the top broken, sticking out from the wood like spindly branches, Jack no doubt planning to take it to the tip one day with some of the other rubbish. She feels a sudden sense of pride at her children's accomplishments. Freddy and Paige are both talented musicians, the two of them perhaps now achieving what she and Rosie had failed to, fulfilling their grandmother's dreams of having a musical family. Freddy in particular has shown almost extraordinary prowess in his drumming. His teacher had just stopped short of calling him her star pupil at the last parents' evening she and Jack attended. Paige prefers a gentler sound, the clarinet and guitar her favoured instruments. She's also shown a talent for songwriting, and Bella has often been brought to tears when she's heard her daughter working on one of her own pieces.

She gasps, her abdomen and pelvis suddenly spasming. After the two huge babies she gave birth to – Paige just over nine pounds and Freddy almost ten – none of the organs below her waist function quite as well as they used to. She needs to empty her bladder. Now. She exhales in relief as the door at the top of the stairs opens.

He skips down before pulling the gag from her face.

'I've been trying to shout you …'

'Sorry. I was too busy sending another text to darling hubby. This is so much fun.' He grimaces. 'Besides, you know, you might not have noticed, Bella, but the gag kind of warps your speech. It makes you sound even more whiny than you normally are.'

'Funny.' So much for his supposed love of her. Bella doesn't understand how he can have told her he adores her so many times yet still be so cruel. It doesn't make any sense. She swallows, feeling sweat form on her upper lip. She's so uncomfortable. 'I need to pee. I've been here for hours. Did it not occur to you I might have to use the loo at some point?'

'Of course it did. I'm not a complete monster. Beautiful as you are, you're obviously not a youngster anymore, Bella. A woman of your age, with two kids, has needs; I know that. Which is why you'll be glad to know that the best facilities you could ask for are already here, right where you need them …'

Going to a far corner, he lifts up a plastic sheet. Beneath it is the chemical toilet Jack bought from Argos once, when he intended to take Freddy camping. A plastic throne, the seat down ready for her, unlike the ones in the house, which Freddy always leaves up.

Bella grimaces. 'You're not actually expecting me to use that thing?'

'You don't like it? Oh, Bella.' He pouts. 'I am disappointed.'

She sighs. At least it's an upgrade on last time. During her first abduction, she was given an empty bucket and a bag of sand. She can still remember her feelings of utter humiliation, each time Lawrence unstrapped her, not even turning his back as she hovered unsteadily over the metal rim, as though he was taking pleasure in her embarrassment. She remembers how she thought, numerous times, of attacking him while her arms and legs were free. Perhaps throwing her own piss, or the sand, in his face to blind him while she escaped. But he'd put paid to that plan by holding a knife to her throat each time she relieved herself. 'I suppose I don't have much choice …'

'Aw, come on, Bella, where's your sense of adventure? You seem like the glamping type to me. Imagine you're staying in an exclusive yurt, with a hot tub just outside your door. I've even put a plastic bag in the bottom, easier to clean …'

'Can't I just use the downstairs loo? It's only a few steps from the kitchen. You can watch me the whole time.'

He shakes his head. 'I'm afraid not. You must think I'm soft in the head, if you think I'm going to let you anywhere near the rest of the house. Of course—' he lets the plastic sheet drop into place '—I can always swap it for a bucket. Maybe you'll feel more at home with that. It'll be just like old times.'

'No, no. I'll use it. I will.' If she doesn't go soon, the alternative is that she'll end up soaked.

'That's the spirit. You've got to be positive, Bella, count your blessings.'

Bella squeezes her legs together as he crosses the dusty floor towards her. She can see how much he is relishing being in control, his movements slow and deliberate, as if he's fully aware of her desperation and is taking great delight in making sure she has to wait as long as possible. 'Hurry up, please.'

'All right, all right. Patience is a virtue, didn't you know? Always in such a hurry, Bella. Dashing around ...'

Reaching to his waist, he pulls out the knife he held to her throat earlier, the blade catching the yellow light of the bulb above their heads. 'Now, I'm sure I don't have to tell you not to try any funny business while you're ...' he chuckles '... doing your business. We wouldn't want you to have a nasty accident now, would we? All that blood would leave me with far too much cleaning up to do.'

'Please don't hurt me.'

'Of course I won't. Not if you're a very good girl and do exactly as I say.'

Bella holds her breath, trying to contain her bladder for just a little longer while he brutally rips the tape from her body.

Four and a half weeks earlier

Bella was finally beginning to feel a little more relaxed. In the few days after the arrival of the flowers on her desk, her anxiety had been high, a little voice in the back of her mind constantly trying to convince her that Lawrence was definitely back in her life, that he was going to hurt her and her family, despite what the florist had told her on the phone about it having been a woman who ordered the bouquet to be sent to her office. After all, wouldn't Lawrence have made all sorts of connections while he was in prison? Wouldn't it have been easy for him to recruit someone – a girlfriend, a friend, a fellow ex-con – to have done his dirty work for him, thus giving him the perfect alibi?

Jack had had other ideas. 'I really think it's likely, Bell, that it was simply a relative or visitor who wanted to say thank you for all your hard work. It's easy enough for someone who's busy to just forget to give their name.'

Bella thought about it, remembering how the florist had said something similar. She'd received bouquets on the odd occasion before, the card usually addressed to the office as a whole, rather than just one person. Yet the fact that the arrangement had been so similar to the one Lawrence had once sent, not to mention the card having been signed *with love*, had really spooked her. Was she being oversensitive? 'I suppose you could be right. Don't you think it's a bit strange though, after the Facebook thing?'

Jack had shrugged. 'Maybe, but if it had happened at any other time, we probably wouldn't have thought twice about it. Would have forgotten about it within minutes. Our sense of paranoia is at its peak at the minute, don't forget.'

Bella nodded. She *was* feeling paranoid. She couldn't help it. In the end, she'd taken Rosie's advice and decided not to telephone the Victim Contact Scheme unless something else happened, something she could actually prove had been instigated by Lawrence himself. She didn't want to end up sounding hysterical if it was all nothing to worry about and nothing else happened.

And, in the days that followed, nothing had.

Now, as she waved goodbye to Trish as she left the office, her step was a little lighter than it had been. Even if it had been Lawrence who'd organised the flowers, she thought, which even she was beginning to doubt, perhaps he now regretted it. Had realised that, if he didn't want to go back to jail, he needed to leave her well alone, get on with his own life while he had the chance. She was going to try her best not to worry about it anymore. To forget about the mysterious bouquet, and Facebook, and the missing milk. She needed to move on.

On the drive home, she switched her mobile to hands-free and called her mother's landline.

'Hello …'

'Hi, Mum. Just calling to double-check when you're coming to pick Freddy up? I know it's still a few weeks off but I'm going to try and organise my diary when I get home. Paige is going away with her friend and they both have loads of activities booked in later on in the summer break, so I want to make sure I have everything written down.'

'Of course. It's the Friday, the first week of the holidays. Dad wants to set off early so we should be at yours first thing, if that's okay with you? You know how he worries about the traffic.'

'That's fine.' Bella stopped talking for a few seconds as she nego-tiated the constantly busy Bridgefoot roundabout. Her journey home always took longer than she anticipated. She could under-stand her dad's worries about getting stuck in a jam. 'I'll pack him some snacks for the journey.'

'Oh, no need. We'll probably make a stop on the way. Just make sure he brings a raincoat. I remember him having to borrow your father's last year and it was at least three sizes too big.'

'Sorry ...'

'Anyway, I'll speak to you before then. I'll remind you.' Her mother seems to hesitate. 'How are you doing, darling? Are you okay?'

Bella thought about her visit to her sister's house a few days before. Her anxiety about the bouquet she'd been sent. Telling Rosie about the missing milk. Of course, her sister was bound to tell their mum about any concerns she had for Bella's welfare. She fought a flicker of irritation. Did Rosie think she was being melo-dramatic? Exaggerating her concerns? 'I'm fine, Mum, honestly.'

'Rosie telephoned and said she was a bit worried about you ...'

'Rosie needs to concentrate on her own family.'

Her mum was quiet for a second or two. 'She wants to make sure you're all right, Bella. You know that.'

Bella sighed. She didn't really want to have this conversation now. 'I know, Mum, but really, everything's fine. Nothing for you and Dad to stress about. Let's forget it, shall we?' As she herself was trying to do.

'Well, as long as you-know-who is behaving himself.'

Bella couldn't help but smile. Even all these years later, her mother still couldn't refer to Lawrence by his name. After the abduction, she'd done everything she could to support Bella, getting her daughter appointments with the best therapist she could afford, sitting with her in the middle of the night when Bella's frequent nightmares woke her. Every so often, it struck Bella how much the whole experience must have affected her mum as well. How she must have worried. Must worry still. 'I think so, Mum. Everything's quiet at the minute. You just concentrate on having a good summer. Freddy is looking forward to seeing you.'

'Oh, and us him. Tell him Grandpa has got his fishing gear sorted already.'

'I will. Speak soon, Mum.'

'Bye, love.'

She pulled the car into the driveway, trying to put Lawrence Knox to the back of her mind, to look forward to the summer ahead. Perhaps she and Jack would be able to have a weekend away somewhere by themselves, once the kids had left for their respective destinations. She made a mental note to talk to him when he got back from the business trip he'd gone to the day before. Even though he'd only been away one night this time, for a staff training event, she'd missed him desperately.

She frowned at the car parked directly in front of their house, wondering if someone nearby had a visitor. Jack would need the spot when he came home. As she approached the front door, it opened, Paige standing in the hallway, her eyes wide.

'Thank God you're home. I was just going to call you. You need to come and speak to this man. I can't get rid of him, Mum ...'

'What?' Bella's heart lurched, a sudden image invading her mind of Lawrence, older, prison-ravaged, but still him, inside her house. 'Jesus, Paige, how many times have I told you not to open the door to anyone when I'm not here? Where's your brother?'

'Upstairs.'

Bella pulled her mobile from her bag as she hurried inside, ready to call 999 if she needed to. So much for trying to think positively, not to mention Jack thinking that Freddy and Paige had taken their warnings to be careful seriously. In one ear and out the other, it seemed. She braced herself as she entered the living room.

A man she'd never seen before turned and smiled at her. Handsome and well-dressed, he looked to be in his mid-twenties, his hair gelled back, possibly to hide a potential bald spot. Bella had no idea who he was, but there was one thing she did know: he wasn't Lawrence Knox.

'Mrs Anderson?' He held out a hand. 'Great to meet you. I'm Luke Rushfield. Rushfield Estate Agents?'

Bella kept her own hands by her sides. Despite seeing immediately that the man in her house now wasn't the same man who'd abducted her and strapped her to a chair almost two decades before, her hackles had still risen, her fight-or-flight response heightened. She never trusted anyone until she got to know them. She turned to her daughter behind her. 'Paige, go upstairs.'

'But …'

'Just go.' As she spoke, she noticed a cardboard box sitting on the sideboard, a large white address label above a black-and-white picture of a kettle. Bella presumed it had been delivered while she was at work, one of the kids having brought it in. She couldn't even remember ordering it. She shook her head, turning her attention back to the man. 'I'm sorry. Estate agent, did you say?'

He nodded as he gazed around the room, seeming to be assessing the fixtures and fittings. 'Yep, I must say it's a great place you have here. Love the original features.'

'And you're here because …?'

He focused his attention on Bella. 'Sorry, er, you called us? A few days ago? About coming to do a valuation on the house?'

Bella shook her head, images of unwanted flowers and friend requests and missing milk swirling around her mind again. 'No, I don't think so. There must be some mistake …'

'No, no mistake.' Luke Rushfield looked at the phone in his hand. 'I have all my appointments noted down and you're definitely here. Wednesday, five o'clock.' He looked up at her, eyebrows raised. 'Mrs Bella Anderson. That *is* you, isn't it?'

Bella felt colour rise in her cheeks. This man must have thought she was completely crazy, to be wondering why he was here in her house, after she'd apparently made an appointment with him.

She shook her head. 'No … I mean, yes, I am Bella Anderson, but I didn't make any appointment …'

'You didn't?'

'No. Why would I? I don't even want to sell my house. Why would I want it valued?'

'Maybe *Mr* Anderson …?'

'Believe me, I would know if my husband was interested in selling our house. It doesn't even actually belong to him. It's technically mine, but anyway, Mr Rushfield, that's not the point. The point is, my husband and I don't have secrets from each other, and we most certainly don't go around enquiring about the value of our biggest asset behind the other's back.'

'No, no, of course not.' It was Luke's turn to flush. 'But you did ring the office and make the appointment, Mrs Anderson. My staff are highly efficient. There's no way they would make a mistake with someone's name or address.'

Bella immediately thought of what she thought she'd seen on Facebook, when she was in the garden centre. Exactly that, according to her sister and Jack. A mistake. 'And you know for a fact that it was me, do you? Did you speak to me yourself? Take the call personally? Because I can tell you now that I made no such request, Mr Rushfield.'

'Er …' Luke Rushfield looked at his phone again, apparently checking his appointments.

'Well?'

'Well, I can see now that the appointment was actually made online, via our website booking system. There was no phone call …'

Bella folded her arms. 'Well, there you go then. In that case, it could have been anybody. Maybe you need to improve your system.' She gestured towards the door. 'Now, if you'd kindly follow me, I'd like you to leave my house.'

She was aware she was being rude, a large part of her not knowing how else to treat this unwanted visitor. For years after the abduction, Bella had barely known how to interact with other human beings. While her fellow students behaved in exactly the way students were expected to – getting drunk, turning up to lectures with hangovers – her own social life had been practically non-existent. It was only when she met Jack that she'd learnt how to talk again, how to listen. At least with him. Still, there were times, even now, when the introvert Lawrence Knox had turned her into, the antisocial Bella, made an appearance again.

Luke Rushfield looked at her for a few seconds before shrugging. 'Okay, it's your house. But you should know that I did put off other prospective clients so I could be here today, Mrs Anderson. It's a highly marketable property you have here. You could make a lot of money ...'

'I'll bear that in mind.'

As he passed her, he held out a card. 'Please feel free to contact me if you change your mind.'

Bella snatched the card from him and dropped it onto the hall table before pulling open the front door. 'Goodbye, Mr Rushfield.'

She let out a long breath as she closed the door behind him, making sure to turn the key and test the handle three times before also activating the house alarm. They didn't usually bother until they turned in for the night.

Bella stood in the hall for a few seconds, rubbing the palms of her hands against each other. Even with all the security measures, she didn't quite feel safe.

*

She was sitting at the kitchen table with a large glass of wine when Jack got home.

He raised an eyebrow. 'Drinking on a school night?'

She took a gulp. 'I think we're lucky I'm not drinking every night the way things are going.'

Jack dropped his bags onto the floor and pulled out a chair. His suit was rumpled from the long drive, his tie hanging loose from his collar. He kept his eyes on her as he sat. 'Has something happened? Where are the kids?'

'They're fine. Freddy is already asleep and Paige is FaceTiming Louise.'

'Then what?'

Bella sighed. Not for the first time, she wished she could be the kind of wife who greeted her husband at the door with a wide smile and a warm embrace. Poured him a drink and placed a hot meal in front of him, all the while asking about his day. Instead, her husband was having to tiptoe around her. Walk on eggshells, in case something else had happened to upset her. No wonder he looked tired. 'When I got in from work today, there was someone here, in the house. Paige had let him in.'

Jack paled. 'Not …?'

She shook her head quickly. 'Not Lawrence, no. That's what I thought too, at first. But, no, it was an estate agent. From Rushfield's? He said I'd made an appointment to have the house valued.'

'And did you?'

'Of course I didn't. Don't you think I'd have told you if I'd thought about selling?'

Jack shrugged. 'I guess you could have just been interested. In the value of the place, I mean. You have to admit there's been more than one occasion over the years when you've had a sudden urge to start googling properties in some far-off country in the middle of the night and enthusing about them the next morning when I'm still half asleep.'

Bella felt a surge of frustration. 'Jack, I didn't make any appointment. I love this house. It belonged to my parents and my grandparents before that. It's part of the family, where Rosie and I grew up, even before we actually lived here. Yes, I might look at holiday homes every now and then, and, yes, the house is a place where I experienced a very significant trauma, but I have no intention of ever living anywhere else, despite what happened. You know that.'

'Okay …' Jack stood and rooted in the cupboard for a second wine glass. Sitting back down, he poured himself a large glug. 'So, who did make the appointment?'

'That's the thing. I have no idea. He said it was made on the website, in my name. They have an online booking system.'

Jack took a sip of wine, apparently thinking. 'Maybe it was someone messing about? A prank?'

'A prank?' Bella let her mouth drop open. 'Do you believe that, Jack? Really?'

He shrugged again. 'These things do happen.'

'These things? And I suppose the milk going missing and the friend request and the flowers arriving were just pranks as well, were they?'

'The milk …?' Jack stared at her. 'You mean the milk you forgot to buy? Jesus, Bell, I think you might be overthinking things a bit now, don't you?'

'Overthinking?'

'That's how it seems to me. What will it be next? Lawrence broke in and ate all the bread? Or the cheese? Used up all the loo roll or left the bath running unsupervised as always seems to happen here? These are all part of family life, Bell, *our* family life, which is busy and noisy and chaotic. You forgetting to add milk to the shopping was just an oversight, something that's bound to happen every now and then. It wasn't part of some conspiracy against you.'

'What?'

'Look, I can understand your anxiety. The flowers, the estate agent. Of course it's a bit weird that both of those things happened within days of each other, but, admit it, Bell, neither of those incidents were in any way threatening and it's highly likely that both have a rational explanation. As I said before, if Lawrence hadn't been released, you probably wouldn't think twice about any of this.'

'Wouldn't I? So, you wouldn't be suspicious if this was happening to you? Wouldn't you want to know who it was who'd sent flowers, or who'd been impersonating you online? Well, I'm glad to know I've got my husband's full support. Thanks for that.' Bella lowered her chin, staring at her wine. She was trying not to cry.

Jack sighed. Reaching out a hand, he took Bella's fingers in his. 'I'm sorry. I don't mean to sound harsh. I just think it's possible that everything that's happened to you really is a coincidence. It just doesn't seem like it when you're worrying.'

Bella looked at him. 'Perhaps so. But, Jack, I was *abducted*. Held against my will. And the man who did that is now out of prison. I came home today to find a stranger in our house. A stranger who was here, on his own, with our children. Does that not frighten you?'

He nodded. 'I see your point. I'll have another word with the kids. Make it clear they're not to let anyone in, even speak to anyone, without checking with us first, okay?'

'And you'll not treat me like I'm hysterical if I keep calling the Victim Contact Scheme? You'll take me seriously if something else happens?'

Jack squeezed her hand. 'Of course I will.'

Bella pulled her hand away and took another gulp of her wine. She would ring the scheme again the following day, she thought. She needed to know for sure if Lawrence Knox was breaching the conditions of his release.

Jack now

Jack needs some food, his early evening walk around the town centre leaving his stomach rumbling even more than it had at lunchtime. The need to get out into the fresh air, leave those confining walls, just for a little while, had suddenly overwhelmed him, so, after pulling on a pair of jeans and a casual shirt, he'd enjoyed a meander around the green space that surrounded Warrington's ornate town hall. It isn't often he gets time to himself with two active kids and a full-time job.

Now, he glances up at the sky as he enters the old fish market square, a strong July sun sitting low above him. It's exactly the type of evening when he and Bella might decide to leave Paige in charge and go out and have a cocktail on a terrace somewhere in the cultural quarter. Not tonight though, he thinks sadly. Tonight, he's alone.

He looks around the market square, wondering what he fancies to eat: chicken, pizza? Something different? There are plenty of restaurants to choose from, he and his family having visited most of them at one time or another. Freddy and Paige usually take it in turns to pick. After a few seconds' contemplation, he heads towards a popular Italian, the smell of garlic strong as he approaches the door.

Once seated, Jack orders some pasta and a beer. He isn't a big drinker, some wine with Bella at the weekends and a couple of pints after work on the odd occasion about his limit, but, after the day's events, he thinks some indulgence tonight is justified. Hell, as Bella said to him, just a few weeks ago, it would be no surprise if the two of them had taken to drinking every night after what's happened recently. And so much more has happened since she said those words. Things he can barely bring himself to think about without anxiety prickling at his skin. Who'd have thought his beloved family would end up where it is now? The four of them, distant from each other, not just physically, but emotionally too.

He stares out of the window as he waits for his food, thinking about his wife, wondering how Bella might be feeling now, in the house, without him. They've spent Friday nights together for as long as he can remember, any work commitments, trips away for him, fundraising events for her, usually over and done with by the end of the week. Jack hates the thought of Bella being sad, tears pricking at his eyes at the idea of her loneliness, her guilt about everything that's happened lately. The past few weeks have been so difficult, so stressful, for them both. Has he done everything he can to support her? He hopes so.

He brings his phone to life, reading again the most recent text that came through from Bella's a short while ago:

Just checking in. All still okay here. Thanks so much for giving me this time to think, Jack. It really is what I needed xxx

Jack smiles at the words before scrolling through his contact list until he finds Gail and Brian's landline number.

The line rings for a little while, his mother-in-law sounding breathless as she answers. 'Hello?'

'Hi, Gail, it's Jack.'

'Oh, hi, Jack, sorry, I was in the garden. Freddy and Brian are cleaning up the barbecue. We're going to put some burgers and sausages on. Remember the ones from the local butcher Freddy always liked so much?'

'Sounds good.'

'I've promised him a piece of chocolate cake if he eats some salad as well.' Her laugh is very like Bella's. 'Everything okay there, Jack? There's nothing wrong is there?'

'No, no, everything's fine, Gail. Have you heard from Bella at all?'

'I haven't. I hope she's okay.'

'That's why I'm calling, actually, to reassure you. I had another text from her not too long ago and she seems fine. Says this alone time is just what she needed.'

'That's good. Sounds positive at least.'

'Definitely.'

'You were probably right, Jack. I'm sure she'll be back to her old self again after the weekend. Seeing things with a bit more perspective.'

'Let's hope so.' Jack's stomach rumbles as he catches a rich aroma coming from the restaurant kitchen. 'Well, I'll leave you to your barbecue. Say hi to Freddy for me.'

'Will do. Thanks for keeping me updated, Jack.'

'No problem.'

He ends the call, thinking for a few seconds before connecting to the restaurant's Wi-Fi and bringing up Google's search bar. For a while, when he and Bella first met, when she told him about what had happened to her, Jack didn't want to read any articles about his wife's abduction, the idea of hearing about her terrifying experience from any point of view but hers making him highly uncomfortable. He'd heard the story from Bella herself; he didn't need to hear it from anyone else. Didn't need to hear the sensationalised version, adjusted and exaggerated for the general public.

The first time he did read an article, it was almost by accident. He and Bella had been packing up a small number of belongings that Gail and Brian had left behind, when they came across a collection of newspaper clippings, cut from various local presses and tabloids. Even now, Jack remembers how strange it had seemed to be packing his in-laws' things and unpacking his own in the house where his wife had grown up. It was like a dream come true. From the minute he first saw the four-bedroom stone cottage, as different from where he himself had grown up as chalk was from cheese, he'd been in awe of it. How different his and Bella's childhoods were. His own mother could never have afforded anything like that on her own, and Jack had had no clue what it was like to have any kind of excess money until he was well into his twenties, when the commission started coming in at the beginning of his sales career. He'd often marvelled at Gail and Brian's generosity in giving Bella the house; a world where parents did such things was like a different planet to him.

He types his wife's name into the search bar on his phone screen, the experience as surreal now as it was when he first saw those newspaper articles all those years ago, before the kids were even born. The stories he'd read then were accompanied by black-and-white pictures of Lawrence Knox. Jack had seen that face in his mind's eye for weeks afterwards, his first sight of the man who had caused Bella such trauma, such fear, filling him with anger, a rage that he'd never experienced before. He clicks on a search result now, the images that suddenly fill the screen showing that face again, the one that has haunted both him and his wife for so many years.

He takes a swig of the beer the waitress has left on his table, the taste acrid as it always is on the first swallow. Staring at his phone, he switches from one article to another about his wife's abduction. At the time, nineteen years ago, the story made local headlines, even one of the bigger national newspapers running a feature on it. Jack had been astounded at how the reporter had got away with making Lawrence out to be some kind of victim, focusing all the article's attention on the fact that Bella had pretended she loved her abductor in order to escape. As if she were some kind of *femme fatale*.

In the past few weeks, though, Lawrence's release seems to have generated little interest, a small article tucked away in the corner of a Leeds local rag's website, the picture this time showing an aged Lawrence as he shops in his local supermarket. Jack has looked at this story before, when the Victim Contact Scheme first told Bella about the board's decision. His feelings now are much as they were when he first saw it online. Derision, disgust. Lawrence Knox looks like someone Jack would cross the road to avoid.

He sighs, putting his phone on the table and sitting back as the waitress brings his bowl of pasta. For some reason he doesn't understand, he's ordered carbonara, the rich and creamy sauce something Bella would usually enjoy, he himself more likely to opt for something spicy. Jack wonders if he's done it deliberately, some strange, subconscious way of paying tribute to the wife who might usually be with him when he eats out. 'Thank you.'

'You're welcome. Can I get you anything else?'

'Another beer would be great, thanks.'

'And, is anyone joining you this evening …?'

Jack looks up. The waitress is younger than he is, attractive, her eyes green like Bella's, hair a few shades lighter, her smile wide. He's used to women flirting with him. When he first started going away for work, he was surprised by the number of his colleagues who gave in to temptation when they weren't at home, seeming to think a casual encounter in another town or city didn't count as being unfaithful. Jack disagrees. He's never been interested in meaningless flings. He believes in commitment. 'To be honest, as a married man with two children, I'm looking forward to enjoying a meal, and the rest of my evening, in some peace and quiet for a change.'

The girl's face reddens. She's got the message.

Jack smiles as he watches her walk away. Picking up his phone again, he clears the screen. Lawrence Knox's face disappears, leaving Jack to enjoy his pasta without his wife's abductor staring at him.

Bella now

She's exhausted, her whole life suddenly seeming to catch up with her, sitting on her shoulders like a dead weight. Bella slumps in her chair, chin almost on her chest, the few salted crackers and strongly flavoured cheese he brought her a few hours ago still sitting in her stomach undigested and congealing. It's an effort not to retch.

She sniffs, looking at the room around her. She wonders if it seems somehow darker now than it was before. It must be evening, she thinks, the summer sun outside perhaps beginning to fade, readying itself to sink slowly towards the horizon that sits to the west of the house. She jumps as the bulb above her suddenly fizzes and blinks, her heart pounding as she's plunged into darkness for just a split second before it comes back on again. She hopes it holds out; the idea of sitting here alone, in the dark, is more than she can bear. How many times has Jack talked about replacing the old light fitting? Too many, she imagines. When it comes to jobs around the house – the leaky tap in the utility room, the plastering in Freddy's bedroom – she's usually inclined to nag her husband, but any jobs that have needed addressing in the basement are way down her list of priorities.

Before long, it will be nighttime, the long hours until morning seeming infinite, stretching endlessly ahead. Will she be cold, the temperature of the air around her plunging as the sun outside disappears, her thin sportswear little protection even at this time of year? She wonders if he'll think to bring her a blanket or warm sweater. Last time she was here, Lawrence had draped a thin duvet over her after she'd told him she was freezing, only her short summer pyjamas covering her that time. Her skin prickles now. That first night alone, all those years ago, had been the worst of her life, tears running down her cheeks as she'd begun to wonder if Lawrence would ever come back, or if he'd left her alone forever. She'd hated being reliant on him, feeling weak and feeble. What would have happened to her if he'd simply decided to abandon her? Had thought better of his plan to convince her to love him? Would she have survived until her parents and Rosie came home and found her? Or would that have been the end of her journey, never meeting Jack; Freddy and Paige, her future children, never existing?

She moves her feet around in her trainers, pins and needles stabbing at her toes. She's thankful that at least she has shoes on this time, a small blessing, a help if she somehow manages to escape. Her circulation is beginning to suffer now, her muscles feeling weak, legs alternating between hot tingles and a numbness that suggests they're giving up. Lips dry from being forced into an unnatural smile by the scarf. How on earth can someone who has claimed to love her put her in this position?

She thinks back to the first time she was here, Lawrence kneeling in front of her, begging, pleading, for her to at least try and see the situation from his point of view. To see that he simply didn't have any choice, that he couldn't, just *couldn't*, let her slip away, leave his life as if she'd never been in it. The knife he held constantly in one hand was an ironic reminder of the way his mind worked, the way he viewed love. They barely knew each other, she'd told him. No, *screamed* at him. Why didn't he find someone else? Find someone who was willing to love him back? That wasn't an option, he'd told her. Not. An. Option.

She remembers the first time she'd met him, her life changing forever in that moment without her even knowing it. If only she'd been able to see into the future. She could have avoided so much pain. She'd been in the crowded students' union bar in Leeds, not long after she started her degree. She was supposed to have been meeting someone else, a guy from her business class having asked her out a couple of days before, the two of them arranging to meet when they had a free night. She'd liked this guy, Pete, she remembers. He was a lot like Jack, she realises now. Confident and capable. Good-looking in that same worldly-wise sort of way. Bella was gutted when he hadn't turned up, wondering what it was that had changed his mind when he'd seemed so keen, so interested in spending time with her. Was there something about her that had put him off? That had made him think twice about meeting up with her?

When Lawrence had approached her at the bar that night, she'd been glad of the company, irritated at having been stood up, happy to be widening her friendship circle in her first awkward few weeks at uni. *Stuff Pete,* she'd thought. It was his loss. Lawrence made her smile, his tendency towards self-deprecation a refreshing change after some of the other, more arrogant boys she'd met so far. This new friend of hers was quite cute, in a nerdy-little-brother kind of way. Like a funny film sidekick. Or so she'd thought at first. When she'd agreed to meet him for another drink, perhaps something to eat, later the same week, she already knew that she'd unlikely ever be attracted to Lawrence romantically, and a large part of her presumed he felt the same way. That he'd be happy for the two of them simply to pass some spare time together. Be friends.

It was the third time they met that Bella had felt something wasn't quite right. Lawrence had turned up to their casual drink together overdressed and looking nervous, as if he were a potential groom getting ready to propose. God forbid. It was when he started calling her *beautiful Bella,* producing a velvet box with an expensive necklace inside and telling her he'd spent most of his term's grant on it, that Bella knew she had to retreat, distance herself, and quickly, from this strange boy, before his behaviour became even more intense. It was only later, after she'd been through her ordeal in the basement, Lawrence locked away and Bella struggling to settle back into uni life, that she found out Pete hadn't stood her up at all. Approaching her as she waited to go into a lecture, the guy she'd really liked once had told her Lawrence had warned him off, claiming Bella was already spoken for. Her stalker had been watching her even before they'd met in the bar.

She bites her lip now, wondering, if she'd done something different, right at the beginning, whether her life might not have gone the way it had, whether she might not be where she is now. If only she'd gone home after she thought Pete had let her down. Spurned Lawrence's company in favour of a night in front of the telly, eating chocolate and feeling sorry for herself. Would it have made any difference? Would it have encouraged him to give up on his pursuit of her, knowing she hadn't shown the slightest bit of interest in him? After eventually rejecting his advances, she'd tried so hard to ignore him, turning the other way when he began to turn up where she was: at the uni coffee shop, the pub, loitering in the corridor outside her halls of residence room.

After a week or so, the flowers began to turn up, the first bunch of lilies swiftly followed by three dozen expensive white roses. That was when Bella knew she might need some help.

Her friends had rallied round, keeping her company whenever she had to go anywhere, circling her like a pack of protective wolves, shouting in Lawrence's direction on her behalf, threatening him with the police. She suddenly feels sad that she's lost touch with most of them now, her friendships dwindling, as often happens, after she married and had children. Would her uni mates do the same for her now if they could? Come to her aid if they knew what was happening to her, protect her as they had then? She likes to think they would.

She likes to think there's someone out there who would help her. If only she could reach them.

Four weeks earlier

She'd come home from work early, feigning a headache. Though Friday was usually her day off, her manager had asked her to go in to cover for an absent colleague, but as soon as she got there, Bella had known it was a mistake to say yes. She couldn't concentrate. In the few days since she'd returned home to find a strange man in her house – not only in her house but *alone with her children* – she hadn't been able to stop thinking about what could have happened. How Paige and Freddy could have ended up as vulnerable as she herself had once been. In the end, she'd asked Irish to take on some of the excess emails, to organise the tombola prizes. She'd pay her back when she was feeling better.

The house was quiet when she got home, no mysterious cars parked on the pavement outside, no strangers hanging around the driveway. The kids were both at school, the two of them becoming impatient as the summer holidays drew close, Freddy seeming to be more anxious than he usually was as he practised for his drumming exam. Bella was glad the holidays were nearly here. The kids had both worked hard and needed a break. Not to mention that she herself needed a change from the routine of early mornings and packed lunches. Homework and music lessons. Again, she wondered if she and Jack might get away for a few days. As long as nothing else strange, nothing for her to worry about, happened in the meantime. At the minute, she had to admit, she didn't feel too hopeful it wouldn't.

The day before, she'd called at her sister's house on the way home, part of her needing an objective viewpoint, someone to tell her she wasn't being melodramatic in the way she was feeling. That she was right to have called the Victim Contact Scheme twice in the last two days.

'Oh my God ...' Rosie's mouth had fallen open when Bella had told her about Luke Rushfield. 'And Paige let him in? After everything you told her about Lawrence?'

'Yep. Jack had a stern word with her. Told her she needed to be taking the situation a bit more seriously.'

'Definitely. Jeez, someone coming to check out your house without you knowing is just plain creepy.'

'And, to add insult to injury, I received a valuation through the post this morning. Luke Rushfield must have sent it out straight away, thinking he could persuade me to sell, make him a hefty commission, even though I'd made it perfectly clear I wasn't interested.'

'And have you rung the Victim Contact Scheme?'

'Yep. A couple of times. They've assured me that Lawrence is being watched very carefully. He has to report regularly to his named contact and they have no reason to believe that he's broken his conditions or left the area at any point.'

'Let's hope they're right and this is all just some silly mix-up.'

'Do you really think that could be what it is? After everything?'

Rosie had shrugged, looking as helpless as Bella felt.

Now, she dumped her bag on the kitchen table before walking through the house to make sure everything was in order, checking the windows in all the bedrooms, pulling the shower curtain back to be sure there wasn't a stranger, or, even worse, someone she recognised, lurking in the bathroom. In the weeks after her abduction, before she decided to go back to uni, her dad had used to check every corner of the house before he went to bed, his last job of the night to knock on her bedroom door and assure her all was well. The routine had continued even after the trial, after Lawrence had been locked away, her dad knowing that his daughter couldn't sleep unless she knew the house was secure. When she eventually returned to her studies, the following year, her first step back to independence, she'd spent quite some time worrying about the fact that she no longer had anyone to do that for her. Not until she'd met Jack in her final year and eventually moved into the small flat he rented above a Leeds city centre kebab shop.

Heading back down to the kitchen, she wished Jack didn't have to go away so often for work; the training courses the company organised seemed to have become more frequent recently, and her husband was a mentor for any new recruits starting on the sales team. The night he'd been away earlier in the week, Bella had stayed up late to double- and triple-check the doors and windows, unable to resist popping her head into the kids' bedrooms numerous times before she could settle. She was glad Jack was back to working in the office now, for a little while at least.

She put the kettle on for tea, leaning against the counter as she pictured the estate agent looking around her home a few days before. After Lawrence had abducted her, after she'd managed to escape and her ordeal was over, her parents had thought about selling the house, thinking it the best way to ensure their daughter recovered from her ordeal, the best way for the whole family to move on. *We can start again, all four of us, somewhere new,* she remembered her mum saying. They'd even gone so far as having the house valued themselves; it was worth quite a bit more than they'd anticipated, even then. No doubt a fortune compared to what her grandparents had originally paid, even with the surrounding land.

But Bella had seen immediately how much the thought of letting the house go had pained her mother. Mum wasn't ready then, to abandon the home that had formed such a huge part of her family history, that she'd already been hoping she could pass down the line at some point to one of her daughters, perhaps her future grandchildren. Bella was devastated to see how much they were in danger of losing due to Lawrence Knox's actions. As much as part of her had wanted to try and forget the whole experience, move on, she couldn't bear the thought of Lawrence taking so much away, not just from her, but from all of them. She couldn't let it happen. *We'll stay,* she'd told her mum and dad. *This is our home. We'll get past this. Together.*

As she waited for the kettle to boil, she stared at the basement door, the hairs on her arms prickling. The police had found it difficult to say how long Lawrence had been hiding there, all those years ago. Now, the door was always kept locked, Bella insisting it was secured when they moved in, even more vigilant about it after the children were born, never intending to go down there again. There was no other way to access the room below the house. No way Lawrence could get in there now without her or Jack noticing. Was there?

She straightened, heading over to her bag on the table, pulling out her keys and then her phone. She scrolled through her list of contacts before clicking on her sister's name.

Rosie answered immediately. 'Hi, everything okay? Not often I see or hear from you two days in a row ...'

'Yeah. Sorry, I know I'm a pest. You must be busy.'

'It's fine, honestly. The twins are playing nicely for a change. You know I've always got time for my favourite sister.'

Bella smiled. 'Funny.' She fiddled with the bunch of keys in her other hand. 'Remember when I tried to go down to the basement that time, after my therapist suggested it would bring me closure?'

'I do. I remember how unimpressed you were with the idea. *How is spending time in the place that is the subject of my worst nightmares supposed to help me?* I think were your exact words.'

Bella had never forgotten. The very thought of stepping foot on the wooden stairs that led down from the kitchen had made sweat break out on her forehead, her heart beating so fast she'd feared it would leap out of her chest. She'd stood looking at the door for over twenty minutes, Rosie holding her hand, assuring her she'd stay with her the whole time if that was what Bella wanted. In the end, she hadn't been able to do it, too terrified to even step over the threshold. She'd never been down beneath the house once in all these years. 'I did try.'

'I know you did. Hold on …' The line went quiet for a few seconds. 'Sorry, Katie's looking for her snuggle blanket. So, why are we talking about your aborted trip to the basement now?'

Bella swallowed. Was this a really bad idea? Probably. 'I want to try and go down there now. If you'll stay with me. Be on the other end of the phone, I mean.'

'Oh, I see. Bella, are you sure? Is this really a good …?'

'I have to check, Rosie. To see for myself.'

Her sister was quiet for a second. 'You mean, see if Lawrence is down there? Bella …'

'I know, I know, it sounds ridiculous. But he was down there last time, wasn't he? For all that time, and none of us knew?'

'That doesn't mean he's down there now, Bell. You and Jack would know. Of course you would. Don't you keep the door locked all the time these days?'

'Yes, but …'

'But what?'

'You know how sneaky Lawrence can be. He got down there last time and no one noticed.'

'Yes, he did, but Mum and Dad weren't as vigilant about the door then, were they? Not before everything happened. They had no need to be. And we didn't go down there much, not as we got older and stopped bothering with those silly games we used to play. When you came back from uni, after Lawrence started pestering you, I suspect we didn't even go down there once. We spent most of our time gossiping together in one of our bedrooms.'

'And all the time, Lawrence was slipping in and out of the basement effortlessly when we weren't in the house. Feeding himself, using the loo. Remember the huge argument we had about you stealing my last sweet and sour Pot Noodle? And Mum nagging Dad about leaving the toilet seat up when we all knew it was something he never did?' Bella shivered. 'Is it any wonder I freaked out a bit when I thought the milk had gone missing?'

'Of course it's not. Not at all. But, Bella, it simply isn't possible that Lawrence Knox is hiding in your basement again. You and Jack are too vigilant. You monitor the door, the kids have been warned to keep an eye out for any danger, and the authorities have assured you Lawrence is behaving himself. You're okay.'

'I know, but …'

'Not to mention the fact that creeping around a dark basement, for the first time since you were held there, when you're on your own in the house, with no support, is hardly going to give you the peace of mind you're looking for, is it? Do you really think that will help with how jittery you're already feeling?'

'I'm not on my own. You're with me.'

'Look, Bella, I can't stop you going down into your own basement. God knows you've never shown any desire to go down there before, and I don't blame you, but if that's what you really want now, then I'm happy to stay on the phone with you … Cameron, give that back to your sister, please. Sorry, he's going through a phase of wanting everything Katie has.'

Bella looked again at the bunch of keys in her hand, the large copper-coloured one she barely ever used standing out against the smaller, silver ones. She looked at the basement door. Rosie was right. Of course she was. Surely if Lawrence was hiding down there, someone would have noticed? Would have suspected that something was amiss? As much as he'd been clever last time, hiding down there for so long, Lawrence Knox wasn't a magician. Even someone as desperate as he was had his limitations when it came to tricking people. She sighed. 'Maybe you're right.'

'Of course I am.'

Bella turned as she heard a noise outside, a clattering of wood very nearby. 'Hold on, Rosie. I just need to see what's happening outside.'

'Is something wrong?'

'I'm not sure. It's probably nothing.'

She headed through the hallway, the noise increasing as she moved further away from the kitchen. She wondered if there was utility work going on in the lane. If so, they could have warned her. She had enough going on at the minute.

She pulled open the front door, a gasp escaping her. As she stared at the man who was standing in her garden, she realised her sister was speaking on the phone she was still holding to her ear.

'Bell, what's going on?'

Bella shook her head, a large part of her wanting to cry. 'I've no idea. There's a man in my garden putting up a *For Sale* sign.'

*

'Are you okay?' Jack was slightly breathless after running from the car and into the house. 'Jeez, when I heard how hysterical you were on the phone, I thought something really bad had happened.'

Bella looked at him. 'So, you think someone trying to put our house up for sale isn't bad? What would you rather happen, Jack? For you to come home and find me tied up in the basement again?'

He sighed, putting his hands on her shoulders. 'Of course I wouldn't. I just thought, when you insisted I come home from work … Never mind. I can understand why you're upset. But are you sure this isn't just some mistake, Bell? Something you might have thought about ages ago and then forgotten, like the new kettle that arrived the other day you didn't remember ordering?'

'This isn't a *kettle*, Jack. This is our home. I don't think it's quite the same.'

'Could you have just queried something and the estate agent has misunderstood?'

Bella felt her frustration building. 'So you're saying I might have accidentally asked someone to put my own house on the market, the one I've lived in for almost my whole life, that my parents and grandparents lived in, and not remember?'

Jack eyed the bottle of brandy standing on the table.

'Oh, for goodness' sake, Jack!' She waved him away. 'I had a tiny tot in my cup of tea. I was in shock.' What she'd poured into her hot drink had barely even been a measure. Bella's mum and dad had always sworn by a tot of brandy for shock.

'All right …'

'You don't believe me?'

He shook his head. 'Of course I do. I didn't mean to imply … Look, forget it.' Jack began to pace the kitchen. 'Just tell me again, exactly what happened.'

Bella sat down, relating to him the events of the morning, how she'd been on the phone to her sister when she heard a noise outside. How she'd opened the front door to find a man in overalls erecting a tall *For Sale* sign by the front fence. She'd shouted at him, been rude in the same way she'd been to Luke Rushfield a few days before. Despite his insistence that he'd get into trouble if the sign didn't go up, she'd stopped him in his tracks. No way in hell, she'd said, was that sign going up in her garden.

'And did you ring the estate agent?'

'I did. Luke Rushfield left me his card the other day, even though I didn't want it, so I rang him directly. The first thing he said was how pleased he was that I'd changed my mind about the sale. He'd thought I would once I'd seen the valuation he sent through the post.' Bella thought back to her conversation with the estate agent. Like she had when she first met him, she'd found him overly friendly and more than a little smarmy. She hoped Jack didn't employ similar techniques when he was trying to make a sale.

Jack raised an eyebrow. 'Well, this place is worth quite a lot more now than it was when your parents gave it to you. Even I was surprised when you told me how much the agency was thinking of asking for it.'

'That's not the point, Jack. I'm not remotely interested in how much the house is worth. It's our home.'

'Of course it is. So, what else did he say?'

'That the sale had been requested by email. That he received an email from me when he got to work first thing this morning saying I was happy with the quote and wanted the house to go up for sale immediately, that I was hoping to move out as soon as possible and would be happy to come to *an arrangement* if he could guarantee me a quick sale.'

'Christ ...' Jack seemed to think for a few seconds. 'But, Bell, this can't be Lawrence. You told me yourself what the Victim Contact Scheme said the last time you rang them. That he's being monitored very closely. It's the authorities' job to make sure he's doing what he's supposed to be doing. Do you really have reason to not believe them? To think that he's manipulating you again without them knowing?'

Bella rubbed a hand across her face, struggling to think straight. 'I don't know what to think, but, if I'm honest, yes, I do think I have reason not to believe them. Don't you? *Someone* contacted Luke Rushfield on my behalf, asking him to put my house up for sale. And all I know for sure is that it wasn't me.'

She looked at her phone on the kitchen table in front of her, a thought suddenly occurring to her. Why hadn't she thought to check straight away? She picked it up, a shiver running down her spine as she accessed her email account.

'What are you doing?'

'What do you think?' She scrolled through her *sent* list. 'I should have checked my emails as soon as Luke told me the sale had been requested ...' She stopped, clicking on an email. 'Jack, it's there.'

'What is?' He sat down opposite her.

'The email. It's there. From me to Rushfield's estate agents, saying exactly what Luke told me it did. I didn't write this, Jack.'

'Bella ...'

'I'm sure I didn't!'

He held up his hands. 'It's okay, Bell, I'm not saying I don't believe you. When was it sent exactly? Can you check?'

She looked at her phone again. 'Last night. Two-thirty-nine a.m.'

Jack looked at her without speaking.

'What?'

'Look, Bell—' he pursed his lips '—like I said, I'm not saying I don't believe you, but weren't you up and about again last night? I seem to remember you getting up not long after we went to bed. And the laptop was on this morning.'

'I was just browsing.'

'And correct me if I'm wrong ...' He looked at the bottle on the table again. 'But wasn't that brandy bottle a bit fuller yesterday? I seem to remember there was at least half a litre left. Now there's barely a quarter.'

Bella felt her cheeks flush, remembering how she went through each room of the house the night before, eventually settling at the laptop and scrolling through various online shopping sites before going back to bed sometime after three. She'd only had a few hours' sleep before she had to get up again. She tried to think back. She'd had a small brandy to help her relax, but she was sure it had only been the one. She most certainly hadn't been drunk. Not like Jack was suggesting.

Jack was watching her wide-eyed. 'And if you didn't send the email, then who did? I really don't think Lawrence could have accessed your phone or laptop without you noticing, do you? Especially as you've already been told, more than once, he hasn't left his own area.'

Bella stared at her phone, thoughts tumbling around her mind as if they were in a washing machine: the obvious PIN she used,

122

her date of birth, to access all her devices, her email account just one touch of the screen or the mouse away. She'd always been so strict about her physical safety, so aware of her surroundings, always on the lookout for danger, but she hadn't been quite so vigilant, she realised now, with her phone or her laptop. She wouldn't have known where to start in keeping either of them completely secure. 'He could have done it remotely.'

Jack puffed out his cheeks. 'Well, yes, he could have, but I use a computer every day and I'd have no idea how to get into someone else's phone or laptop without all their details. Would you? Unless Lawrence is some kind of IT genius?'

'I've no idea if he is or not, but, Jack, if that isn't the case, then he *must* have been in the house. They can't be watching him every second. Leeds is an hour away, two at the most. He could easily make the journey here and back without being noticed.' She thought about what the florist had told her on the phone. How the person who'd ordered the bouquet she received was a woman, not a man as she'd thought. They'd all assumed it was some kind of mix-up. 'Either that or he sent someone else. An accomplice? That's not a totally unfeasible idea, is it?'

'But, Bell, the email was sent in *the middle of the night*. You've just told me that yourself. Not only that, but at a time when *you* were awake and at your laptop. Don't you think you'd have noticed?'

Bella shook her head, frustrated. 'That's not the point. Everyone knows you can preschedule emails. All you have to do is check the *Do Not Deliver* box and then select a date and time that you want it sent. You must have done it yourself at work. This one could have been written anytime.'

Jack leant forward, making deliberate eye contact with her, as if he were about to explain something to a child, help one of the kids work out a difficult maths problem. 'Okay, I get what you're saying, but, Bell, think about it. Even if, by some remote, far-fetched possibility Lawrence Knox, or someone he's recruited

123

to help him, managed to get into our house without us noticing, gained access to your phone, or laptop, without you seeing, and prescheduled an email to the estate agent, what on earth could he possibly hope to gain by putting our house on the market? I know he did some weird things in the past, but, even for Lawrence …'

'Remember the flat?'

'The flat?'

Bella nodded. 'The one I told you about, remember? When Lawrence was stalking me at uni, before the abduction, I had a visit from the supervisor at my halls of residence, saying how sorry she was to hear that I was moving out. Lawrence had rented a flat and put my name down as his co-tenant, and then called the halls pretending to be my dad, saying I'd found somewhere else to live and my room wouldn't be needed any longer. He'd even told the new landlord that I was expecting his baby and that we wanted to move in as soon as possible, before the non-existent child was born.' She shivered at the thought. Everything he'd done that she didn't know about at the time, as if another version of herself existed in a parallel universe. Lawrence's universe, where he was convinced the two of them were going to live happily ever after. The idea still filled her with horror.

Jack sighed. 'I'd forgotten about that, but that still doesn't mean …'

'Don't you see? If he convinces himself he can get us to sell the house, then maybe part of him thinks he can convince me to go and live with him. To leave you and the life I've got now behind. He actually still thinks he has a chance, even after everything that's happened. After going to prison.'

'I don't know, Bell …'

Bella stood up. 'You need to check the basement.'

Jack's eyes widened. He looked bewildered, tired. 'Sorry?'

'I was about to make an attempt to go down there and check it myself when the guy with the sign turned up.'

'But you never go down to the basement, Bell.'

'I know, but I was willing to try! We need to see if anything is going on down there, Jack. I don't care what anyone says about how far-fetched this all sounds, about how much a certain someone is behaving himself.'

'But, surely we'd have …'

'Yes, that's what Rosie said, but what if we didn't? What if we let our guard down, just for a moment? If you went down there to fetch something and left the door unlocked, just for five minutes, while you nipped out to the garage or the car.'

'I don't think I did …'

'But you could have, Jack! And Lawrence himself could be sitting down there right now laughing his head off at the fact he's fooled us again.'

'I'm sure that's not very likely.'

'We need to check, Jack.'

'Okay.' Jack stood up. 'Okay, I'll check. If it'll make you feel better, I'll check the basement.'

'It's not about making me feel better. It's about being safe. Keeping our family safe.'

Jack nodded. He picked up her keys from the table and, after sorting through them, slipped the copper-coloured one into the basement door lock. The door opened easily.

Following him, Bella stood at the top of the stairs and watched Jack switch on the dim light before descending. 'Be careful.'

'I'm fine.'

She rubbed away the goose bumps on her arms, trying not to picture Lawrence waiting for Jack in the shadows, perhaps leaping out at him from under the stairs, in the same way he'd once leapt out at her in the darkness of her bedroom. Sometimes, she'd find herself briefly wondering if her mum and dad were right in what they'd said all those years ago, when they suggested leaving the house, moving to another town. Yet, in her heart, Bella knew she would have struggled to do that. She loved this house and always would. She wanted her children to love it in the future. Even the basement, if that was what it took to have a normal life.

Jack moved slowly as he reached the bottom of the stairs, looking around him.

'Can you see anything?'

'Just the usual so far.'

'Have a look in the corners. The dark places that you wouldn't normally go to …' Dark places indeed, she thought. In more ways than one. Over the last few weeks, she'd had to revisit some very dark places in her own mind. She heard a rustle as Jack disappeared from her sight. 'What was that?'

'Just checking under the tarps, where the camping equipment is.'

She raised her voice. 'Any signs of anything having moved?'

'Nope … ah, shit …'

'What?' Her heart thudded in her chest. 'What is it? Are you okay?'

'Yeah, just a ton of spiderwebs, I really should have a proper tidy-up down here at some point.'

Bella exhaled. She wondered how she would have reacted if Jack had gone down to the basement and got into real trouble. Was she relieved that all seemed to be well so far? Or was a large part of her hoping that Lawrence really was in the basement, so she could prove that her fears were well-founded? That something was going on, even though no one else seemed to think so?

Jack appeared at the bottom of the stairs again, looking up at her. 'There's no one down here, Bell. Nothing out of order. No sign of anyone living here. Nothing. Just the kids' old instruments and all the other crap we never use.'

Bella pursed her lips as she watched him climb back up. 'But someone wrote that email.' She turned back to the table and picked up her phone. 'Someone pretending to be me. If Lawrence isn't hiding in the basement, that doesn't mean he hasn't been in the house. Or accessed my devices some other way.' She made a mental note to look into some better security options, to change her PIN and maybe invest in a decent protection programme that covered everything.

Jack brushed cobwebs from his hair. 'I honestly don't know, Bell,' he said again. 'All I can tell you is the basement is always locked, the house has an up-to-date alarm system that only you and I and close family know the code to, and no one else seems to think that Lawrence is up to his old tricks again …'

'So you still think it was me?'

'I hate to say it, but it just seems like the most likely answer to me.' He shrugged. 'I'm sorry. I know that sounds harsh.'

Bella sat down, part of her wishing she could get away with having another tot of brandy to calm her nerves. She knew Jack wouldn't be happy if she did. As she tried to think about what had happened this morning, how it had happened, she moved her phone around in her hands, the rhythm of it soothing her. Despite what Jack was saying, the pressure she was under, she knew she would remember something as big as this. That her mind wasn't so troubled she'd forget discussing her beloved house with someone.

She stopped moving, a sudden thought beginning to form in her mind.

Bella shook her head, trying to dismiss it, the attempt only causing her to focus on the idea more, bring it more to the forefront, in the same way someone who tries to cut out a certain food might constantly crave it. As Jack locked the basement door again, she thought about where she'd been the day before, taking a detour on her way home from work. How she'd nipped to the loo quickly, leaving her phone on the table.

She frowned.

Surely all this couldn't have anything to do with *her sister*?

Bella took a breath and stood up, smiling at Jack. 'Maybe you're right.'

She decided she'd keep any further thoughts to herself for now.

Bella now

It must be around midnight when she sees him again, his gait seeming lethargic as he descends the stairs. Removing the gag, he offers her a sip of water, unstraps her so she can use the loo again, the knife constantly hovering at her throat. Her embarrassment is less intense than the first time, Bella figuring that a person could no doubt get used to anything in a situation like this. She learnt that last time.

She looks at his face as he straps her to the chair again, determined now not to shy away from him, to meet his gaze with her own each time she sees him, no matter how exhausted, how defeated, she feels. Shadows darken the area beneath his eyes, the scar on his cheek seeming to stand out against his pale skin. 'You look tired.'

He nods, puffing out air. 'I'm exhausted, to be honest.'

'Maybe you should get some rest.'

He pulls at the reams of fresh tape to test them. 'We both should.'

'Easier said than done when I'm tied to a chair. It would be nice if I could sleep lying down tonight.'

Straightening, he seems to suddenly remember the persona he's supposed to be adopting in front of her, their most normal conversation since she's been in the basement again forgotten before it's barely started. 'I see what you're doing, beautiful Bella.'

'What? What am I doing? I'm just saying it would be nice to lie down. This chair isn't the most comfortable thing I've ever sat on.'

He waggles a finger at her, chuckling quietly. 'What you're doing is trying to get me on side. Trying to get me to feel sorry for you. I told you, Bella, your tricks won't work this time. I know them all, don't forget.'

She sighs. 'All I'm saying is, it would be nice if you treated me like a human being. One you've claimed many times to care for. To love.'

He crouches down in front of her, stretching out a hand and putting it to her cheek. His fingers gently caress her skin. 'Oh, but I do love you, Bella. You know that, don't you? I always have. Since the moment I first saw you, I've wanted to take care of you, protect you.'

She feels a tear roll down her cheek. 'Then, why? Why are you doing this to me?'

He hesitates before standing up. 'I have my reasons. You'll find them out yourself soon enough.'

'Can't we talk about it?'

He stuffs the scarf back into her mouth, testing the knot at the back before heading for the stairs. 'Enough talking, Bella. I told you, I'm tired. Oh, before I forget …' He pulls her phone from his back pocket, head bowed as he ascends. 'Better text darling hubby again to say goodnight.'

Bella begins to struggle again, trying to speak. All that comes out are muffled sounds.

'Shush, Bella, you'll be fine. Long as there's no hungry rats hanging about. Night, night, see you in the morning.'

She watches as he opens the top door, a feeling of complete panic consuming her, starting in her chest and spreading down each limb like an electric current. The last time she was held down here, the nights were the worst time, a desperate voice inside her head screaming, screaming, that she can't go through this, not again. She just can't. Why would anyone be so cruel as to make her?

Three and a half weeks earlier

Since she'd sat in the kitchen and had the thought about Rosie, Bella hadn't had a chance to speak to her sister, the weekend and the couple of days afterwards passing in a hectic flurry of music practice, lessons and exams, Freddy worrying incessantly that he wasn't ready for his drum grading and Paige sitting three end-of-year papers in two days. Add to that the shopping for the kids' upcoming holidays and the constant phone calls she was getting from her mum to remind her about what she needed to pack, and Bella wasn't surprised she was feeling a bit overwhelmed.

It was midweek before she finally had any free time, her nerves beginning to tingle as soon as she allowed thoughts of everything that had happened the week before to fill her head again. Another headache pushing at her temples as soon as she'd woken from her restless sleep, she'd decided first thing to ring the office and tell them she wasn't going to make it in today. She really couldn't face it, not until she'd sorted out some of the things that were on her mind. After forcing down half a piece of toast, she grabbed her keys and bag and set the alarm before heading out to the car, pressing the handle down firmly two or three times to make sure the front door was locked. Perhaps they should get a dog, she thought as she walked down the driveway. The kids would love that.

As she climbed into the car, she felt a twinge of guilt as she remembered the confused tone of her sister's voice on the phone the night before.

'Of course you can come round, I'm free all morning tomorrow, but can you tell me why? You sound, I don't know, a bit *off*, Bell.'

This wasn't a conversation Bella wanted to have over the phone, especially when Rosie was distracted getting the twins to bed. She'd assured her sister they'd talk the next day.

Jack wasn't happy with her that morning, when she'd eventually voiced the thoughts she'd been harbouring since insisting he investigate the space beneath the house. 'Christ, Bell, I can't keep up with this.' He'd thrown things into his briefcase, rushing to try and beat the traffic on the way to the office. 'One minute you're convinced Lawrence is hiding in the basement again, the next, you think your sister is out to turn your life upside down by trying to sell your house. You're not making any sense.'

'It makes perfect sense to me, Jack. I've told you. I was *at her house*. I left my phone on the table. She was the only one who ...'

Jack stopped what he was doing for a second, staring at her. When he spoke, his voice was loud. 'So, what you're saying is that, in the few minutes you were in the loo, your sister, the two of you always as close as any siblings could be, has unlocked your phone, compiled an email to a local estate agent telling him you want to sell your house immediately, prescheduled it, and then put your phone back exactly where you left it? All while watching her *two-year-old twins*?'

'I know it sounds ridiculous—'

'*Ridiculous?*' He opened the fridge and grabbed the sandwiches he'd made the night before. 'That's an understatement if ever there was one. I mean, why the hell would she?'

'Because she's jealous!' Bella had almost shouted the words, glad that Paige and Freddy had already gone to school and couldn't hear their mother. She'd tried to calm herself. 'As much as Rosie and I are close, Jack, there's always been an underlying friction between us. We both know I got a lot more attention from our parents because they felt so bad about what happened to me. Rosie barely got a look-in. And then, as if that wasn't bad enough, they decided to give me the *family home*.'

'But Rosie got money instead!'

'It doesn't matter, Jack. Money isn't a replacement for the house we both grew up in, that we'd spent time in since we were babies. Rosie felt like she was second best and we've both always known it. We just don't talk about it. Don't want to complicate things by dragging it all out into the open.'

Jack had stood with his hands on his hips, shaking his head. 'Jeez, Bell, even for you, this sounds completely bonkers.'

'*Even for me?*'

'Even for you.' Glancing at the empty wine bottle she'd forgotten to put in the recycling bin the night before, he'd raised an eyebrow. 'No wonder you're popping headache pills this morning.'

As Bella drove now, she felt a surge of anger at the way Jack had spoken to her. Yes, he had a point. Why would her sister, her lovely Rosie, want to hurt her? Want to put her through more trauma than she'd already been through? And, yes, she *had* been adamant that Lawrence was behind everything that had happened over the past few weeks, that he might have been hiding in the basement and had accessed her phone or computer. She was confused. Wasn't that allowed under the circumstances? Who wouldn't be, in her shoes? If she could at least speak to Rosie, find out for definite if her sister had any involvement in what had happened with the house, then at least she could put one theory to sleep. Be able to think more clearly. Then Jack would have to take her seriously regarding her fears about Lawrence. Wouldn't he?

As she pulled up outside Rosie's house, she felt suddenly very unkind, wondering if she really was being ridiculous, suspecting that her sister was in any way involved. Rosie had enough on her plate already with the twins, without Bella accusing her of all sorts. Much like Jack, Martin was away from home a lot with work, his job too well paid to currently consider giving up so he could spend more time with his family. Rosie didn't have it easy, essentially a single parent the majority of the time, all the hard work, the sleep training, the weaning and dealing with tantrums, down to her alone. Bella had tried to help as much as she could, but she knew it wasn't the same as having a husband by your side to share the load. And now, here she was, about to add to her sister's woes.

She climbed out of the car, seeing the curtain twitch at the front window as she made her way up the path. The door opened before she reached it, Martin smiling at her as she approached, his eyes slightly wary behind his glasses.

'Hey, Bella.'

'Martin, hi.' Bella was taken aback; she hadn't expected Martin to be here on a weekday. 'Not working?'

'I've taken a few days' leave. See if we can crack this toilet training once and for all, before we need to take all the carpets up and replace them. I'm adamant a puppy would have been easier.'

Now Bella felt even more guilty for intruding. She stepped into the hall, moving around a pile of toy cars on the floor. 'I won't stay long. I just need to speak to Rosie for a few minutes.'

'No problem. She's upstairs with the twins. Can I get you a drink? Tea? Coffee?'

'I'm good, thanks.'

She sprinted up the stairs, heading into the twins' bedroom. Martin had always thought Cameron and Katie should sleep in separate rooms, but Rosie wouldn't hear of it. They'd been together for nine months before they were born, she insisted time and again. It was too soon to separate them.

Bella stood in the doorway, watching for a few seconds as her sister wrestled a sock onto her son, only for him to pull it off again as soon as she started the next one. In one corner of the room, Katie was sitting facing the wall, singing to herself, wearing nothing more than one of her mum's sunhats over her full head of hair, a few shades darker than Rosie's. 'Need some help?'

Rosie looked around. 'Oh, hi. If you fancy wrestling with an octopus …'

Bella crossed the room, sitting on the edge of the bed, next to her nephew. She picked up one of the small blue socks before gently taking hold of Cameron's chunky right leg. 'Maybe some teamwork will do the trick.'

'Worth a try.'

Working together, they got Cameron into his underwear and socks, swiftly followed by a T-shirt and shorts, a mischievous smile crossing his face as he finally wriggled off the bed and headed towards his sister.

Rosie straightened, hands on her hips. She blew her fringe from her eyes, looking as if she'd just done ten rounds in a boxing ring. 'He'll probably take it all off again as soon as I turn my back. I swear my children are destined to spend their entire lives naked.'

Bella chuckled.

Rosie began to fold excess clothes. 'Anyway, what's so urgent that you needed to come round on a Wednesday? Aren't you supposed to be at work?'

'I called in sick.'

'Okay. Everything all right? Nothing else weird has happened, has it?'

Bella fiddled with a pair of dinosaur-decorated socks on her lap. She looked around the small room her nephew and niece spent so much time in, imagining what their lives might have been like if her and Rosie's parents had made a different decision about who they gave their house and their money to. Both she and her sister knew full well why their mum and dad had gifted the house to Bella: they felt guilty about what had happened to her there. About going on holiday when they did and leaving her to her fate. It was their way of trying to make amends.

She kept her voice low, not wanting the twins to pick up on any tension. 'Was it you?'

Rosie looked at her. 'What?'

'Was it you who emailed the estate agent from my phone? Asking for my house to be put up for sale?'

Rosie's mouth fell open. She dropped the T-shirt she was folding and sat down on the bed, facing her sister. 'Are you kidding me?'

'I was here, the day before the guy turned up with the *For Sale* sign. I went to the loo and left my phone on the table. The email was actually sent later, but you'd easily know how to preschedule it; it's not difficult. Not to mention the fact that you know my access PIN is my birthday. You and Jack always laugh at my halfhearted attempts at digital security.'

'So, that means …?'

Bella took a breath. She had to know. 'Rosie, you always hated that Mum and Dad gave the house to me. You objected, remember? Thought it was the wrong decision. You said so.'

'Yes. Because I wasn't sure you should be living there after what you'd been through! I thought you might need a fresh start, somewhere else, not a reminder of what had happened to you every time you got up in the morning.' Rosie glanced behind her to make sure the twins weren't listening.

'No, that wasn't the only reason.' Bella shook her head. 'You were jealous. That Mum had given her family home to me and not to you. You thought it should have been the other way around. Or that they should have waited and given it to both of us after they die …'

Rosie was quiet for a few seconds, staring wide-eyed at Bella, as if she was trying to take in what her sister was telling her. She opened her mouth and closed it again before seeming to find the words. 'So, that's what you think of me, is it? What you think I'm capable of? Do you think I sent you the mysterious flowers as well? Or faked a Facebook account and pretended I was *Larry Knox*? Drank your milk?'

'No, I … I don't know.' Jack had been right with what he'd

136

said that morning. It did sound ridiculous. She was being stupid. 'I'm sorry, I just don't know what to think. Jack and you have both said that Lawrence can't possibly have been in the house without us noticing. Nor could he have accessed my phone or laptop remotely unless he's suddenly become some kind of technical wizard while he was in prison, so what am I supposed to think? You are the only person I've left my phone with.'

Rosie turned away and began to fold clothes again, her movements slow and deliberate. 'I don't know whether to be worried about you or offended, Bell. At the minute, I'm leaning towards the latter.'

'I'm sorry.' Bella stood up. 'Jack said it was a bad idea, coming around here to confront you.'

'He was right.' Rosie looked back at her. 'And what is Jack's theory about the origins of this mysterious email? Does *he* think I sent it as well?'

Bella shook her head. 'No, he ...'

'What?'

'He thinks *I* sent it, in the middle of the night, when I couldn't sleep and was on my laptop. That I've forgotten because ...'

'Because what?'

Bella shook her head again.

Martin appeared in the doorway, a frown creasing his forehead. He glanced at the twins. 'Everything okay?'

Rosie pursed her lips. 'You mean, apart from my sister suggesting I'm the person she thinks is playing tricks on her?'

'What?' Martin looked at Bella. 'Rosie told me about some of the things you think have happened, but I thought you were saying that Lawrence ...?'

'She was,' Rosie interrupted. 'Until she decided the only rational explanation for someone trying to put her house on the market is that it was me. Because I'm so jealous of her and her lifestyle ...'

'Bella …' Martin looked disappointed, like a teacher who'd discovered his favourite pupil had been playing hooky.

'I said I'm sorry.' Bella held her hands up. She was close to tears, as she seemed to be a lot lately. 'I was wrong, okay? But please bear in mind that I'm finding it very difficult to think straight at the minute. No matter what I say, no one seems to believe me.'

Rosie sighed. 'Of course we do. We love you, Bell, you know that. It's just …'

'It's fine. I'll go.' Bella felt bad enough without her sister feeling sorry for her. She headed out of the room and down the stairs. As she descended, she heard Rosie talking to Martin in a low voice, the words muffled behind the bedroom door. As she stopped to listen for a second, she was sure she heard her sister say the words *Jack said*, quickly followed by the word *drinking*.

*

As she drove home, she felt exhausted, all the emotions she'd been trying to suppress over the last few weeks, since Lawrence's release, coming to the surface, as if she were a pot left too long on the stove, in danger of bubbling over. She hadn't felt this alone for a long time. Not since she'd been trapped in the basement all those years ago, with none of her loved ones knowing she was there.

When she'd first been told Lawrence Knox was getting out of prison, she'd known she would feel unsure, that she'd be frightened of him entering her life again, scared that he still harboured feelings for her after all this time. She'd been prepared for that. But what she hadn't been prepared for was this uncertainty. This feeling of being lost, that she was wandering around her own home, her own life, like a stranger, not knowing who she could trust. Not knowing who she could talk to that might take her seriously. She didn't know where to turn.

Her eyes brimming over, she pulled the car into a side street near the town centre, frightened she might have an accident. Swiping at her tears, she took her phone from her bag and wrote a quick text to her sister:

I'm soooo sorry. I'm just not coping very well with everything that's going on. Really sorry I upset you both xxx

She stared at the screen for a minute or two, waiting for an answer that didn't arrive. Either Rosie was busy with her family, or she wasn't ready to communicate yet. No doubt, Bella had deeply hurt her sister's feelings by accusing her. She knew now that she hadn't been thinking straight. That Jack was right in what he'd said about her theory being far-fetched, even under the current circumstances.

Running her hand over her wet cheeks, she suddenly wondered if her mum and dad had been justified in the guilt they'd felt all these years about what had happened, which had led them to giving their eldest daughter the house. Perhaps Bella *did* bear some kind of grudge against her parents and sister for abandoning her. For going on their holiday and leaving her unprotected. Despite her own insistence that they go, enjoy themselves, live their lives as normal, maybe what she'd really wanted was for them to disagree with her. To insist on staying and keeping her safe. Perhaps it was only now, when she felt unsafe again, that her feelings about being left were beginning to come to the surface, clouding the remorse she often thought she should have about accepting the house?

She jumped as her phone vibrated in her hand, a text suddenly coming through. Not from Rosie as she'd expected, but from Jack:

Going to be late home tonight. Fancy meeting for dinner? Just the two of us? If you could call and book our usual place for 8, I'll meet you there. Might take your mind off things xx

Bella smiled. Trust her husband to instinctively know when she'd had a bad day. Although he'd been cross with her, even exasperated, that morning, he was now offering an olive branch, obviously knowing she needed cheering up. A quiet dinner, a chat, would likely do her the world of good.

She fished a tissue out of her bag and wiped her eyes before starting the car. She'd ring the restaurant as soon as she got home.

Jack now

Jack stretches his arms as he looks out of the window, a layer of thin net curtain and two of toughened glass between himself and the outside world. It's early, the town not quite awake, just the occasional bleary-eyed dog walker or keen commuter passing on the pavement below. The sun is bright even at this hour, the darkness of the short summer night already having made way for a clear blue sky. It's going to be a nice day.

He heads to the hospitality tray, turning over a clean mug and flicking through the sachets of coffee until he finds a full-strength. Despite his wife wanting him to cut down on his caffeine intake over the past few years, he knows decaf just won't cut it this morning. He hasn't slept well, his worries about Bella resulting in numerous dreams that kept waking him, leaving him tossing and turning in the unfamiliar hotel bed, the meticulously clean sheets tucked in too tightly, making him feel suffocated. At one point, he remembers, he woke thinking he'd heard a banging in the corridor, a fist hammering at a door perhaps. Falling asleep again, he dreamt of his wife, his mind conjuring up images of a younger Bella, trapped in the basement of their house when she wasn't much more than a girl. Had she felt trapped again the past few weeks? When the life she'd so carefully cultivated began to unravel?

He pours boiling water into the too-small cup and adds two tiny cartons of milk, smiling suddenly as he remembers Bella's habit of taking her own herbal teabags and jar of instant coffee every time they stay anywhere away from home. It's always made the kids cringe, the way their mother packs so many home luxuries when they go on holiday: biscuits and packs of treats, little packets of washing powder, even the iron one year. She likes to feel at home, she's always said. Even when she's not. That's part of the reason they never got around to using the camping equipment he bought, the expensive tent and gas stove, even a chemical loo, still sitting mostly unused in the basement. Bella hadn't much liked the idea of roughing it beneath flimsy, not to mention insecure, canvas and, after his initial enthusiasm for the idea, Freddy had soon lost interest too.

Jack has always fully understood Bella's decision to stay in the house after what happened to her there, despite the way her fear of the basement overwhelms her sometimes, on her worst days. He remembers talking to Rosie about it once, the two of them in the kitchen together one Christmas. Their house has always been the chosen spot to celebrate the festive season, Gail and Brian and their youngest daughter seeming to enjoy *coming home*, as they call it, despite the trauma they'd all gone through there. Leaning against the counter in the kitchen she'd grown up in, Rosie had told him she'd sometimes had doubts about him and Bella living in the house, bringing up their family in the same place where she'd been held hostage. *It's where she feels she belongs,* he'd told his sister-in-law. *Didn't Lawrence take enough without taking this too?*

Was Rosie right? he wonders now. Should they simply have said no to the house and lived somewhere else, somewhere where Bella could attempt to completely forget about what had happened to her? Or would the ghost of Lawrence Knox simply have followed her wherever she went, even if they'd moved to the other end of the earth? He suspects it would have; Bella seems to have carried her trauma inside her, the rather uneasy peace they'd both managed to achieve over the years now completely disrupted with Lawrence's release.

He sips at his coffee, sitting on the bed and rubbing his fingers across his eyes, trying to wake himself up. He needs to shower and get his day going. As much as the thought of lying around in the hotel room and watching TV all day is appealing, he knows he needs to keep himself occupied, perhaps tackle some of the paperwork he brought with him from the office. Withdrawing from the world and feeling sorry for himself won't do him, or Bella, any good. He picks his phone up from the bedside table, clicking again on the message that came through late last night. He's already read it more than once:

Goodnight, Jack. Hope you're okay xxx

Is he okay? Considering the circumstances, he thinks he's holding up pretty well. He scrolls through his list of contacts, wondering if he should try to forward Bella's message to Gail or Brian to reassure them their daughter is still okay and coping. He's aware they have no signal at the cottage but thinks the message might reach them when they're out and about. Just as he's about to click on his mother-in-law's name, another text comes through. He frowns as he sees it's from Jazz, unusual on a Saturday:

Hi, sorry, sorry, sorry, I know it's the weekend (and very early!), but I totally forgot to get your signature on those invoices for the Walker job! Couldn't sleep for thinking about it! Could I bring them to you? It won't take a second!

Jack rolls his eyes. He remembers Jazz telling him she had some things for him to sign before he left but they both must have let it slip their minds after their chat about Bella. He texts back:

Can't it wait?

Jazz's next message comes through immediately:

I'll be in sooooo much trouble if the boss doesn't have them on his desk before opening Mon!

Jack sighs. He looks down at the insipid coffee he's drinking. Perhaps an hour or so out of the hotel and something hot and frothy in a gigantic cup will do him good. Help the time pass if nothing else. He touches his phone screen again:

Okay, I've got a bit of paperwork here to go through first that will need filing after. Meet me in town around 10 and we can grab a coffee and do a swap?

He downs the rest of his weak coffee and heads to the bathroom for a shower.

Bella now

She jerks awake, her eyes blinking rapidly, panic fluttering in her chest as she tries to work out where she is. Looking around, she's expecting the room that slowly comes into focus around her to be the large bedroom she shares with Jack, the John Lewis curtains she chose but that he's always hated hanging lifeless in front of the closed windows she insists on, even in the summer months. She frowns. She's not in her bedroom but somewhere that's only vaguely familiar, a room she knows but in which she wouldn't normally wake up. A hotel? Her parents' house? She shakes her head. No. There is nothing clean or luxurious or homely about her surroundings. There are no curtains, no windows. No comfortable bed sheets or smell of an inviting breakfast. Just dust-filled air and a trapped fly buzzing somewhere around the ceiling. The flickering bulb still just about on above her head.

She's still in the basement. Day two of her second confinement.

The realisation hits her like bricks falling from a high building. She isn't sure what time it is, but she knows she's slept, her cricked neck stiff, almost immovable, the rest of her body screaming out for a change in position, for some relief. If it's morning, and she thinks it is, she's now been here for approximately twenty-four hours. A whole day. The thought of spending as many days down here as she did the last time is almost enough to send her mind over the edge, to drive her completely insane. This can't be happening, she tells herself. Can't. Be. She tries to open her mouth, ready to scream into the damp void that is the room beneath her house. Instead, she coughs around the gag, almost chokes. Her throat is too dry.

She wriggles around on the chair, the tape once again chafing at her skin as she tries to shift her position, give her aching muscles some freedom. As she circles her feet, attempting once again to revive her circulation, she remembers a dream she had sometime in the night, images popping into her mind as if from a vaguely remembered film. She dreamt about her sister.

In the dream, Rosie was younger, round-faced and pink-cheeked, the two of them together in the garden just beyond the kitchen at the top of the stairs, the house, she seems to know instinctively, still belonging to their grandparents. Behind them, in front of the tall back hedge, stands a summer house their grandad once built from pieces of leftover decking, makeshift plant boxes attached to the rudimentary windowsills. She and Rosie had loved it, the structure lasting until she and her sister were well into their teens. Their father had eventually pulled it out, plank by rotting plank.

Bella frowns, the dream bringing tears to her eyes now, the more she remembers of it. She and Rosie were playing, the two of them being silly in the way they used to be so often, twirling around the garden, doing cartwheels and handstands, something her sister was always good at. As Bella put her hands to the grass, she fell, her legs twisting awkwardly above her, the ground coming up to meet her like a truck on a busy road. Within seconds, Rosie was at her side – *There, there, Bella, you're okay. I'm here* – suddenly morphing into their grandma, armed with plasters and bandages, a bowl of hot water and a cloth.

She tries to stretch her aching neck, wishing her sister were here with her now. Rosie is practical and pragmatic, would know how to get her out of this situation. Would have a list of tricks they could try, to get the better of their abductor. Rosie wouldn't be crying and fretting. Instead, she would remain positive, would be determined to find a way out.

Feeling her muscles creak, her thoughts still jumbled from broken sleep, Bella suddenly remembers a party she and Rosie went to when they were teenagers, just a few months before Bella left home, before Lawrence Knox changed her life forever. A typical gathering of belligerent kids who thought they could hold their drink but who invariably ended up puking on the lawn at the front of whoever's house they were at. Like many there, Bella had also overindulged, the idea that this was the last night for a while that she and Rosie would have some fun together making her giddy. Much more sober, Rosie had taken charge, behaving more like the older sister than the younger, making sure they both got home safely in a taxi and, more importantly, that neither of them got into trouble with Mum and Dad.

Rosie is sensible, always has been. Perhaps if what had happened to Bella happened to her, she would have found a different way to deal with it. Would have put a stop to the situation before it escalated to the point where she found herself captured and helpless.

Bella feels an intense sadness settle around her, a feeling of such complete and utter isolation like she's never known, as if she's the only person left in the entire world. The last time she was here, she realises, even after four or five days, she still had a sense of hope. A sense that someone would find her eventually, that she *would* get out of this situation, no matter how dire it seemed. Now, she feels as if she'll never see the light of day again. As if, after her recent behaviour, her accusations, her family don't really care if she completely disappears from their lives. That they'd be happier without her.

She squeezes her eyes shut in frustration. If only she hadn't fought with her sister over the past few weeks, pushing her away and accusing her of all sorts. Getting it into her head that Rosie was conspiring against her. Despite the tension between them about the house, about their parents' decision to hand it to Bella, they barely ever argued. Had always been there for each other. Jack had warned her. *If you take this out on the people closest to you,* he'd said recently, *you'll end up pushing everyone away. Surely that's not what you want?* Well, look at her now. All alone and with no one coming to rescue her. No one worrying about her. Jack was right. Of course he was.

She attempts a deep breath, trying to wake herself up, shuffling her wrists and ankles again against the tape. She imagines she can feel it loosening, the binding perhaps not as tight as it was yesterday, strapped around her a little less vigorously after she went to the loo last night and he struggled a little to tie her down again while still holding the knife. He'd said he was tired. Maybe she's just thinking wishfully.

She looks up at the door at the top of the stairs. Even if she could move, shed her gag and sticky binding, where would she go? The door is locked. She doesn't have to try it to know. Bella's insistence on the basement being kept as secure as possible since they lived in the house is now working against her, the key clicking in the lock every time he leaves her alone. Even if she could reach it, rattle the hinges, bang her fists against the wood, who would hear her? The answer is no one. No one apart from the one person who knows she's down here. The person who knows how terrified, how traumatised she was the last time she was here. Who has insisted on putting her through this ordeal again.

Even now, he must be up there, perhaps on the other side of the door, listening to her struggling, grunting in frustration as she tries to free herself. Smirking to himself at her pointless efforts.

She stills for a few seconds, trying to swallow, her throat seeming even more sore and dry than it was when she first woke. She needs water, and she wonders when he'll see fit to come down here and stop her becoming seriously dehydrated. The fact that she hasn't needed to pee for hours says it all. Her body's usual functions are beginning to shut down, much like they did last time. Will he offer her breakfast, she wonders, or leave her to go hungry? Eat in front of her like he did yesterday, as a punishment for her rebuttal of what he saw as his kindness? What if he's still asleep? Has slept late, on the sofa or upstairs, oblivious to her discomfort, her desperation. Dreaming of the future while she's down here, forgotten and suffering.

Bella feels suddenly cross. She *has* to stop feeling sorry for herself. Has to be more positive. More like Rosie might be, even if the two of them have barely been speaking lately.

Lifting her chin, she feels her stomach churn as the key clicks in the lock and the door above her opens again.

Three and a half weeks earlier

Bella felt twitchy and anxious. As much as she liked the idea of spending the evening with Jack, enjoying some nice food and perhaps a bottle or two of wine, her stomach was unsettled. She was worried about leaving Paige and Freddy in the house alone. Despite the fact that Jack had found no signs of life in the basement and Paige being old enough to be left in charge, she couldn't stop her mind wandering back to the day when she'd found Luke Rushfield in her living room, her daughter having let him in, and then panicking because he didn't seem to want to leave. What if Lawrence himself turned up when she and Jack weren't there? Spun the kids some lie about being a friend of the family or a long-lost relative? Would Paige be on her guard now she'd been warned a second time? Or would she simply let him in?

Before she made the restaurant booking, Bella had done a Google search and pulled up an online article from a Leeds local newspaper's archive. The piece was accompanied by a small picture of Lawrence as he was led into court. Looking at his face, even after so many years had passed, still made the hair on the back of her neck stand up. Made her want to look over her shoulder, even in her own home. *Especially* in her own home.

She showed the picture to Paige. 'I should have done this before. I don't want to frighten you, or Freddy, but I need to know you're listening to me and Dad and taking this situation seriously. Chances are you'll be fine, but, just in case, this man in the picture is who you need to be on the lookout for. Do not let him, or anyone else, into the house when Dad and I aren't here. Okay?'

Paige gave the picture a cursory glance. 'Looks like a proper weirdo to me. Don't know why you had anything to do with him in the first place. Look at what he's wearing.'

'Well, obviously they're not his normal clothes. He was held on remand before the trial.'

'Nah, still not feeling it.' Paige screwed up her face.

Bella looked at the picture more closely, trying to see Lawrence as she had when she first spoke to him that fateful night in the students' union. She thought about what Paige had said. 'Well, I know it sounds strange now, after everything, but I actually quite liked him when we first met. He was funny and charming in a quirky sort of way. And, of course, I was a bit lonely in my first term at uni, feeling homesick. I thought we'd be friends.'

'And look how that turned out.'

'Anyway …' Bella clicked off the article, suddenly not wanting to look at the person who had caused her so much pain for a second longer than she had to '… bear in mind he's older now. He might look a little different, have grey hair, or a beard, or …'

'Yeah, yeah, I get the message. No one allowed in the house. Got it.' Paige gave her a thumbs up. 'Can't speak for Freddy though. You know how weird he is about trying to get to the door before I do. In case it's one of his weirdo friends wanting to play weirdo video games with him.'

Bella rolled her eyes. 'I'll show him later, but, for now, you're in charge. I'm depending on you, Paige. I can't book this table unless I know you're going to be okay.'

*

She sighed now as she paid the taxi driver and climbed out, looking around her nervously in the same way she did whenever she met Rosie for coffee or went out for a run. She crossed the road, heading towards the mixed-cuisine restaurant she and Jack had always liked so much. They'd spent many of their date nights there, the two of them always able to find something on the menu to suit their different tastes. When she'd called to make the booking, Bella had been worried it might be too short notice, that their favourite eatery might be full and they'd have to go somewhere else, but the young girl who answered the phone had been more than happy to accommodate them. She pulled open the door and stepped inside.

The restaurant's host was standing in the reception area, in front of a wooden podium, a booking log open in front of him.

Bella lifted a hand in greeting, the staff familiar and friendly with her, she'd been here so many times. 'Hi, I booked a table for eight o'clock? Bella Anderson?'

'Ah, yes.' The host glanced down at the open book in front of him. 'Lovely to see you again, Mrs Anderson. If you'd like to follow me, I'll show you to your table.'

Bella followed him through the busy restaurant, her nerves still tingling as she looked around her at the other diners. She was lucky to have got in, she thought. The restaurant was almost full, large groups sitting at the huge round tables in between couples, both on their own and with children. Under normal circumstances, when she wasn't feeling so anxious, Bella loved this place: the beautiful décor; rich, colourful fabrics hanging from the walls; elaborate, beaded chandeliers. The tiny details the staff used to welcome their guests. She particularly loved the little cards placed on each table, the names of each and every diner handwritten in elaborate old-fashioned lettering. She tried to focus as the host spoke to her again.

'I'm sorry that Mr Anderson isn't joining us tonight.'

Bella frowned. 'Oh, he'll be along shortly. He's probably just been delayed at work again.' She shrugged and smiled.

'Er, I see. The booking was for two though, wasn't it?' He pulled out a chair for her. 'Well, the table we've given you is big enough for four, so no problem.'

Bella took her seat. She had no idea what the host was talking about. Of course she'd made a booking for two. For her and Jack. Perhaps they were just overly busy.

She slipped off her jacket and ordered a large glass of white wine while she waited. She presumed Jack would be happy to drive them home if he was coming straight from the office, and the alcohol would help calm her nerves, meaning her husband might enjoy her company a bit more than he had recently. She picked up the stiff, white card in front of her place setting: *Bella Anderson*. The name seemed almost odd, as if the Bella Anderson she'd once been was now a stranger to her. How she wished she could get back to being the wife Jack knew and loved. She would, she thought to herself. They would sort this out and get past it. Get back to living the life they deserved.

She accepted her drink, taking a large gulp as she gazed out of the window, hoping Jack wouldn't be too long. She wanted to speak to him, to try and explain a little bit about how she'd been feeling recently. How frightened she'd been and how that had led her to being a little erratic. Acting in a way that, no doubt, seemed out of character, being unkind to her sister in a way she wouldn't normally dream of. She was sure that, if she explained it all to Jack over dinner, in a calm and rational way, she would be able to get him to see the situation from her point of view. Get him to imagine what it must be like to be in her shoes.

Watching a young couple walk hand in hand along the pavement, she thought about the early days of their relationship. How careful Jack had been not to pressure her or move things along too quickly. How he'd made her feel safe from the very beginning, always slipping his arm around her if they were in a crowded space, patient if she was having a bad day. There were lots of those then. Days when she could barely concentrate, couldn't focus on anything else but what had happened to her. As if she were there, in the basement, all over again.

For a while, perhaps years afterwards, there had been bad dreams, Bella often waking in the night soaked in sweat, her screams fading as she slowly became aware of her surroundings. Jack had never once complained about his sleep being disturbed, and didn't now on the nights when she still preferred roaming the house to being in their bed. When Paige was born, this tiny, completely vulnerable being suddenly needing to be kept safe at all times, the dreams had returned for a while. Bella had been terrified that her night terrors hadn't gone for good, even all these years later. Who knew what was lurking in the future for anyone? None of them – not she herself, nor Jack, nor her parents – were capable of controlling the actions of other people, no matter how much they'd have liked to.

She took another gulp of wine, glancing at the time on her phone and looking around her. Jack was late. The awkward feeling of being stood up by Pete all those years ago, and what that situation had led to, suddenly came back to her. Her heart began to race, the familiar prickle of panic, which she'd felt so many times in the past, agitating her empty stomach. *Calm down,* she told herself sternly. *It's only been ten minutes or so.* Jack had never let her down before. He wouldn't dream of leaving her stranded here on her own, not when he knew how anxious she'd been lately. She felt herself beginning to shake, her body no longer her own, not under her control.

'Bella?'

Bella looked up, the numerous lights from a nearby chandelier blinding her. She screwed up her eyes, trying to focus on the person standing over her. Part of her felt dazed, as if she'd consumed much more alcohol than she actually had. She could barely breathe. What on earth was happening to her?

She shaded her eyes with her hand. 'Oh … Jazz …?'

'Yes, hi, I'm sitting over there with a friend and I spotted you.'

Jazz indicated a table in a far corner, a gregarious-looking young woman in a bright orange outfit and huge earrings smiling over at them. 'Bella, are you okay?'

Bella looked down at her hands, realising how much they were quivering, as if she were freezing cold. She could feel beads of sweat on her top lip. It had been a long time since she'd had a panic attack, her therapist once telling her she might experience them on and off for the rest of her life. 'I, er ... I'm not sure I am, to be honest.'

Jazz bent towards her, frowning. 'You're as white as a sheet. Do you need a doctor?' She turned to look around the restaurant. 'Are you on your own, Bella? Do you have someone with you?'

Bella shook her head, trying to focus on keeping her breathing even. 'I was supposed to be meeting Jack, but ...' She glanced at her phone. Almost eight-twenty-five. 'He's late. He must have been delayed at work. It's not like him to ...'

Jazz crouched down at the side of the table, her long legs bent at sharp angles. Her eyes showed concern as she spoke, calmly and evenly, as if she were talking to a lost child. 'Jack's in a meeting, Bella.'

'What?'

Jazz nodded. 'It seemed to me that it was going to go on for a while. The big boss is there. I sneaked out of the office myself because I didn't want to end up missing my meal.'

Bella looked at Jack's assistant. When she'd first met Jazz at a Christmas party five or six years ago, she'd felt a spark of envy. Jazz was tall, well over six feet, her stature akin to that of an Amazonian queen, her short, bleached hair surrounding a flaw-lessly made-up face. Not usually someone inclined to feel jealous, it had taken her some time to get used to the idea of this goddess working so closely with her husband, but, the few times they'd met since, she'd come to like Jazz very much, thought they could have even been friends if they'd had the chance to get to know each other better. She shook her head. 'No, he ... He texted me this afternoon. Told me to book a table for eight and that he'd meet me here.'

Jazz frowned again. 'Maybe he got dragged in at the last minute and couldn't get out of it. Are you sure he said to book for tonight?'

'I'm sure. I rang the restaurant as soon as I got home.' Bella picked up her phone, bringing the screen to life and clicking on her message app to check the text Jack had sent earlier. As she did so, the phone buzzed suddenly, the screen going black. Her battery had died. 'Shit.'

'Never mind.' Jazz shifted her position, pulling her own phone from the pocket of her black jeans. 'Maybe he was planning to slip away as soon as he could but it's dragging on. Those meetings can be quite intense sometimes. Would you like me to see if I can get hold of him on my phone?'

Bella shook her head. 'No, no, honestly, there's no need, Jazz. I'm sure he'll be along soon. Jack never lets me down. And I'm sorry if I seemed a bit off when you first came over. I get a bit panicky sometimes.'

'That's understandable, after everything you went through.'

'It's just when I'm on my own. And the man who abducted me—' she still struggled to say the words out loud '—he recently …'

'Jack said.' Jazz put a hand on her arm. 'You don't have to explain, honestly.'

'I'll be fine once Jack gets here.' She looked around the room. 'I love it here, don't you? Have you been before?'

'Lots of times. I always eat far too much though.' Jazz chuckled. 'I'll be half a stone heavier by tomorrow.'

'Oh, me too. I especially love these little name cards they use. Such a nice touch. I always end up taking ours home, got loads in a drawer somewhere.' Bella plucked her own card from its little stand before reaching across the table for Jack's. Swivelling it around in her hand, she examined the neat lettering.

She felt her eyes widen, all of her breath suddenly seeming to leave her body.

The name on the card, written in the same elaborate letters as her own, was *Lawrence Knox*.

Bella couldn't speak. She remembered the host looking confused as he'd led her to the table, when she'd said that her husband would be along soon. *The table was a booking for two though, wasn't it?* Yes, a booking for two. Just not, apparently, the two she'd specified when she'd called earlier in the day.

Jazz looked at the card before looking back at her. 'Lawrence Knox? But, Bella, isn't that …?'

Bella stood quickly, the chair behind her almost tipping over. She swayed on her feet, the few gulps of wine she'd had making her head cloud suddenly. She put a hand to her forehead, hoping the feeling would pass. She couldn't faint, not now. She needed to get out of here.

She grabbed her bag and jacket from a nearby chair, ignoring Jazz's concerned look as she turned and headed towards the door.

'Bella … Bella, wait …'

As she reached the door, Bella felt Jazz's hand on her arm. She stopped briefly, her whole body itching to go outside, to get away, part of her feeling as if she were suddenly trapped in the basement all over again. As if she would never be able to escape her past.

'Bella, wait. You're in no fit state to be going off on your own. Just let me grab my keys and I'll give you a lift home. We can call Jack from my phone, find out what's happened. Where he's got to.'

Bella looked across the restaurant. In the far corner, she could see Jazz's dining companion still watching them, a frown creasing her forehead as one of the waiting staff laid plates of food on the table in front of her. She felt a surge of guilt at how, once again, she'd managed to inconvenience someone, encroach on their time. She'd been so looking forward to tonight. To some normality. 'No, really, Jazz, I just want to get out of here. On my own. I'm not sure what's happened tonight but I'm sure it's just some stupid mix-up. A prank …' She was aware she sounded like Jack. How could this possibly be a *prank*? 'Whatever it is, I've no doubt Jack will get to the bottom of it when I eventually see him. Get back to your meal, and I'll just grab a taxi.'

'Are you sure? I'd be happy to help, to stay with you until …'

Bella didn't think she could bear another second of this lovely girl being kind to her. 'I am. Thank you.'

'Well, if you insist, but, just one more thing …' Reaching behind her, Jazz grabbed one of the restaurant's takeaway menus from the host's podium, as well as a stray pen. 'I know your battery's dead at the minute, but I'll jot my number down for you. If you ever need anything, even if it's just to chat or rant at someone, just call. It's not a problem.'

Bella took the menu and slipped it into her bag, speaking over her shoulder as she quickly turned away. 'Thank you, Jazz. Please don't worry, I'll be fine.'

'Take care, Bella.'

She pulled open the door, aware, as she stepped out into the street, that she might never be able to visit her favourite restaurant again. That she would be too embarrassed, too worried that the staff would think her volatile or unhinged after her sudden departure. She hadn't even paid for her wine. Standing on the pavement for a few seconds, she let the night air cool her face, the beads of sweat on her forehead drying as she tried to suppress the shivers that were running through her entire body. What on earth had happened tonight? Whatever it was, it seemed completely surreal. Ever since Lawrence Knox had been released from prison, it was as if she'd been transported into some parallel existence. One in which she'd never managed to build a life without Lawrence in it.

Looking down at her hand, she realised she was still holding the little card she'd picked up off the table, the letters that spelled out Lawrence's name now dampened by the sweat from her fingers. How the hell could Jack and Lawrence's names have been mixed up? Jack had texted her, told her to meet him here at eight. And she'd made the booking *herself*, giving the young girl on the phone the names of both people who would be attending. Herself and her husband. Yet, when she'd got here, the host was clearly expecting her to be meeting up with someone else. More specifically, the man who'd stalked her. Imprisoned her. Tortured her.

What the hell was going on?

Trying to swallow the feelings of panic that were threatening to overwhelm her again, Bella dropped the card into her bag and looked around the dark street, wondering where the nearest taxi rank was. She gasped as she saw a figure hurrying towards her. 'Jack!'

Jack tried to get his breath, his cheeks pink. 'Bell, I'm so sorry I'm late.'

'Where on earth have you been? It's after eight-thirty.' Bella felt a flood of relief. At least now she knew she'd read Jack's text right. That he'd told her to book the restaurant tonight at eight, otherwise he wouldn't have been there, apologising.

'I had a last-minute meeting; it ran over … I tried to call you as soon as I got out, but …'

'My battery died. Jazz thought you must be struggling to get away.'

Jack frowned. 'Jazz? What do you mean? When did you speak to Jazz?'

'Just …' Bella pointed a thumb over her shoulder. 'She's in the restaurant with her friend.'

'Oh.' Jack stood for a few seconds, catching his breath. 'Yeah, she's right, it was totally unavoidable. Anyway, I'm here now. I'm sure they won't mind us eating later than planned. Let's go in and …'

Bella shook her head. She was tired and confused. All she wanted now was to go home and have a soak in the bath before bed. 'No, I don't think I want to. I've lost my appetite.'

'What do you mean? You love it here.'

'I know, but …' Bella took a breath. She was trying to sound calm. At least she had a witness to what had happened tonight. Jazz would back her up about what had gone on in the restaurant, then Jack wouldn't think she was completely crazy. 'Something happened in there, while I was waiting for you. Something really weird. I don't want to go back in, Jack.'

Jack hesitated before sighing. 'Okay …' He put his hand to her elbow. 'Well, the car's not far away. Come on, you can tell me about it on the way home.'

Bella nodded. Pulling her jacket more tightly around her, she followed her husband along the dark street.

*

'So, tell me again, Bell. I'm not sure I'm getting my head around this. You're telling me there was an actual card?' Jack laid his laptop bag on the table and pulled off his jacket and tie. 'With *Lawrence's* name on it?'

Bella flopped down onto a chair. She felt dazed, her head spinning, as if she'd been in a wrestling match, or had drunk a whole bottle of wine rather than half a glass. 'Yes.'

'You didn't just imagine it? In your panic?'

'Of course I didn't!' She'd told Jack how she'd begun to panic when she'd realised he was late. 'I'm not completely crazy, Jack.'

'Of course not. I didn't mean …'

'What *did* you mean?' Bella rooted around in her bag for the little name card, pulling it out and holding it up for Jack to see. 'Happy now?'

He sighed as he sat down opposite her. 'I'm sorry. I didn't mean to doubt you.'

'Didn't you?' Bella felt as if that was all Jack did at the minute. He and everyone else. Even now, as she held the card in her hand, the evidence of what had happened, she felt as if she still needed to convince her husband. 'Jazz was there when I picked it up.'

'So, she was there? In the restaurant?'

160

'I told you, she was having a meal with her friend. She said she'd left work early so she wouldn't be caught up in the meeting herself.' *Unlike you*, she stopped herself from adding.

'I vaguely remember her saying something about going out, but I was only half listening. I'm so sorry I left you waiting. I know we didn't part on the best of terms this morning and I didn't want you to think … I did try to call. You're normally so vigilant at keeping your phone charged.'

Bella remembered how cross Jack was with her after she'd told him she was intending to confront her sister this morning. It seemed like forever ago. She shook her head. 'I didn't bother tonight. I was showing pictures of Lawrence to Paige and then I called the restaurant … Anyway, it doesn't seem so important to have a full battery if I know you're going to be with me.'

Jack's eyes widened. 'You were showing pictures of Lawrence to Paige? Why?'

'Because I was worried about leaving her and Freddy alone. That she might still not have listened to us and might end up letting someone in the house again.'

'I'm sure she wouldn't.'

'I wanted her to know what he looked like, just in case …'

'Fair enough.' Jack seemed to stop and think for a few seconds. 'And this was before you rang the restaurant to book the table?'

Bella looked at him. 'Yes, just before. Why?'

'Nothing.' Jack shook his head.

Bella watched him. She knew when her husband was thinking, possibly about something he thought might upset her. 'What, Jack? Tell me …'

Jack sighed. He fiddled with the bunch of keys in front of him. 'It's just … Well, have you thought there might be a really simple explanation to what happened? A more simple one than we think?'

'Like what?'

'Like, Lawrence was on your mind, after you'd been showing pictures of him to Paige.'

'What on earth do you mean?'

Jack shifted in his seat. 'It would be very easily done, Bell. I've done it myself at work enough times. I've been talking to someone, then I write an email or text and end up putting the name of the person I've just been talking to in the email instead of the person I'm actually supposed to be talking about or to.'

'You mean ...?' Bella felt her eyes widen.

Jack shrugged. 'Like I said, it's easily done. You're thinking about Lawrence, he's on your mind, like he has been a lot lately, then you ring the restaurant and ...'

'You think *I* gave them Lawrence's name?' Bella couldn't believe what she was hearing.

'Not deliberately, of course.'

'Not deliberately? Jack, how stupid do you think I ...?'

Jack reached a hand across the table. 'I don't think you're stupid at all. You know I don't. I just think you've had a lot on your mind lately.'

'So, you think I would book a table for myself and the man who stalked me? So we could have dinner together?'

Jack scoffed. 'You know that's not what I mean. I just know how easy it is to say the wrong name, that's all. Especially when you're distracted. When your mind is on other things.'

'Nice to know you have so much faith in me.'

'It's nothing to do with having faith in you.'

'Isn't it?' Bella bit her lip. Was Jack right? Could she really have said Lawrence's name instead of that of her own husband? Was she completely losing the plot?

'Look, forget I said anything. It was just a thought.'

Bella looked him in the eye. She felt angry now. She was sure she hadn't done what Jack was accusing her of. She'd said *his* name. Hadn't she? 'Because you'd rather think I'm going crazy than think Lawrence Knox is stalking me again? Consider the fact that he could have somehow changed the booking? Cancelled it and made another in his own name?'

Jack's shoulders slumped. 'Bella, think about it. How on earth would he know? How would Lawrence know we'd made arrangements for tonight? That we'd booked a table, that he'd have the opportunity to rearrange it? It's impossible.'

'Not if he's somehow accessed my phone, like I said before! If he's been in the house, or … or planted some kind of listening device.'

'Listen to yourself! Lawrence isn't a secret agent, Bell. This isn't the set of a Hollywood movie!'

Bella wanted to cry, a large part of her aware of how ridiculous she sounded. She didn't know what else to think. How could *she* be the one at fault here? She wasn't. She hadn't done anything wrong, but now her husband was mocking her. 'I know that, Lawrence! Shit … I …' She put her hands to her face for a few seconds before looking back up. 'You're getting me all confused. *Jack*, I meant *Jack*. Of course I did.'

Jack looked at her, without speaking.

Bella tried to adjust her tone. She needed to stay calm. 'I know that, Jack. I know Lawrence isn't a secret agent, but that doesn't mean …'

'Bell, we checked the basement. You've spoken to the people who are monitoring him.'

'Yes, yes, I know, he's behaving himself. Hasn't put a foot wrong since he left prison.'

Jack stood, moving around the table before crouching in front of her. He put his hands on hers. 'Look, I can understand why you're upset. You've had a shock. But I really don't think this was anything to do with Lawrence, sweetheart.'

'How can you say that?'

'Because I know how upset you've been recently. Understandably so. And it's easy to make mistakes in those kinds of circumstances. As you've just demonstrated.' He straightened, taking her hand to pull her to her feet. 'Why don't you go and have a soak in the bath? I'll plug your phone in then we both know it's fully charged and then I'll make you a nice hot chocolate, okay?'

Bella sighed and nodded. 'I'd rather have a glass of wine.'

Jack looked at her. 'If that's what you'd prefer.'

Bella slowly headed for the stairs, her feet feeling as if they were glued to the floor, they were so heavy. She hadn't felt so low for quite a long time.

Bella now

'Morning, my beautiful Bella. How are we on this fine day? Did you sleep well?' He reaches towards her. 'Let me take this horrible gag off you for a minute. Can't answer all my questions with that thing on now, can you?'

She takes a breath, scoffs. 'You know very well I didn't sleep.'

'Aw, that's a shame. I thought you'd be nice and cosy down here in your very own room. No kids pestering you, none of your usual chores to do. Surely you should be counting your blessings?'

Bella rolls her eyes. 'So, tell me, did you?'

'Did I what?' He saunters back and forth in front of her. He's enjoying every moment of this.

'Did *you* sleep well? Were you comfortable? Or did your guilty conscience keep you awake?'

'Ah, beautiful Bella ...' He smiles, the scar on his face stretching like a cat. 'Always thinking of others. Don't you worry about me. I was very comfortable last night. Slept like a baby.'

'I bet you did.'

'Of course, I did worry about you. Just a teeny-tiny bit.' He holds his thumb and forefinger half an inch apart.

'Don't lie. You don't care about me. No matter what you say or have said in the past. All you care about is yourself.'

He shrugs. 'Maybe you don't know me as well as you think you do, Bella.'

Bella feels a flash of anger. 'Oh, I know you. Probably better than you know yourself. You've been in my life long enough for me to understand what kind of person you are.'

He smiles. 'The type of person who has come to offer you breakfast? Can't complain at that now, can you, Bella? Now, what would you like?' He marks off items on his fingers. 'Toast? Cereal? A nice fruit salad? Can't have you getting scurvy down here while you're being deprived of all that lovely sunshine now, can we?'

At his mention of the sun, Bella feels her stomach lurch. Even though she's only been down here for a day, it seems like so much longer since she's seen any natural light. Her run yesterday morning feels like weeks ago. She swallows drily. 'I just want some water. It's so hot down here. I'm dehydrated.'

He holds a finger under his nose. 'I thought I could smell something. Must be all that sweating you've been doing.' He turns on his heel. 'One glass of water coming up. Anything for my beautiful Bella.'

She watches him walk back up the stairs, a sense of hate like she's never known travelling through her body like a tsunami. She wants to fling herself from the chair she's strapped to and jump on his back. Grab the knife from his belt and jam it into his body over and over again, up to the hilt. Stab him until he's more holes than flesh. Make him feel the pain that she herself is feeling …

She closes her eyes. She should be outside now, enjoying the nice weather like everyone else, not having thoughts of murder. She wonders what the kids are doing. She pictures Paige, in France with Louise and her family, her smooth skin sun-kissed, her usually dark hair a few shades lighter; Freddy fishing with his grandfather, his too-big waders baggy around his small frame. She hopes they're having the time of their lives, that they're oblivious to what's going on at home, she herself not even entering their thoughts. No matter how much she wants, hopes, to be rescued, she prefers to be as far from her children's minds as it's possible to be.

She looks up as he reappears at the top of the stairs, a glass of water in his hand, the other resting lightly on the knife at his belt. A reminder of what he will do to her if she tries anything, if she even thinks about screaming when he's not next to her. 'Doesn't look like a very substantial breakfast, Bella, even for you. Sure I can't tempt you to a big fat bacon sandwich? Wouldn't take me a minute to nip to the café …'

Bella thinks for a few seconds, all her nighttime thoughts of escape coming back to her. If she sent him out, would that give her an opportunity? Would he perhaps be less vigilant now than he was yesterday? Maybe leave the basement door unlocked?

He chuckles. 'Ah, the look on your face, Bella. I always know what you're thinking, don't forget.'

Her shoulders slump. Of course he's not going to go out and get her a sandwich. Leave the door open. Her captor may be a lot of things, but he's certainly not stupid. 'I'll just have the water, thank you.'

'Wise choice, Bella.' He approaches slowly before holding the glass to her lips. 'There we go, all better. Can't have your beautiful skin drying out now, can we?'

She swallows, her throat painful, perhaps more than simply dry. 'Thank you.'

'You're very welcome. Sure I can't get you anything else?'

Bella thinks hard. Looking at him, she realises how different her situation is now to how it was the last time she was here. Her captor is older, more mature. Escape will not be so easy this time around; she's aware of that. 'Actually, there is something I wanted to ask you. If that's okay?'

He gives a little bow. 'Your wish is my command, Bella. Just name it. Within reason, of course.'

'Please could you think about unstrapping me from the chair?'

She tries to speak quickly, to get the words out before he stops her. Or gags her again. 'I mean, you know I can't go anywhere. I'm trapped down here. The door is firmly locked – you see to that every time you leave. Even if I banged on it, I doubt anyone would be near enough to notice. Believe me, I'm completely aware of my limitations. What harm could it do to release me from the chair? At least let me stretch my legs?'

He looks at her for a few seconds before chuckling again. 'Bella, even you know that's a request too far. After what happened last time you were down here? You must think I'm a gullible idiot ...'

'Please. I promise I won't try to escape. I'm just so uncomfortable.'

He shakes his head, reaching forward to pull her gag back up. 'I'll see you in a little while, Bella. When I'm sure you'll be regretting not having taken me up on my offer of breakfast. Don't get too hungry now.'

'Please ...' Bella tries to form the word around the scarf as he walks back up the stairs, her throat more painful with each sound she makes. 'Please ...'

He gives her a final glance over his shoulder before shutting the door and locking it.

Three weeks earlier

'But surely you can tell me if someone else rang after I'd booked the table? If someone claimed the details had changed?' Bella paced the kitchen, her mobile pressed firmly to her ear. She was glad it was finally the weekend, that she had some time off work. She'd been struggling to focus on anything other than what had happened at the restaurant and wasn't sure she could cope with going into the office much longer. Not when she was feeling as she was.

'I'm sorry, Mrs Anderson. We have so many bookings each week, all taken over the phone by different members of staff; it really would be impossible to tell you. If someone did change your booking, it likely would have been a different member of staff who dealt with it than the one who took your original call.'

Bella grunted in frustration. She looked down at the name card she'd been rolling around between her fingers almost constantly in the three days since she'd leant across the table and seen Lawrence's name on it. This wasn't the first occasion she'd called the restaurant, her frustration growing every time she was fobbed off by a junior member of staff. Today, she'd insisted on speaking to the manager, a glamorous, red-haired woman she'd seen in there a few times when she'd been in with Jack. 'Someone must have written the new details down though? If someone had changed the booking? Perhaps done something as simple as scribbled out one name and replaced it with another?'

'You're probably right, Mrs Anderson. But once a booking has been fulfilled, we shred all the details of the previous day's visitors, firstly due to data protection, and, secondly, because, otherwise, we'd have mounds of paperwork. I'm afraid there'll no longer be any record of any changes made to your booking on Wednesday.'

Bella stopped pacing, trying to think. 'Surely there must be some way of finding out if someone changed that booking without me knowing ...' If that was what had actually happened, she thought to herself. Jack was adamant, even now, that she had simply made the mistake herself. The more time passed, the more she'd begun to wonder if he was right. But she'd been so sure ...

'I'm afraid not, Mrs Anderson. I'm so sorry I can't help you any further. I'm aware that you and your husband are regular customers here and we'd hate to lose you because of a silly mix-up. Please accept our offer of a free ...'

Bella moved the phone away from her ear and ended the call. She was angry. Angry and embarrassed. She'd looked like such a fool: walking out of a restaurant she visited regularly in such a state, not even paying for her drink, though the manager had assured her on the phone that the cost of her wine had been covered after she left. Jazz, she presumed. She sat down at the table, thinking about what Jack had said to her after they'd got home on Wednesday night. How it was such an easy mistake to make, one he'd made many times himself at work. Was he right? Had she really been so distracted after showing pictures of Lawrence to Paige that she'd automatically said *his* name instead of her own husband's? Thinking about how happy Lawrence would have been at the idea made her want to throw up.

She flushes as she remembers how she'd kind of proved Jack's point, saying her stalker's name in the heat of the moment, her mind muddled from all the stress. It wasn't the first time it had happened. Bella had once called Jack *Lawrence* when they'd not long been seeing each other, after they'd both had a bad day and had got into a petty argument about something she couldn't remember: what they were going to eat for supper, or which film they might watch on TV. She pictured his young face as he tried his best not to show how much the mistake had upset him. Had her husband felt the same on Wednesday but again attempted to hide his pain? Focusing his concern on her rather than on himself and his own feelings?

She looked up as Paige came into the kitchen.

'You ready?'

Bella sighed. The last thing she felt like doing was shopping for holiday clothes for her daughter, dealing with Paige thinking nothing suited her and taking ages to try everything out on a busy Saturday. 'Sure.'

Feeling like she didn't have much choice, she grabbed her car keys and bag, dropping the restaurant name card back inside along with her phone. She couldn't imagine how she would be able to concentrate on the task in hand this afternoon, but she'd try. She'd spent little enough time with the kids as it was lately. Been too distracted by other things.

She shouted up to Jack that she was leaving, asking that he please make sure all the doors were kept firmly locked. She wasn't sure he'd even heard. He and Freddy, as well as an assortment of Freddy's friends, were absorbed in a new video game in her son's bedroom. Perhaps he simply didn't feel the same need she currently did to be extra conscious of security.

The roads were full of traffic, and Bella found it difficult to keep her patience, tooting her horn more than once. When a pedestrian stepped out in front of her as she tried to turn into the multi-storey car park, she swore sharply.

'Mum, calm down.'

'I'll calm down when people stop being so stupid.' She felt Paige looking at her. 'Sorry, I'm sorry, sweetheart. I'm just tired, that's all.'

'You haven't been yourself for weeks. Dad said he's worried about you.'

Bella glanced at her daughter as she drove up the steep ramp. 'He said that?'

'He did. He told us we have to be *mindful* around you, because you're so anxious all the time. Apparently, you're not coping very well after that Lawrence guy was released.'

Not coping? Was that how Jack worded it? Putting the responsibility on *her*? Making it clear to the kids that what was happening, her recent distress, was down to her alone? That it was nothing to do with Lawrence, but simply how she was reacting to him re-entering the world? She tried to concentrate on finding a space, pulling the car into a tight spot between two others on what seemed to be the busiest floor. She didn't want the car park to be empty when they returned.

They took the lift down to the mall, Bella making sure they waited for an empty carriage, just the two of them inside. As they stood quietly, she took a deep breath. For her daughter's sake, she was going to try her best to put Lawrence Knox to the back of her mind. At least for a few hours. 'So, are you looking forward to the holiday?'

'Can't wait.' Paige smiled. 'Louise says there's a huge pool in the villa and a cool bar just down the road.'

'A bar, eh? Well, I hope Louise's parents are going to be keeping a close eye on both of you.'

Paige chuckled as they reached the ground floor. 'Yeah, right.'

They walked through the mall, Bella constantly looking over her shoulder as Paige meandered in and out of various shops. Looking around each one, she checked the positions of the security guards, searched for the fire exits, scrutinised as many other customers as she could, her heart thudding at one point as a man in a red baseball cap caught her attention. It wasn't Lawrence. Even so, Bella felt inclined to move closer to her daughter, constantly checking the whistle she'd slipped around her neck before she left, usually reserved for when she was running alone. She hoped Paige hadn't noticed she was wearing it.

As they left River Island, Bella jumped as she heard someone say her name. Turning warily, she saw her sister standing outside the shop next door, Cameron in the double pushchair in front and Katie walking alongside, holding her mother's hand.

Bella took a deep breath, remembering how upset Rosie was the last time they spoke. She hadn't told her sister about what had happened at the restaurant, knowing it would simply add fuel to the fire of their argument. 'Rosie, hi.'

Paige dropped her shopping bags, moving towards Katie and holding out her arms. 'How're my favourite cousins?'

Katie giggled, her arms in the air as she waited to be picked up. She loved spending time with Paige, the two of them so alike, it was clear to Bella that Rosie's daughter was practically going to be her own daughter's twin as she grew older.

Rosie was looking at her. 'How's things?'

Bella shrugged. 'You know, okay …' She wasn't sure what else to say, not used to an awkward atmosphere when she was with her sister. 'Are you doing some shopping?' Of course she was. Why else would Rosie be in town?

'Just picking up a few bits for the twins.'

Bella nodded, watching as Paige played with Katie's hair. She looked back at Rosie. 'Maybe we could all go for a …?'

'We'd better get going.' Rosie shook her head, reaching for her daughter's hand. 'Cameron's getting tired.'

'Okay …'

'Bye, Paige.'

Bella watched as her sister walked away, the twins gesturing towards a toy shop as they passed.

The rest of the afternoon passed quickly, Paige being surprisingly less choosy with her outfits than she usually was, perhaps something to do with Bella's agreement to spend a bit more money than she normally would, a way of coping with her guilt at not taking as much interest as she would have liked in her daughter's holiday attire. She'd been a dreadful mother lately, she thought, as she nervously watched Paige stand at the counter in Next, using Bella's card to pay for her goods. Always on edge, never relaxed or interested in doing the fun things she normally at least tried to enjoy. When was the last time they'd all got together on a Friday evening and watched a film? Played a board game? Not for quite a few weeks, she realised.

She smiled as her daughter approached, bags over each arm. 'How about a milkshake? I can't remember the last time we sat and had a drink together.' She wished she'd insisted on her sister coming with them.

'Ooh, yum. And one of those scrummy cookies?'

Bella's heart tightened at Paige's wide eyes. Sometimes it was as if her baby had never grown up from the sweet little girl she once was. 'Sure, as many cookies as you'd like.'

They walked back through the mall, Bella's arm at Paige's back as they negotiated the crowds. At times like these, Bella couldn't help but remember the numerous times when she was at uni and she or one of her friends had spotted Lawrence lurking in the distance. Standing on a corner of the street or hiding in the shadows of a doorway, watching her. Usually he would be smirking, as if to let her know that he was never going to do what she wanted. Never going to let her get on with her life without him being a part of it. With how she was feeling lately, it looked like he'd been right, didn't it? How could he have had such a hold on her for so long?

As they neared Paige's favourite milkshake stall, Bella automatically glanced over her shoulder as they queued. As she scanned the crowds, she stopped, her gaze resting on a figure quite a distance away, her heart feeling as if it were suddenly going to burst out of her chest.

No.

It was him. She was sure of it.

Was it?

She squinted, studying the darkly clothed man who was loitering by a far glass door that led to the street. His face was covered by a baseball cap, pulled low in exactly the same way Lawrence used to wear, his black or navy long-sleeved T-shirt looking as if it carried some kind of sporting logo. He was standing very still, staring in her direction. Although she couldn't see his eyes, Bella could feel them on her. It was as if she'd travelled back in time.

She stepped away from her daughter. 'Paige, stay here ...'

Bella could barely hear Paige's protests as she walked back through the mall, all her attention focused on the figure that she knew, *knew*, was watching her. Anger roared through her like a blazing fire. This man had done enough, ruining her life in the past, at a time when she should have been enjoying herself, having fun like the other students. Now, he was daring to try and ruin it again. After all she'd done to try and move on, get over him, all the therapy, all the nights waking up covered in sweat, her family constantly worrying about her, he was here, in her home town. Which meant she'd been right all along. Lawrence Knox had been stalking her again. He'd sent her flowers, a friend request, could have been in her house. He had changed her restaurant booking after she'd made it.

She began to jog, dodging around the other shoppers, some of them frowning at her as she only narrowly avoided bumping into them, determined to reach Lawrence before he attempted to escape. This time, she wasn't going to be afraid. She was going to confront him, end this stupid game once and for all.

Within seconds, the man moved, Bella watching as, head bowed, face in shadow, he pulled open the glass door, obviously intending to head outside. She began to run faster, determined not to let him get away from her. Not now she had him in her sights. Little did Lawrence Knox know, she wasn't that meek young girl anymore, the one he could control so easily. She was an adult now. She was ready to fight.

She reached the doors just as he slipped out, Lawrence jogging down the steep steps in front of her and disappearing around the edge of a building. Quickening her pace, Bella pulled the heavy door open and ran down the steps herself. She paused briefly at the bottom, looking up at the street in front of her. Lawrence was in the distance, seeming to be heading for the main road, his arms swinging as he walked quickly, proficiently. She wondered how he'd got so far in such a short time. Perhaps he'd spent his time in prison working out.

She began to run after him, trying to maintain her breathing as she shouted as loudly as she could. 'Hey, hey, you … Don't think you can run away from me.' She was aware of people turning their heads to look at her, a crowd at a nearby bus stop ceasing their conversations as she ran past.

As she reached the top of the street, she watched Lawrence jog across the main road, integrating himself into the crowds of shoppers on the other side, briefly dropping out of sight. Spotting a police car parked further down, outside a block of offices, Bella lifted her whistle to her lips, the blue, backwards letters on the white bonnet like a beacon she had to reach. She had to attract someone's attention, let them know what was happening.

She was determined she wasn't going to lose the man who had caused her and her family so much harm.

She blew as hard as she could, the shrill sound piercing the afternoon air. This was only the second time she'd used the whistle in nineteen years, the first when she'd thought a gang of youths was following her as she jogged through her local park. She remembers how the community support officer who'd come to investigate had raised his eyebrows at her, his attitude patronising, as so many people had been over the years, the kids simply behaving, he said, as kids often do when they're out and about. The way her own kids probably had on many an occasion when she wasn't there to chide them. Now, she ran across the road, narrowly avoiding being hit by a taxi as she continued to shout and blow her whistle. By this time, she was attracting more than a little attention, some of the shop doors along the road opening as the staff came out to see what all the fuss was about.

Bella waved her arms in the direction of the police car, the two officers standing near it looking in her direction. She shouted at the top of her voice. 'Stop that man, stop him.' She blew her whistle again, an elderly lady standing nearby gasping and putting her hands over her ears, as if the sound was causing her pain. A dog further up the road began to bark frantically.

One of the police officers jogged towards Bella. 'Er, madam, can we help you?'

Bella stopped in her tracks, seeing the officer wince as she blew her whistle again in frustration. There was a crowd gathering around her now, some people even filming her on their mobile phones, grinning as they did so. Great, now she was going to be all over the internet. Just what she needed. She felt her cheeks burn. 'That man—' she pointed up the road, trying to catch her breath '—he's been stalking me …'

The police officer followed her gaze, his colleague talking to someone on her radio. The first officer looked back at Bella. 'Just calm down and take a breath. Which man are you talking about, madam?'

'That one … The one with …' Bella stopped, squinting her eyes. Moving her head from side to side, she tried to see around the people closest to her. The street was so busy now that all the pedestrians seemed to be blending into each other, making her feel as if she were looking for a single fish in a sea of a million others. No matter how hard, how far she looked, there was no sign of a red baseball cap, a dark sports shirt, anywhere.

She squealed in frustration, stamping her feet on the pavement as a toddler might.

Lawrence Knox had completely disappeared.

*

Bella walked back up the stone steps towards the mall, her shoulders slumped. She was cross with herself. If she hadn't caught the attention of the police, been hindered by the passers-by crowding around her, she might have easily caught up with Lawrence. She was a fast runner, years of practice keeping her fit, preparing her for an occasion such as this. And yet she'd failed to reach him. To stop him. He'd simply got away from her.

She guessed she was lucky that the police officers let her go after giving her a talking-to, instead of taking her to the police station, accusing her of disturbing the peace or some such. They hadn't shown much understanding of what she was saying anyway. When she'd tried to explain about Lawrence, about who he was and what he'd done, they'd looked at her in the same way her family had seemed to be looking at her recently. In the same way the authorities had the other times she'd thought she was in danger. As if she were making up fairy tales, like a child with an overactive imagination.

Her stomach lurched as she remembered her daughter. Bella had left Paige by the milkshake stall, hadn't even thought to ask if she could make a quick call when she'd been trying to explain to the police why she was making such a spectacle of herself. The officer had kept her talking for, what? Twenty minutes? More? She pulled her phone from her bag. Six missed calls and a text. She'd been away from her daughter for almost three-quarters of an hour.

Feeling nauseous, she jogged up the last few steps and pulled open the same glass doors she'd exited from, the recent memory of spotting Lawrence standing there sending shivers up her spine, cold sweat drying on her skin. She must have looked a mess. As she walked quickly through the thinning, late-afternoon crowd, she looked around for her daughter. Paige was sitting on a bench a little way from where Bella had left her.

Bella breathed a sigh of relief. At least Paige was okay; the idea that Lawrence could have doubled back on himself after she'd lost him, headed back into the mall while she herself was delayed talking to the police, suddenly filled her with an almost paralysing fear. As she approached the bench, she realised that her sister was sitting alongside her daughter, one arm around Paige's shoulders while she jiggled the twins' pram with the other.

'Paige.' She covered the ground between them as quickly as she could. 'I'm so sorry ...'

'Where have you been?' Paige stood up, her make-up streaked by tears. 'What happened? One minute, you were here, the next, you'd completely vanished. I thought ...'

'Oh, no, Paige.' Bella took her daughter in her arms. 'I'm fine, honestly. I'm really sorry.' She looked at Rosie. 'I'm sorry, you really didn't need to ...'

Rosie pursed her lips. 'Paige called me to see if I was still in town. She was frightened. She didn't know what had happened. What on earth were you thinking, Bella? Where did you go?'

'I ...' Bella was suddenly reluctant to speak, not wanting to aggravate her sister more than she already seemed to have. 'I saw Lawrence.'

'What? Lawrence Knox? Here?' Rosie looked around in alarm.

'Yes.' Bella pointed towards the doors she'd just come through. 'He was standing over there. I chased after him, but he ran away. I ... I lost him.'

Rosie looked at her, her arm still around Paige's shoulders, as if protecting her. But from who? 'And you're sure it was him? You saw him clearly? Spoke to him?'

Bella shook her head. Again, she felt like a child being told off. 'No, I ... He was too far away. And when he ran, I couldn't catch him up. I tried ... But it was him. I know it was.'

'Did you see his face?'

Bella thought back to when she'd first spotted the figure lurking in the distance. Her eyesight wasn't bad for someone her age, the only glasses she needed to wear for close-up reading. Surely that meant she couldn't have been mistaken. Didn't it? 'He was wearing a hat, a baseball cap, like Lawrence used to, pulled low. But, Rosie, I'd know him anywhere. I *know* it was him.'

'Oh, like that guy wearing a hat over there?' Rosie gestured to a young man walking past. Two spots of pink had appeared on her cheeks. 'Or that one there? Are they Lawrence too? And what if it had been, Bell? What if it had been Lawrence? Which I'm sincerely beginning to doubt … You left Paige *alone*. After everything you've said about the kids needing to keep themselves safe.' She pulled her niece closer to her.

'I … I didn't think.' Bella felt confused. Her sister was angry with her. Paige was upset. She could see now that she should have stayed. Perhaps alerted a security guard, called the Victim Contact Scheme as soon as she got home to tell them she thought she'd seen Lawrence. Yet, at the same time, this was happening to *her*, wasn't it? This man was torturing *her*, wrecking any chance she had of living a normal life, making her behave in ways she wouldn't usually. And, for the first time in as long as she could remember, her family, her loved ones, didn't seem to understand.

'No, you didn't.' Rosie pulled her arm from around Paige. 'I've told Paige to make sure she calls me if there's any time she feels unsafe again in the future. Any time at all. Day or night. Which I'm hoping she won't. For now, I suggest you take your daughter home, Bella.' She kissed Paige's cheek.

Bella watched her sister walk away, an ache sitting low in her stomach. She hadn't eaten much recently and her head felt light from the running. She turned to Paige. 'I'm so sorry, sweetheart. You're fine, no harm done. Let's get you that milkshake and cookie.'

'Too late. The stall's closing.' Paige gathered up her bags and began to walk towards the lift.

Jack now

Jack makes his way through the town centre, the sun above him strong enough to burn, making his scalp tingle. The old market square is busy, most of the weekend shoppers wearing shorts and T-shirts, sunglasses and floppy hats. Jack stands for a moment, watching a group of excited children queue for a mini funfair ride, remembering when his own were that age. He used to love bringing them out in the summertime, taking them to parks and on bike rides, taking the train into Chester and riding the river boats. It was the family life he never thought he'd have.

He remembers the last time he spoke to his own mum, perhaps eight or nine years ago now, just before she passed. The conversation, like many they'd had, had been fraught with tension, their countless unresolved disputes always simmering between them. She and Bella had never got on, the two of them only meeting once or twice in the early days, Mum not even bothering to send an apology or make an excuse when she didn't turn up for the wedding. She'd never met Freddy or Paige, her only grandchildren apparently of little interest to her.

Jack has never told Bella the truth about how difficult his upbringing was. She's had enough to deal with, without him adding to it. When he first became part of his wife's family, he struggled with how much Bella's parents did for her: giving her the house, lending her money whenever she needed it. Much as Jack has always loved where they lived, he occasionally wondered then if it should have been *his* job, as the so-called man of the house, to provide for his family. To build their future. Bella never thought it mattered. *We'll do the same for our own kids,* she's said more than once. *That's what parents are for.*

It wasn't what *his* parents were for, certainly. When Bella had first come into his life, his mother's latest boyfriend, one of many in Jack's youth, had just moved in with Mum after getting out of prison. *Uncle* this, and *Uncle* that, she'd always called them when he was little. Jack had worked his hardest to get away, to get his career off the ground, make some money and escape from his childhood home. He was determined not to follow in his parents' footsteps, not to be anything like his own dad who he'd only met once when he was very young. Jack was going to be different, to make something of himself. And he's done that, hasn't he? He's made it, changed the course of his journey. Got the job, the respect, the family. And, at least, when his time comes, hopefully later rather than sooner, he won't exit the world in the same way his mother did: in a stupor, surrounded by empty booze bottles and dirty takeaway cartons. The detritus of the life she didn't even have the awareness to regret.

He makes his way across the square, heading for the small café bar where he's arranged to meet Jazz, hoping whatever paperwork she needs him to sign won't take very long. Seeing that she hasn't arrived yet, he picks a table in one corner, remembering how concerned Jazz had been after the incident in the restaurant, when Bella had a panic attack and claimed the booking had been sabotaged. What must his PA have thought of his frantic wife? Of the fact she'd said she was waiting for Jack while the name cards on her table implied she'd be sharing dinner with Lawrence instead? Had Jazz believed Bella to be coherent and stable? That she was telling the truth when she said she didn't know what had happened? Or had she seen what the rest of the outside world had been seeing recently? That his wife was a little fragile and not quite thinking straight, not coping with the idea of her abductor being out of prison.

It was entirely feasible to anyone who knew what Bella had been through that she could have made a mistake when she'd made the restaurant booking. Used Lawrence's name instead of his own. In fact, it was obvious to anyone who'd seen the state Bella was in recently that that was what had happened. It was a simple mistake, one anyone could have made, but one that had had a huge knock-on effect on Bella's relationship with the people around her, especially after she'd gone on to abandon Paige in town, claiming she'd seen Lawrence lurking nearby.

Jack feels sad as he remembers how Paige called her mother a complete hypocrite, getting cross when that estate agent had turned up at the house but then running off herself without a word. How could she have claimed she wanted to keep the kids safe if she was willing to go chasing some random stranger through the town centre, leaving her daughter alone and vulnerable? Jack has tried his utmost to be sympathetic to Bella over the years, but he agreed that her behaviour didn't look so good then. She'd claimed she'd seen Lawrence, that she'd tried to attract the attention of the police so she could prove he was stalking her again, but the episode hadn't come to anything. No one really believed the person his wife had spotted was anyone other than a man in a baseball cap, an innocent bystander.

He stands briefly as Jazz walks through the door. As usual she's dressed as if she's just left some trendy fashion show, her summer jeans dazzling white, her bright green sleeveless blouse complimented by a chunky silver necklace. 'Hi, Jazz.'

She sits down opposite him, putting her bags on the chair next to her. 'Sorry I'm late. I got distracted by the chocolate shop. I only intended to nip in, but who knew gift wrapping took so long?'

'No problem. Buying for someone special?'

'Just a gift for Lana. It's her birthday next week and she has a real sweet tooth.'

Jack smiles. It's suddenly nice to be talking about normal things for a change, things that don't involve stalkers and kidnappers. It feels like it's been a long time. 'How are things going between you two?'

Jazz shrugs. 'It's still early days, but we do get on.'

'When your dates aren't being interrupted by my wife's panic attacks ...'

'That wasn't Bella's fault.' She raises an eyebrow as she adjusts her chair. 'I was glad I was there, not that I was much help.'

'I think we've all been struggling to support her these past few weeks.' He glances at the menu on the wall. 'Would you prefer tea or coffee?'

'Coffee definitely. And I'm famished. Are you eating?'

'I probably should while I'm here. I've been up for hours but have only managed hotel coffee so far.' He waves her away as she pulls her purse out. 'Don't worry, I'll get it.'

They make their choices: eggs on toast for Jack, crushed avocado for Jazz. Jack goes to the counter to order, wondering, as he waits, when he and Bella last had breakfast together. Not for a while, he thinks. He remembers how, in the early days, before the kids, they used to lounge in bed together on their days off with cup after cup of strong coffee and flaky croissants. He misses those days.

He takes their coffees back to the table. 'So, shall we get this paperwork sorted? I've brought some invoices for you to file, if that's okay. I thought I might as well make use of my sudden free time.' He opens the folder he's left on the table, feeling Jazz's eyes on him. He looks up at her. 'What?'

'Nothing. You look tired, that's all.'

He shrugs. 'I haven't been sleeping too well. You could say it's been one of those weeks.'

'How are the kids coping?'

Jack sighs. 'They're both on holiday, which I'm grateful for. They've been fully aware that Bella and I aren't getting on so well lately, especially Paige, but I wouldn't want them to know I'm not at home. That things have got quite so bad between their mum and me. Not unless …'

'Unless?'

'Unless I have to tell them.'

Jazz pulls sheets of paper from the leather work bag she's brought with her. She passes them across the table. 'I need signatures on all these, I'm afraid. I don't know how I missed them yesterday …'

'No problem. Did you bring a pen?'

She passes him a black biro, watching as he begins to write. 'Is that what you see happening then? That you'll have to tell the kids? That you and Bella will split up eventually?'

Jack takes a sip of his coffee, the heat stinging his tongue. 'I honestly don't know. Maybe. Bella's not been the easiest person in the world to live with recently. Even talking to her has become more and more difficult. For all of us.' He signs another sheet.

'She's been through a lot.'

'We all have.'

'Bella more than most, I would say.'

They sit back as their food arrives, Jack shifting the pile of paper to the other side of the table.

Jazz sprinkles salt over her avocado before freeing her knife and fork from a rolled-up napkin. 'What I mean is, it's completely understandable that she's not herself.'

Jack nods. 'You're right. There aren't many people who can say they've been through what she has. It breaks my heart, to be honest. I feel so helpless sometimes.'

'Have you spoken to her since yesterday?'

He shakes his head. 'She's texted me a few times.' He brings his phone screen to life and holds it up, showing Jazz the goodnight message that came from his wife's phone last night.

'At least she's thinking about you.'

'Yep.'

'You must be worried though.'

Jack cuts into his granary toast. 'I feel like I've done nothing *but* worry for weeks, but what can I do?' He shrugs again. 'As frustrated as I feel, I can't make her want me to be at home. I guess I should be grateful it's only a couple of days.'

Jazz swallows a mouthful of food. 'She did seem to make it very clear she needed this time alone. I just ...'

'What?'

Jazz seems to think for a few seconds. 'Have you ever thought, what if she's right? What if it *is* Lawrence Knox behind everything that's going on? Is she safe there, in the house on her own?'

Jack sighs, more heavily this time. He puts down his knife and fork. 'If you want me to be completely honest, Jazz, I do not think for one minute that Bella is in any danger from Lawrence Knox. We've looked into it and, according to the people who are monitoring him, he's not put a foot wrong since his release. Not once. And they really do know what they're doing.' He picks up the pen and signs another sheet. 'I genuinely appreciate your concern, of course I do, but do you really think I would have left her alone this weekend if I thought he was still stalking her? If I thought there was any remote chance?'

'I suppose not.'

'I've spent weeks trying to look at this from every angle, and I think the truth is that Lawrence is doing exactly what the authorities have said he is: abiding by the rules of his release, staying in his own area. Getting on with his life. Just like Bella should be doing.'

'But from the bits and bobs you've told me at work, she seems so sure ...'

Jack takes another slurp of coffee, thinking about the times he's gone into the office feeling low after another *incident*, as he and the kids have come to call them, at home. 'Yes, but this isn't the first time she's felt like this. Nor is it the first time she's wanted me nowhere near her when news of Lawrence Knox has popped into our lives yet again. The kids and I have seen it numerous times over the years: when there's a parole hearing, the anniversary, even when she's seen something on a TV show or the news that's triggered unhappy memories. Then Bella's stress gets the better of her and she starts to feel anxious, stops taking care of herself, starts drinking a little too much. Even begins to see things that aren't there. Imagines things. At times like this, she becomes completely unaware of her own behaviour and how it affects everyone around her.'

Jazz rests her cutlery on her plate. 'And you think her having some time alone will help?'

He scrapes his own plate. 'I hope so. Fingers crossed, once she's had some thinking time, she'll be able to see things more clearly and we can get her the help she needs. Lawrence's release has been a massive shock, but I'm praying that, with some therapy and support, she'll be able to move on eventually. We all will. Together, as a family.'

'I hope so, Jack. I really do. I've felt so sorry for her these past few weeks.'

Jack smiles. Jazz is obviously a very caring person, so much more mature now than the shy intern he'd once given an opportunity to. 'Anyway, enough about my problems. Let's get this paperwork sorted, shall we?'

Jazz drains her coffee and, pushing her plate and cup to one side, begins to sort through the remainder of the sheets in front of her.

Bella now

She needs to think, to calm her racing brain and work out a way to get out of here. Her throat is burning now, sharp needles of pain pricking at the inside of her mouth every time she tries to swallow. She wonders if she's getting some kind of summer flu or other virus. If she weren't trapped down here, she'd probably think about talking to a doctor or pharmacist. Some chance.

She wonders what he's doing upstairs. It seems like ages since he came down and brought her the glass of water, her stomach rumbling as she knew it would after she refused food again. She knows she should eat something, *keep up her strength* as her mother used to say when she struggled with food after the first abduction, but she doesn't think she could stomach it. She's frightened she'd be sick around the gag and end up choking, or sitting here covered in her own waste. She swallows again, tears springing to her eyes with the pain.

She hates being ill, any sense of being incapacitated making her feel weak. She remembers once, four or five years ago, when a particularly bad flu virus was doing the rounds, the kids both catching it at school, Freddy first, then Paige. After thinking she'd escaped its clutches, Bella had started to feel not quite right herself just as the kids were recovering. She'd spent the next two weeks in bed, barely able to lift her head, let alone do any cooking or anything around the house. Jack was brilliant, taking time off work to look after her, running back and forth to the pharmacy, making her soup. She remembers being so grateful at the time that she had him to look after her. That she could rest easy knowing he wasn't the type of husband, the type of father, who needed detailed instructions before he could do anything.

That was what had first attracted her to Jack. The minute she met him, she had a feeling she'd be able to rely on him for anything. Be able to ask him anything and he'd be there, immediately at her side. It was as if he wanted to prove to her that he would take care of her. That her place next to Jack was her safe zone. And he'd done that, hadn't he? He'd looked after her for all of their married life.

She wonders if her family are thinking about her, worrying about her. Or if she's simply pushed them too far away recently. She didn't mean to. Her family mean everything to her, her children the best things in her life. She's just been so frightened of everything that's been happening. And she was right, wasn't she? That's the silliest thing about the whole situation. She was right that she was in danger. Yet she feels no satisfaction at having been proved so. What difference does it make? Her family have still been hurt, her children traumatised.

As soon as she gets out of here, she'll apologise to them for all the hurt they've been through. Try and make amends with Freddy and Paige, as well as her sister. It might take time, but they'll get over it, she's sure. They'll be a family again eventually.

And she *will* get out, she just knows it. She *has* to.

She looks around the room. If only she could persuade him to unstrap her, release her from the chair, she is sure she'd be able to use something in the basement to overpower him. When she'd suggested to him that he at least make her a little more comfortable, give her a little more freedom, he'd smirked at her in that irritating way he has. As if he were laughing at her silly ideas. Treating her like a dumb female. It doesn't matter to her what he thinks of her. The next time he comes down, she's going to ask him again. Try and wear him down, like a persistent child badgering a tired parent for a new toy.

If only she had some idea of what he's planning. What he's hoping to achieve by holding her in the basement for a second time. Surely, he must have thought ahead. Must know he can't keep her down here indefinitely without someone noticing. Not for the first time, she wishes she could see into the future. Then perhaps she could come up with a plan of her own.

She rests her chin on her chest, suddenly feeling dizzy. She knows her blood sugars are low, the feeling the same as when she was pregnant and her body was struggling to process what she was eating. She hopes that, when she eventually stands up, she won't be too weak. That her muscles won't fail her. Moving her head around to clear it, her skin scrapes against something beneath the collar of her T-shirt. Something hard that she'd completely forgotten was there.

For the first time in many hours, Bella feels a sudden sense of warmth, of comfort.

Her whistle is still around her neck.

Two and a half weeks earlier

Bella sat at her desk, struggling to focus on the computer screen in front of her. She'd been at work for over two hours already and had barely done a thing. When she'd got out of bed this morning, a large part of her had been tempted to call in sick again, ring her manager and make some excuse about not feeling very well. Yet, an even larger part of her didn't want to be at home either. She didn't feel safe anywhere.

She'd tried to explain it to Jack before she left.

'I feel like, everywhere I look, he's going to be there. Just like he was the first time around. As if, every time I look over my shoulder, he's going to be behind me, laughing at me, delighted that he's getting away with this all over again.'

Jack had looked exasperated. 'And yet, as we keep pointing out to you, you haven't actually seen him at all. You've just *thought* you have. I totally get where you're coming from, Bell, I really do, but you have to rein your imagination in, for your own sake. You're just going to make yourself ill.'

She knew he was getting cross with her, especially after the incident with Paige in town, but was Jack really expecting her not to be frightened?

She looked up as the door opened, part of her expecting to see Lawrence now, strolling into the office as if he belonged there, a huge bunch of flowers in his arms, her stalker wanting to deliver them personally this time. Instead, she saw Trish, smiling widely as she came in to start her shift.

'Morning, everyone, lovely day out there. Shame we're stuck in here ...' She hesitated as she saw Bella. 'Everything okay, Bells?'

Bella nodded, trying to hide behind her screen. She knew everyone in the office was talking about her. Just this morning, she'd overheard Cath, her manager, talking to someone on the phone, saying how she was feeling overburdened after a member of her team had recently *let her down*. Bella knew exactly who Cath had meant. She hadn't been as focused recently as she usually was. Did anyone blame her? How could she concentrate on her job, on *anything*, knowing that Lawrence Knox was in her life again? Was planning to ruin it the same way he had before?

After she thought, was *sure*, she'd seen Lawrence in town, as she'd told Jack this morning, Bella was convinced he was now going to be everywhere she went. Even when she was driving into work, she'd been constantly looking in the rear-view mirror, expecting to see him following her, keeping a car or two behind, like in the movies. She'd found herself carefully watching the pedestrians through the windscreen as she waited impatiently at a crossing, hating to be still for more than a few seconds. At any moment, one of them could have turned around and smirked at her. *I'm still here,* Lawrence would silently say as he looked at her. *You can't get rid of me. No matter how hard you try.*

And she had tried, hadn't she? She'd tried so hard to rid herself of him, to lead a normal life.

She wondered what she'd do if her worst-case scenario actually happened. If she came face to face with the man who'd imprisoned her. If she'd caught up with him that day in town. Would she scream at him to leave her alone? Make a citizen's arrest? She seemed hysterical enough as it was, Jack spending most of the night before begging her to come to bed after she'd checked the front and back doors, the windows, the basement, for what seemed like the thousandth time. She'd ignored him, spending much of the remaining dark hours keeping a vigil at the bedroom window. Just in case. Lawrence could have been out there, hiding in the lane. Watching her as she looked out for him.

She stifled a yawn as Trish approached her desk.

'Have you heard the rumours?'

Bella frowned. 'Rumours?'

'Cath is talking about redundancies. I *accidentally*—' she made quote marks in the air with her fingers '—saw an email on her computer the other day. At least three members of the team have to go.'

'I haven't heard anything.' Bella wasn't sure she'd have remembered if she had. Work was the last thing on her mind at the minute.

Trish smiled smugly. 'I did ask her about it and Cath's assured me my job is safe. She couldn't manage without me, were her exact words. Don't know about anyone else though. You had any more flowers delivered lately?'

Bella ignored the question. She'd liked Trish when they'd both first started the job within months of each other. Now, she could see that her colleague would probably step over her own mother to get a promotion. 'I've got work to do, Trish.'

'No problem. I'll leave you to it. Suppose everyone's going to have to work extra hard now to prove themselves. No room for slacking …'

Bella shook her head, putting her fingers to her keyboard and trying to at least look as if she was doing some work. She started an email before deleting it and trying again, the words seeming to be swimming across the screen in front of her.

'Bella?'

She looked up to see Cath standing at her desk. 'Hi, Cath. Everything okay?' Shit, Cath hardly ever came to speak to her unless it was bad news. Maybe she'd come to tell her she was one of the ones whose job was at risk. She felt strangely numb at the idea. Would she be so bothered if she was told she had to go? A few months ago, the thought would have devastated her. Now, she wasn't so sure.

Cath frowned. 'Wasn't it today you wanted the afternoon off? I've got it down in my diary that the new intern is covering you for a few hours?'

Bella sat still, searching her brain for some recollection of what Cath was talking about. Afternoon off? She remembered how she'd thought about calling in sick this morning; she'd had no inkling then that she was supposed to be off anyway. 'Today?'

'That's what it says. You're in ten 'til noon and then Lucy takes over.'

Bella reached across her desk for her phone. She usually left it in her bag but had used it this morning numerous times already to call the Victim Contact Scheme, each time being told the same thing, that, of course, her concerns would be looked into, but the right people were currently more than satisfied that Lawrence was behaving exactly as he should be, her stalker even seeming to have an alibi for the day she was sure she saw him in town: an appointment with his probation officer. She wondered if Cath knew she'd been making personal calls on work time. They were supposed to wait for their breaks.

She brought up her calendar, her stomach flipping when she focused on the day's date. 'Shit! Freddy's drum exam ...' She jumped up from her desk, almost tipping her chair back in the same way she had in the restaurant when she'd seen Lawrence's name on the place card. 'I completely forgot ...'

Cath frowned at her. 'You forgot you were supposed to be picking your son up?'

'I ...' Bella felt her cheeks colour. She began to collect her things together, trying to work out how late she was. She couldn't believe she'd forgotten, a vague memory lurking at the edges of her mind of Freddy talking to her about something this morning. She hadn't been listening, instead looking at old articles about Lawrence on her phone. 'I've had other things on my mind.'

'It would seem so.' Cath reached out a hand as she rushed past, resting it on Bella's arm. 'Bella, I know you've got a lot on at the minute and I totally understand how difficult things must be at home right now, but do I need to worry about you? Should I do a referral to occupational health?'

Bella shook her head. After what Trish had said, she was guessing her position was already fragile enough. 'I'm fine, Cath, honestly. It just slipped my mind that it was today. I'll see you tomorrow.' Even as she said it, she wasn't sure it was true. She couldn't imagine ever being able to focus on work again.

Cath nodded. 'We'll schedule a chat.'

Bella rushed out of the door, glancing at the time on her phone. If the traffic and lights were on her side, she'd just be in time to collect Freddy from school and make it to the music studio. She might have to push it a bit regarding the speed limit though. As she climbed into the car, the ringtone on her phone began to chime loudly. She switched it to hands-free. 'Freddy, I'm on my way.'

'Where are you, Mum? You're supposed to be here by now. I'm going to be …'

'We'll be fine, Freddy. Honestly, don't worry. I just got caught up at work, but I'll be there any minute now.'

'Any minute? How far away are you?'

Bella could hear the anxiety in her son's voice. She hated causing him to worry. She seemed to be doing that to her family a lot lately, Paige barely having spoken to her since they'd had words in town. 'Not far at all. Where are you waiting?'

'I'm in reception. The secretary keeps looking at me as if I've been abandoned. The head's given me time off especially and if I don't go …'

Bella bit her lip. 'We're going, I promise. We're not going to be late.' She silently cheered as the traffic light she was approaching turned green. 'I'm almost there. Stay in the reception area until I get there. I don't want you going outside on your own.'

'Why? In case that guy who kidnapped you comes for me? Will he?'

Bella pictured the school receptionist listening in on Freddy's conversation, wondered if she might alert the head as she heard his words. She wanted to reassure her son, to tell him he was going to be fine, but the truth was, that was exactly what she was worried about. Surely Lawrence would know that the way to get to her would be through her children? 'You'll be fine if you just stay right where you are, sweetheart. I'm going to hang up now, but I'll be right there, any second, okay? I promise you won't miss your exam.'

'Okay ...'

She made the rest of the journey in record time, wondering, as she drove, if she would be able to convince Freddy not to say anything to his dad about her arriving late. About her forgetting the exam. Jack would be fuming if he found out, especially with Paige already being frosty with her. Hadn't she caused her husband enough worry recently without him thinking she wasn't capable of looking after her children? She'd heard stories before, read them in the news all the time, of mothers whose fragile mental health had caused them to lose their kids. No way was she going to be one of them. A statistic.

She pulled into the school car park, barely taking the time to close the car door behind her before dashing into the small reception area. She lifted a hand to the receptionist as she tried to catch her breath. 'Thanks ...'

The woman smiled at her, her befuddled expression leaving Bella with little doubt that she'd been listening to Freddy on the phone.

'Come on, Fred, let's go.'

They jogged to the car, Bella half dragging her son behind her.

'You don't have to hold my hand, Mum.' Freddy pulled his arm from her grip.

'Sorry. We just need to hurry, that's all. We've still got to get back through the traffic into town or we won't make it in time.'

'Why were you late? Did you think you saw that Lawrence guy again?' Freddy climbed into the passenger seat and closed the door, pulling the seatbelt over his shoulder. 'Like when you were in town with Paige?'

Bella looked at him. 'No, of course not. I told you, I just got caught up at work. I lost track of time.' She started the engine.

'Dad says there's no way that could have been that Lawrence guy in town. He said he thought you were just seeing things, because you've been so stressed.'

'Dad's spoken to you about it?' She remembered what Paige had told her about Jack, saying the kids had to be mindful of her state of mind. What else had he told them? she wondered. That she'd simply been imagining everything? Undermining the message she'd worked so hard to get through to them that they needed to be vigilant at all times?

'He just said that guy coming out of prison had been a big shock for you. That we have to be patient.'

'Well, Dad's right that it's been a shock.' She drove out of the car park and onto the road, mentally crossing her fingers that the route into town wouldn't be busy. 'But what he should've said was that you and Paige still need to be extra careful with regards to keeping yourselves safe. Lawrence Knox is a very dangerous man and I need to know you're aware of that.'

'Is he going to hurt us? Hurt *you*?'

Bella felt guilty again at her son's anxiety. 'Not if we're very careful. If we all do everything we can to keep ourselves safe, until I can prove that he shouldn't be out of prison ...' *If* I can, she thought.

'It's getting late, Mum.' Freddy glanced at the clock on the dashboard.

'I know, I know ...' Turning left onto the main road, Bella pressed her foot down on the accelerator. She would have to exceed the speed limit if they were going to get there on time. 'I'm so sorry about all this, Freddy. I know I've been really distracted lately. I've had so much on my mind, but if I could ask you to please not tell your dad that I was late …'

'Mum, look out!'

Bella gasped. She pulled the wheel sharply to the right, immediately aware that it was completely the wrong move, her efforts to avoid the pedestrian who'd just stepped into the road meaning she was now heading straight into the path of an oncoming van. She scrabbled for the brake, the pedal seeming to have completely disappeared from the footwell.

Throwing her left arm out to protect Freddy, she closed her eyes as the car skidded across the central white line, swerving first one way, then the other, before coming to a sudden screeching halt against the low front wall that surrounded a nearby house.

Bella sat for a few seconds, retching, her head spinning before the blackness at the edges of her vision began to close in.

The last thing she remembered before she passed out was that the pedestrian she'd just tried to avoid killing was Lawrence Knox.

Jack now

He and Jazz walk next to each other, the Queen's Gardens quiet. Sometimes, on a Sunday, there's a farmer's market here. He and Bella have visited on the odd occasion in the past, buying continental cheese and focaccia for a late weekend supper. Those were the times when he felt most content in his family life. When they were doing normal things, not talking about stalkers and abduction and ex-criminals. When their lives had seemed the same as everyone else's.

Today, the area is almost empty, he and his PA enjoying the late morning sunshine as he walks her to her car, his thoughts still very much with his wife, as they have been since yesterday. He'd known what he was getting into. When Bella had first told him about her experience with Lawrence, Jack had known immediately that the relationship wouldn't be a smooth ride. Although he'd never admitted it to anyone, at first, he'd had a few doubts. Could he look after another broken person when he himself was still healing from his own fractured background? He wasn't sure. After he'd met Bella's family though, got to know her parents and her sister, seen the family life they had, he'd become determined he was going to make this work. He was going to create the family life he could only dream of when he was younger. The way they looked after each other was a million miles away from his own experience.

'Penny for them.' Jazz is watching him closely, as if she's worried about his sudden withdrawal, his pensive mood.

He shakes his head. 'Sorry, I was miles away. Just thinking about Bella. Everything she did to try and heal herself and now … Well, now she seems so fragile. As if she's fallen to pieces all over again.' He moves towards a bench, suddenly feeling weary. A pigeon bobs around on the stone path at his feet.

Jazz sits down next to him. 'It must have been very hard, the accident. Poor Freddy.'

'Yeah, he was badly shaken up. His shoulder was very bruised. We were lucky it wasn't worse. Much worse. It makes me feel sick to even think about it.'

'I guess that must have been the last straw. Bella putting your son in danger like that.'

Jack sighs, thinking about Jazz's words. He was terrified when he found out what had happened, the idea of losing his son his worst nightmare come true. 'I just don't know what she was thinking.'

'Maybe she was just very frightened, very confused, to have let that happen. I'm sure she would never have deliberately allowed Freddy to be hurt …'

'Maybe not deliberately, no, but if she hadn't forgotten about the stupid drum exam in the first place, hadn't been so distracted, she wouldn't have been rushing. Would have been driving more carefully. All she could think about was Lawrence Knox. She just didn't seem to have room in her head for anything else. For her family, even.'

'That must have been very frustrating for you.'

'Even more so when I found out she'd asked Freddy not to tell me. To keep it from me that she was late. What a pressure to put on a young boy.'

Jazz nods. 'What a shock. I couldn't believe it when you rang the office and told me what had happened. I felt so sorry for you. And for Bella. It must have been terrifying for her.'

Jack scoffs. He can't help it. 'Save your sympathy. Bella's her own person. She has to take responsibility for her actions.'

'Is that the real reason why you're willing to be apart from her now? Why you're not insisting on going home? Being with her? I know you said you're sure she's not in any danger, that she's imagining the threat from Lawrence, but still …'

'Maybe. I was very angry with her. Still am, I suppose.' He looks at Jazz. 'I haven't said this to anyone else, but maybe I need this break as much as she does. I'm tired, you know? Of all the drama, all the stress. How could Bella have put thoughts of Lawrence before the safety of her own son? I just don't understand it. The kids come first. Always. That's rule number one of parenting.' Although not in the case of his own parents, he's willing to admit.

'Well, I don't have kids, but I'd agree with you about that.' Jazz lifts her face to the sunshine. 'But I suppose to really understand Bella's actions, to know what's going on in her head, we'd have to have been through what she's been through, to have experienced it ourselves, otherwise how can we judge?'

'Well, I've lived with Bella for a long time and I'm still baffled sometimes by the way her mind works.'

'Yes, but going through that, having that experience, especially at such a formative time in her life, is completely different. I don't think even those closest to her will ever know what an impact it must have had.'

'I don't know. I guess not … I've tried so hard to understand over the years, but maybe you're right. Maybe I'll never really get it.'

Jazz shifts her position on the bench. After pulling a pair of designer sunglasses from her bag, she slips them on. 'Anyway, what have you got planned for the rest of the day? It's such nice weather, your wife wants to be alone, your kids are away enjoying themselves. Surely you're not going to sit in that hotel room all on your own?'

Jack chuckles. 'Not sure I have much choice, to be honest.'

'You could keep me company? Lana's working, so I'm free all day. We could catch a film?'

Jack shakes his head. 'Thanks, Jazz, but I'm not sure I could concentrate to be honest. I'd probably just end up sitting there brooding.' He stands up. 'I've got a load more paperwork in the hotel that needs sorting through. I might as well use the opportunity and it'll keep my mind off things. I hope …'

'Okay …' Jazz chews on her bottom lip. 'Well, how about we meet for some food later then? If I eat on my own, I'll just end up bingeing on junk.'

Jack thinks for a few seconds. He has to eat. 'How about I drop you a text when I start to get hungry?'

'Fine by me.'

'Great. Now, come on, let's get you to your car before this sun fries us both to a crisp.'

Jazz smiles as they continue to the car park.

One week earlier

Bella had spent most of the past week and a half hiding in her bedroom, using the accident as an excuse to spend much of her day alone, despite her injuries healing quickly, her body back to normal within three or four days. Jack had taken time off work to sort out the car repairs, as well as look after Freddy. To make toast and tea, delivering them to his wife and his son in the same way he always had when anyone in the family was ill. Only, this time, when Jack brought supplies to her, he'd done it with barely a word, the loving smiles he usually reserved for the supposed love of his life now seeming to have disappeared, like melting snow. The doctors had said the damage was fairly minor. They'd both be fine with a little rest. Bella wasn't sure. She felt as if part of her would never heal. Not now.

She moved slowly around the kitchen, putting a chamomile teabag into a mug and filling the kettle, her lethargy more to do with her sadness than anything physical. Alone in the house for the first time since the accident – Jack back at work, the kids hopefully enjoying their final day in school before the summer holidays – she felt her isolation like a weight sitting on her shoulders.

She sat down at the kitchen table as she waited for the water to boil, pulling her dressing gown more tightly around her and staring at the basement door. The room where it all started.

Where her life changed. What kind of person would she be now if she'd never known Lawrence Knox? A better one? A more successful and caring mother? Would she still have met Jack, had her children, if Lawrence had never come into her life? She'd never know, but what she did know was that she blamed Lawrence completely for the rift that had opened up between her and her family these past few weeks. It was no one's fault but his.

She remembered how upset Jack was when he arrived at the hospital, the fear in his eyes something she'd never seen before, not in all the years they'd been together.

'What the hell happened, Bell?' He'd already been to see his son on the children's ward, the flush in his cheeks telling her how agitated, how shocked, he was by what had happened. 'Freddy said you were rushing. That you were late …'

Bella had felt herself tense, the fresh bruising on her own shoulder and abdomen painful. Thank God they'd been wearing seatbelts. She remembered her last words to Freddy before the car swerved, how she'd been asking him not to tell Jack that she'd almost forgotten, *had* forgotten, to pick him up. 'The exam slipped my mind. It came to me when I was at work, when Cath reminded me that I'd booked the afternoon off.'

'How on earth did you forget? Freddy's been going on about this exam for weeks. So, you were speeding? You lost control?'

Bella could see clearly how Jack's fear was dissipating, turning to anger now that he knew she and Freddy were okay apart from their minor injuries. 'Not exactly …'

'*Not exactly?*' He'd taken a deep breath, apparently trying to control his voice in the quiet of the accident and emergency bay. 'What does that even mean, Bell?'

She remembered now that she hadn't wanted to say. Paige had still been frosty with her since the incident in town, Jack distant. Even Rosie had missed the regular phone calls they usually enjoyed every few days. What would her family think when she told them what had happened? Would they believe her? She swallowed heavily. 'I saw Lawrence again.'

Jack had looked at her, standing by the A&E bed with his hands on his hips, the cubicles on the other sides of the curtains all full of patients. The hospital was busy. 'Shit, Bell ...' His shoulders had slumped, in the same way they did when one of the kids had done something that really disappointed him.

'Jack, it was *him*! It happened so fast, in a blur, but I *know* it was. He stepped out into the road as I was driving past, right in front of my car. Wearing that same baseball cap pulled over his face, that same sports-type T-shirt. It was *Lawrence Knox* who caused the accident. Ask Freddy.'

'Freddy says he can barely remember anything about what happened. He's too shocked.'

'But this can't be a coincidence, Jack.'

Jack held up his hands, as if desperate. 'But, Bell, think about it. What the hell else could it be? Even if it was Lawrence, how the fuck would he know you were going to drive past? At that exact moment? How would he know where you were going to be?' Jack's voice had risen a notch before he tried to control it once again. 'Are you telling me, he'd been standing there for hours, in case you happened to drive by? Do you even know what you're saying? Are you concussed?'

She shook her head. 'I don't have concussion.'

'This has got to stop, Bell. It really has—'

'It was him, Jack. And he was near the school. Don't you see? He's homing in on Freddy and Paige as a way to get to me.'

'What are you talking about?'

'He's trying to get nearer to them so he can get closer to me. Hanging around in town, where Paige is, practically every weekend. Hovering near the school where they both are every weekday. He'll probably try to befriend them. Remember how I told you he chatted up my friend Laura, when he first started stalking me?'

'Who?' Jack looked confused.

'My uni friend. Laura. He approached her in the students' union one night, not long after I met him. Tried to make friends with her. She only realised who it was when one of my other friends walked in and recognised him as the guy who'd begun to bother me. It's what he does, Jack. He tries to get close to the people who *I'm* close to.'

'Except that would only make sense, Bell, if we didn't all know what he looked like. Not to mention the fact that you've been told time and time again that Lawrence hasn't left Leeds. Even the police reckon you must have been going so fast, that you simply misjudged the road, lost concentration …'

'What do you mean?'

'I spoke to them earlier. There wasn't anybody else at the scene when they got there. No one hurt apart from you and Freddy. No one claiming you'd nearly run them over. So …' He put his forefinger to the fingers of his other hand. 'Either A, it seems to me as if you simply imagined someone stepping into the road because you were rushing and not concentrating on your driving like you should have been. Or, B, if someone did step into the road, like you claim, it was just someone who made a quick getaway because they didn't want any hassle. Either way, it most definitely was *not* Lawrence Knox! It's as if you're obsessed, Bell.'

Bella had begun to cry. 'It was him, Jack.'

'No, it wasn't.'

'I want to take the kids out of school.'

'What?'

'I want to take them out of school. They're not safe there.'

Jack had stared at her wide-eyed. 'It's only a week or so 'til they break up for summer.'

'All the more reason for them to finish now. I need to know they're okay, just until they go on their holidays, and then I can relax. I'll know Lawrence won't be able to reach Paige in France and that Freddy will be safe with Mum and Dad. Then I'll be able to focus on finding out how he's getting away with fooling the authorities and proving to you that he's stalking me again, once and for all.'

'Christ, Bella.'

'I mean it, Jack.'

In the end, Jack had had little choice but to give in to her demands, Freddy and Paige staying at home, where Bella could see them, in the days after the accident. When they'd both insisted they wanted to go in for the last day of term, the most fun day of the whole year, she'd been reluctant to say the least, her fear of what might happen threatening to overwhelm her as it had so many times recently. She'd eventually agreed, on the condition that Jack drove them both in this morning and that he would pick them up later on, as well as insisting they both had fully charged phones with them and that they texted her every break and at lunchtime to let her know all was well. She wasn't sure she'd be able to relax until they were home.

She poured her tea. She and Jack had barely spoken since the accident. The kids seemed to be avoiding both of them by staying in their bedrooms, knowing the relationship between their parents was strained. Once Bella's bruising had begun to subside, she'd taken to walking along the lane to get out of the house for a little while, phone in her hand in case she needed it. The doctors had advised her to avoid exercise for at least a couple of weeks, but she was looking forward to being able to run again. It was the only way she knew how to clear her head. How to get her thoughts in some kind of order.

She sat down again, sipping at her hot tea and playing with the whistle she'd taken to wearing even while she was in the house, despite the logical part of her knowing there was no one nearby likely to hear if she used it. She didn't feel safe without it. She looked at the basement door again, staring at the knotted wood as if it were a television screen showing the story of her life, all episodes passing before her eyes in quick succession: Lawrence,

Jack, the kids. Work. The redundancy consultation process was due to begin in just a few weeks. Were they missing her after the doctor at the hospital had signed her off for a fortnight? Or was her absence simply a precursor to them letting her go? A chance for Trish to show Cath how much she could do, how she could be relied on more than her colleague?

She reached across the table for her mobile and scrolled through her contact list, wondering if she should ring the Victim Contact Scheme again. Just one more time, to see if they could tell her anything different. If they'd found anything out about Lawrence's movements over the past few weeks, anything that would suggest he'd been lying. Jack had said they'd get fed up with her. That they might even start screening her calls, if she phoned them too many times. She needed to stop, he'd said, on the few occasions over the past week when he'd been able to bring himself to speak to her. No doubt, he knew she wouldn't. Couldn't.

She stopped scrolling as she reached her sister's name. The last time she'd actually spoken to Rosie was the day she'd seen her in town, when Bella was sure she'd spotted Lawrence lurking in the distance and had set off in pursuit. She knew her sister had telephoned Jack a few times over the past week to check how Freddy was doing, hearing her husband talking on his mobile, downstairs in the kitchen, when she'd got up to go to the loo one night. He must have thought she was asleep.

'Tell Martin thanks for asking, but we don't need anything. Freddy's just mostly shaken up, struggling with the idea of his mum losing it so much that she ended up crashing the car, but he'll get over it in time.'

Listening at the top of the stairs, Bella had bitten her lip to stop herself crying out loud. How much it hurt to hear her husband say she was *losing it*.

Jack had continued. 'She's convinced it was Lawrence she saw. I've told her it's all ridiculous, and I'll keep telling her that. She's pushing me away, of course she is ... I can see what's coming ...'

What was it he could see coming? A complete breakdown? The end of their marriage?

'We just need to keep on at her. It won't be easy, but we have to keep trying.'

At least he seemed to still want to support her, she thought now. She supposed she should be grateful for that, even if her husband did seem to think she was imagining things. She clicked on Rosie's name with her thumb, holding the phone to her ear as it rung at the other end.

'Bella ...' As usual, Rosie sounded out of breath, harassed, tired, even with that one word. 'Hold on, just let me put Cameron down.'

'I just wanted to hear your voice. We haven't spoken for a while.'

'I know.' Rosie's tone was frosty, in the same way Paige's had been recently. 'Are you surprised? Honestly, Bella, I'm not sure I can speak to you at the minute without losing my temper.'

'But, Rosie ...'

'No, don't ... don't make excuses. You upset Paige and you put Freddy in real danger. I'm surprised Jack is still with you, to be honest. If Martin did anything like that to my kids, I'd be out the door like a shot.'

Bella felt a stab of hurt in her chest. Surely children belonged to both parents, Freddy and Paige hers as well as Jack's? She loved them more than she could say, always had done. She would never deliberately hurt her son. What had happened was an accident. An accident caused by none other than Lawrence Knox. 'I didn't put Freddy in danger, Rosie, I promise you. It was Lawrence, he ...'

'Don't even go there, Bella. Jack's right, this needs to stop. You know you're going to end up losing them, don't you? Losing all of your family if you're not careful.'

Bella couldn't believe what she was hearing. How could Rosie, her own sister, say such awful things to her? Was she right? Had her own behaviour been so bad that she might end up pushing away everyone she loved? The thought almost took her breath away. She couldn't speak.

'Look, Bell, why don't you just concentrate on getting yourself together? Katie, can you please stop that …? Come and stand with Mummy … Just concentrate on sorting yourself out and we'll speak another time, okay? I really can't deal with this right now. Martin's gone away again this morning and I'm up to my eyeballs.'

'Okay …'

'But, Bella, no more about Lawrence Knox, okay? Or flowers, or friend requests … or you really might not like the consequences of your actions. I'm hanging up now.'

Bella stared at the phone as it went dead. She knew her sister had been angry with her, but she hadn't realised that Rosie's resentment of her actions ran so deep. She felt completely and utterly alone.

Standing up suddenly, she scrabbled in her bag for her bunch of keys, quickly rustling through them to find the large copper-coloured one. She approached the basement door and then stabbed the key into the lock and pulled it open, a shiver running up and down her spine as she stared into the dark space. The place that had been so complicit in holding her against her will all those years ago. When she'd tried to come down here last, a few weeks ago, asking Rosie to stay on the phone with her while she checked to see if her stalker had been hiding beneath her house again, their conversation had been interrupted by the man who came to put an unwarranted *For Sale* sign in her garden. Her attempts to reconcile herself with her past had been thwarted, put on hold. *Well, not this time,* she said to herself. *Not anymore.*

Anger rose within her as she put a hesitant foot forward, resting it on the top of the first wooden step as if she were about to walk on hot coals, the darkness below seeming to pull at her, wanting to capture her, hold her within its grasp once again. Reaching a shaky hand towards the light switch, she flicked it on, watching as the items in the basement came into view: the children's old and broken instruments, camping equipment. Shadowy tarpaulins that rose and dipped like the surface of the sea.

Bella may have been alone this time, may have pushed her husband and sister away with her insistence that her stalker was still in her life, but there was one thing she now knew for sure. She was going to gain back power over her own life. And the first thing she needed to do in order to achieve that was what her therapist had told her so many times she had to face. The thing she'd never managed before, even with her sister's help. Her husband's.

She needed to go down into the basement for the first time in nineteen years.

She took another step down the stairs.

She was not going to let Lawrence Knox control her any longer. She was going to face her demons. End this game of cat and mouse once and for all. And, this time, she was going to win.

Bella now

She's beginning to shiver, her skin pimpling beneath her running clothes, her throat feeling as if it's on fire. A bead of sweat forms on her forehead and runs down into her eye, blurring her vision. She moves her head from side to side, the scarf in her mouth now wet and tasting mildewy. If only she could get out of this blasted chair.

She has a fever, her body alternating between hot sweats and cold tremors as it tries to cope with the alien invader that's spreading its virus-carrying tentacles deep within her. Cursing silently, she wonders if it's anything to do with the car accident. If she perhaps had a missed infection or forced herself to recover too quickly. Going out walking and not giving herself time to rest as the doctors told her to.

Over the past couple of hours, she's sure she has fallen asleep numerous times, her eyes closing despite her using all her strength to try and keep them open. She's been seeing things, she thinks. At one point she thought Jack was here, wiping her brow in the same gentle way he had when she was in painful labour with both Paige and Freddy, the image making her want to weep. Another time, she was adamant her children were with her, both of them excitedly telling her about their holidays, Freddy full of stories about fishing and barbecues, Paige showing off her tan.

212

Bella wishes the fever would break, the hallucinations simply bringing wave after wave of fresh anguish as she comes to and realises she's been imagining things. Just like Jack has been saying she has for weeks. She wants her family back. Wants the life she's been denied so many times, so many obstacles getting in her way. What has she done to deserve so much pain?

She tries to swallow, her mouth too dry, as she wonders, as she has so many times already, what time it is. Late morning? Lunchtime? Later? Her stomach feels empty in a way it never has since those five days in the basement nineteen years ago. Her mind is muddled, no longer sure of when she last ate, last had a sip of water or used the loo. How many days has she been here now? Is it still just the one? Or have more passed while she's been drifting in and out of sleep?

She wonders if her captor ever intends to come back, or if he has chosen the ultimate form of torture to carry out on her. If he has abandoned her completely.

She looks at the door at the top of the stairs, imagining him behind it, in the house she's lived in most of her life, her home, laughing to himself at what he's putting her through. How he's got away with keeping her down here without anyone suspecting. The deep scar on his face will be curling in on itself while he grins, coiling against his skin like a snake. She shakes her head in frustration, ridding herself of the image. What the fuck is he planning to do with her? Keep her down here forever, like some kind of slave? Why won't he tell her what's going to happen?

She tries to shout. 'Hey ...'

Her voice isn't working properly, the word coming out as little more than a croak, even if she wasn't gagged. She can sense him listening to her weak sounds, ear to the door as he enjoys her distress.

She tries again, desperate to gain his attention, for him to come down and tell her what he's going to do with her. *To* her. 'Hey ...'

She has to stop; it hurts too much. She hangs her head and

coughs weakly, almost ready to give up. Give up on everything. Her dreams. Her life. Her family. She hopes whatever it is that's making her bones ache, her head hurt, isn't too serious.

Otherwise, she could die a very painful death down here and no one would know.

Jack now

'Are you sure you're going to be okay, Jack? I hate to leave you when you're feeling low. That hotel room must be miserable.'

Jack looks at his PA. The heeled sandals she's wearing make her seem taller than ever, her gangly limbs seeming far too long to fit into the small Peugeot she's been driving for as long as he's known her. 'Thanks, Jazz. I'll be fine as long as I have something to keep me occupied. Dinner would be good though. Eating alone is the worst – I'm not used to it.'

'I bet.' Jazz leans against the car, seeming in no hurry to leave. 'I'm just worried about you, to be honest. About Bella too. Asking for some space when she's obviously so vulnerable. Maybe, when she said she needed some time alone, she was really trying to tell you she needed some help, that she wanted you to come home and be with her.'

Jack shakes his head. 'You heard her voicemail. She doesn't want me there. And I need to respect that. You were right in what you said: we all need time out sometimes.'

'To tell you the truth, after you played me the message, part of me was expecting you to do the exact opposite of what Bella had asked. To go straight to her and try and put things right.'

Jack chuckles. 'Oh, I know what's good for me, Jazz. I've learnt to listen when a woman tells me what she wants.'

'Well, all credit to you. I haven't been with Lana anywhere near as long as you two have been together and I'm not sure I could be so strong. Despite it being the right thing to do to respect her wishes, I think I would probably be banging on the door and begging her to let me in.'

Jack raises an eyebrow. 'Like you say, Bell and I have been together a long time. I know when she means what she says.'

'Well, you know her best, I guess.' Straightening, Jazz pulls her car keys from her bag, pressing the fob to open the car door before looking at him again, as though she's had an idea. 'Would you like *me* to try calling her? I gave her my number once, when I saw her that night in the restaurant, but I don't know if she kept it. I never heard anything from her. You could give me hers? I'm sure she wouldn't mind …'

'Thanks, Jazz.' Jack starts to turn away. He's beginning to feel twitchy, anxiety tightening his chest. Jazz is only trying to help, but it suddenly feels as if she's a leech, clinging to him, asking question after question, not seeming to want to let him go. He didn't know his wife had her number; Bella had never mentioned it. 'But I wouldn't want to give Bell's number out without her permission. You know, just in case. I'll tell her you were asking after her though, when I see her after the weekend …'

'Do that.'

Jack looks back at her, sensing her watching him. There's something different about Jazz's demeanour suddenly, her attitude towards him not quite so friendly. She's looked after him at work for so many years. Now, she's looking at him like she might a teenager who's planning to sneak out after dark. 'Everything okay, Jazz?'

'Sure …' She takes a breath. 'I was just thinking …'

'About what?'

Jazz laughs softly. 'That I've never noticed before what a catch you are, Jack. I can see why Bella was so attracted to you when you met.' She studies him. 'That scar on your face makes you look like some kind of movie star. What is it they say, *rugged good looks*?'

Jack smiles. 'Thanks, Jazz. I'll see you later.' He walks quickly away. He doesn't have paperwork to do. He has an appointment to keep.

A day and a half earlier

Her morning run had done her good, Bella glad that her body was functioning more normally now. She was feeling stronger, more determined, her mind focused on the task ahead of her, and she couldn't afford to waste any more time. She had to prove to Jack and her sister that she was right about what was happening. That she wasn't imagining things. That Lawrence Knox wasn't abiding by the conditions of his release. She was going to do this. She was going to take back control.

Entering the house, she headed straight for the kitchen, pulling off her bumbag and dropping her keys and phone into her handbag as she always did, so she knew exactly where they were if she needed them. If she at any point felt herself in danger and needed to make a quick exit. She kept the whistle around her neck, wearing it practically twenty-four hours a day now, only removing it when she showered. She knew Jack thought she was being silly, being extreme in her attempts to protect herself, but she didn't care. She'd do what she had to do to keep herself safe, even if everyone else thought she was losing her mind.

She ran water into a glass, guzzling it down, her throat feeling dry. She hoped she wasn't coming down with something. She had a busy day ahead, now that the kids were safely out of the way, Paige in France since earlier in the week, Freddy currently on the road to the Lakes with her parents. She hoped they were okay. Her relationship with her daughter had started to thaw a little over the past few days, the start of better times to come, with any luck. Freddy had been anxious this morning before he left. The car accident had had quite an impact on his state of mind. Bella hoped the time with her mum and dad, the fresh air and outdoor activities, would help. She didn't think she'd ever not feel guilty at what he'd been through. Yet, despite how angry Jack and Rosie had been with her, she was adamant the accident wasn't her fault. Lawrence Knox had stepped out in front of her car. She hadn't had any choice but to swerve. Perhaps she should have simply run him down and suffered the consequences.

She leant against the sink, mentally ticking off the list of what she had to do. First, she was going to ring the Victim Contact Scheme and demand that someone in charge speak to her. Despite knowing how busy they were, she needed to be absolutely certain Lawrence was being watched carefully, needed someone to look again at what he'd been doing, where he'd been, over the past few weeks, to see if anything had been missed. She wasn't going to take no for an answer this time.

After that, she was going to talk to the local police, walk down to the station that was just a few minutes away and see if the officer on duty could give her some advice about her situation. She'd read somewhere that her county force had some kind of unit set up, especially to deal with stalking. To address the fact that it wasn't always taken seriously, that the women, and men, she supposed, who were victims were often dismissed as hysterical. Just like she'd been recently. She would find out the details and see if she could get someone from the unit to ring her. Once she'd done that, she might call Rosie again to see if she could try and build some bridges with her sister, perhaps offer to help with the twins while Martin was away. She missed the time they usually spent together.

And, last but not least, she would ring Jack at work. Ask her husband to come home early and spend some time with her. They needed to talk, just the two of them, so she could tell him how she was going to sort this situation out, win back his affection. They couldn't put it off any longer. Couldn't let things carry on as they were. If they both tried really hard, they would get past this; she knew they would. Get back to the loving relationship they'd had before things went so wrong.

She looked at the basement door, thinking about her journey beneath the house a few days before, the first time in almost two decades that she'd ventured down there. It might not have seemed so to the outside world, but it was one of the bravest things she'd done in her life. Perhaps even braver than escaping the clutches of Lawrence Knox when she was just a girl. Confronting the past, placing herself directly into the memories she'd worked so hard to avoid, had seemed impossible even just a few weeks ago. Her therapist would have been proud of her. So would Jack be when this was all sorted out. When he realised what she'd had to put herself through to sort her life out all over again.

She straightened, the hairs on the back of her neck standing up suddenly as she looked more closely at the basement door.

Something wasn't right.

Putting her glass down on the counter, she crept across the kitchen, approaching the door like a cat stalking its prey. Standing in front of it, she felt anxiety begin to build in her chest. She shook her head. She'd been so vigilant. Ever since she'd seen Lawrence in town, since the car accident, she'd double- and triple-checked every lock, made sure every single window and door was completely secure. Before she went for her run this morning, after Freddy and her parents had left, she'd locked the back, examined all the windows, checked the handle of the front door as she went out. And, as always, she'd checked the basement was locked. She *knew* she had.

Yet the door was now slightly ajar, the tiniest gap showing around the wooden frame.

Bella tried to move quickly, heading towards the table to grab her bag. She needed her phone and her keys. She needed to get out of the house. Now.

She was stopped in her tracks before she'd barely taken three steps.

As the needle entered her neck, as she began to lose consciousness, Bella frowned to herself. She was confused. In her peripheral vision, she could see the outline of the man who had grabbed her, one side of his face near to her own, a familiar savage scar running the length of it.

The man who was attacking her wasn't Lawrence Knox after all.

Bella now

Bella looks up as the door that leads into the kitchen opens and Jack slowly descends the stairs.

She watches him, the way he seems to saunter towards her, his whole body radiating an attitude she's been struggling to reconcile with the man she thought loved her. Her mind reels, as it has done each and every time he's come to the basement to see her over the past day and a half. She's still completely in shock that her husband could do this to her. That he could imprison her in the basement of her own home in the exact same way Lawrence Knox did nineteen years ago. Re-enact the most traumatic experience of her life almost down to the last detail.

Of course, he's the one who would do it. Jack knows everything that happened to her over the course of those five days when she was here last time. And she's the one who told him, isn't she? Their conversations about what happened to her, in the early days of their relationship, helped shift a huge burden from her shoulders. She told him everything: how Lawrence had grabbed and drugged her, gagged her with a scarf. Strapped her to a kitchen chair using builders' tape. Even how she'd had to use a bucket when she needed the loo. At least he made an upgrade in that department. She supposes she should be grateful.

'How are we doing, beautiful Bella?' He smiles as he pulls the gag away from her mouth again, the scar he's had since a childhood accident, a fall from the second-hand bike his mum bought him from a charity shop, curling upwards. She found it attractive once, the mark seeming to enhance his face, lend it a certain unique charm. Now, she simply associates it with fear. Fear of her own husband, the man who she's been married to for almost sixteen years.

'Please can you stop calling me that?' Her throat is hoarser than ever, her words coming out as a harsh whisper. 'You know that's what *he* used to call me. How much I hate it ...'

Jack crouches down in front of her. 'Your voice sounds strange. Are you ill?'

She thinks about denying it, but then nods, wanting to cry. It seems like such a long time since anyone has asked after her welfare. Is Jack genuinely concerned? 'I think I have an infection.'

'Ah, I'm sorry to hear that. What a shame no one was here to take care of you while you've been suffering.'

'Don't mock me!' She tries to kick out at him, her foot bound by the tape. 'You used to love me, take care of me ... What happened?'

'Aw, Bella.' Jack stands up again. 'You know I still love you, of course I do. It's just ...'

'Just what? You don't love me any more than Lawrence Knox did!' She tries to shout, the pain too intense. She's sure she needs antibiotics before the infection does some serious damage, travels to other parts of her body. She needs to see a doctor. 'You're no better than he is.'

When she opened her eyes yesterday morning, emerging from the grip of the drug in her system, Bella had struggled to get her head around what she could see in front of her. Her beloved husband, standing over her with a knife in his hand after strapping her to a chair, making all her worst nightmares come true. All that time, all those weeks, she thought it was Lawrence who was ruining her life again, Jack trying to convince her she was losing her mind. That she was imagining things. Ironic, in a way, that her husband was right. It wasn't Lawrence behind what was happening at all.

'Oh, I think you'll find I am.'

Bella shakes her head. 'You think you're so clever, don't you? Forcing me to make that phone call yesterday morning, making me leave you a voicemail so that it would look like I didn't want you to be at home. Telling you to book into a hotel so that everyone would know we're not together, so you have an alibi. I bet you've really enjoyed letting everyone listen to that message, telling them I didn't want you here.'

Jack seems to think for a few seconds. 'Well, everyone did seem pretty convinced, especially after your dreadful behaviour over the past few weeks. Your mum, my work colleagues. Everyone now knows that you're so cross with me, you don't want me anywhere near you this weekend.'

'And those voicemails *you* left, saying how much you loved me, saying you'd come home if I needed you? The texts you sent from *my* phone, making out I was being nice to you, saying goodnight? Wow, all such good moves, Jack. A two-way conversation you created all by yourself.' Bella makes no effort to hide her sarcastic tone. 'Seems like you thought of everything.'

'Well, we wouldn't want everyone to think our relationship had completely broken down, would we? Not after we've been together so long, been through so much. That would be no good at all.'

'Even though you made it look to everyone as if I was practically going mad? Convinced everyone I was seeing things? That I was never in any danger?'

'Well, let's face it, Bella. I'd be a pretty poor husband if your ex-stalker *had* actually begun to threaten you after he got out of prison and I just left you in the house on your own, to defend yourself, wouldn't I? But, once you started making allegations that everyone, including the authorities, could see were blatantly

224

untrue, it came as no surprise that we ended up parting ways, just for a little while. Me confined to that dreadful hotel, all on my own …'

'So the Victim Contact Scheme was right. Lawrence has been behaving himself all along.'

'Of course he has.' Jack points a finger at her. 'And the scheme were very interested when I told them what a difficult time *you* were having recently.'

'You rang them?'

'More than once. Someone had to apologise for how much you'd been pestering them. I told them to be patient with you, if you rang again, but that it was very clear to me that everyone involved was doing their job properly and that Lawrence hadn't done anything wrong. It was just you who couldn't see it.' He grimaces. 'Probably due to the fact that you'd been drinking a little more than usual.'

Bella feels sick. 'I was so sure it was Lawrence I'd seen. In town. But, if I'd looked more closely, run through the mall a bit faster, I'd have seen it was you all along. You were supposed to be at home with Freddy. You left him.'

'He was fine; he had his friends over.'

'And when we had the accident …' She pictures the person who stepped out from the pavement as she drove, his face hidden, the whole incident passing so quickly she barely had time to register any details. 'That was you too. If I'd managed to get out of the car sooner …'

'It wasn't much of a disguise, to be honest.' Jack chuckles. 'A red cap, hiding my face, and a sports shirt. But I knew you were so obsessed with Lawrence stalking you again, you'd immediately assume it was him, just like you have every other time someone in a baseball cap has come a little too close to you. I'm afraid you only have yourself to blame for making yourself an easy target, Bella.'

'But Freddy was hurt.'

Jack's face flushes red, as if he's angry. Perhaps with himself rather than her this time. 'That wasn't supposed to happen. What I'd intended was to be hovering at the side of the road somewhere, so you'd see me *after* you returned from dropping Fred at his exam. How was I supposed to know you'd forget and be running late? Be passing, not to mention driving too fast and far too close to the pavement, at a time when you were supposed to be at the studio already and Freddy was safe? What happened actually *was* an accident, Bella, just as you said, and you've no idea how difficult it was for me not to do more than just hang around for a few minutes to check Freddy got out okay.'

'We could have been killed.'

'Again, your fault, Bella. *Your* fault our son was hurt. Not mine.'

Bella looks at the floor, still bewildered by everything she's learnt since yesterday. It's a minute or two before she speaks again. 'But what I don't get is why, Jack? *Why* are you doing this? What the hell are you hoping to gain?'

Jack shakes his head, as if her confusion is making him sad. 'Oh, Bella, you're disappointing me. I used to think you were so clever. I could swear that's where the kids got their brains from. Maybe they take after me more than I thought ...' He puts a finger to his lips.

'What do you mean?'

'Haven't you worked it out yet?'

Bella tries to think. She's been so tired and confused, the drug Jack injected her with yesterday no doubt lingering in her system, her throat obviously infected. She's been in such shock at what her husband, the man who she thought would always protect her, have her back, is doing that she's struggled to work out the motivation behind his actions. What on earth is he hoping to gain by all this? She stops, looks at him, a thought suddenly occurring to her. 'The house. You want the house ...'

Jack holds up a finger. 'Ah, my beautiful Bella, I knew you'd work it out in the end. My clever girl.'

She shakes her head. 'But, Jack, the house is yours anyway. You live there. It's your home. You know I'd never …'

'Never what?' He scowls. 'Never divorce me? Never turf me out? Never leave me with nothing? The house is yours, Bella. It always has been. Not one brick of it belongs to me. If you and I split up, I could end up on the streets or in some dingy bedsit. End up exactly like I was before, when my no-good mother put her useless boyfriends before her own son.'

'But I didn't realise …' Bella frowns. 'Your childhood wasn't that bad, was it?'

'What would *you* know? All you've ever talked about is yourself. The trauma *you* went through, how *your* life was ruined. Never had any time for anyone else's worries, have you, lovely wife?'

'That's not fair.'

'Isn't it?'

Bella is flabbergasted. In all the years they've been married, it's never occurred to her that Jack felt like he'd been left on the sidelines. Of course she wouldn't have left him with nothing. Not even if they split up. 'Why didn't you ever say? About the house? About how you felt?'

Jack shrugs. 'Why should I have to? You don't care about me any more than my mother did.'

'Of course I do, Jack, I love you. We can sort this. Even now, we can talk to a solicitor, forget any of this ever happened.'

'Too late!' He turns towards her, his hand on the knife at his waist, as if to remind her, once again, of the power he has over her. 'It's too late, Bella. You can't make amends now, no matter how hard you try.'

She lifts her chin. Jack's wrong. She can still salvage this situation. 'If you let me go now, I'll give you the house. All our savings as well, if that's what you want. Everything we own. I'll take the kids somewhere far away and I won't mention any of this to anyone. I won't tell anyone what you've …'

Jack crouches down in front of her again, reaching a hand to her face and gently moving her hair away from her eyes. 'You just don't get it, do you?'

'Get what?' Her voice is shaky.

'Of course I want the house, Bella, but do you really think I want to lose my kids?' He shakes his head. 'I want it all. Freddy and Paige. The family life I've always craved, that I didn't have as a child. That I've worked so hard to get. The only thing I don't want anymore, my poor darling, is you. You're too broken, Bella, too much hard work. Even when Lawrence was in prison, I had to look after you, constantly tiptoe around you. And now, it's ten times worse. Have you any idea how exhausting you are to live with?'

Bella stares at him, tears springing to her eyes. 'But the only other way ...' She swallows heavily. 'The only way you'll get the house, the kids, everything, is if ...' She thinks about the will they made only a year or so ago. Everything she owns going to her next of kin. To Jack. So he could take care of the children if anything happened to her. It made so much sense at the time.

'If?' Jack's smile widens.

Bella chokes back a sob. 'If I die.'

'Now you're getting the idea, beautiful Bella.'

'No, Jack. Please don't.' Bella is crying now, her tears unchecked. 'Think about the kids.'

Jack stands up, pacing the room like an animal in a cage. 'Actually, Bella, you're getting the idea now, but you're not quite all there yet.'

'What do you mean?'

'Well, I'm not actually going to kill you.'

Bella feels her eyes widen, a surge of relief, of new hope, travelling through her. 'Oh, Jack, thank you, thank you so ...'

'You're not listening, Bella.' Jack turns to face her, pulling the knife from its sheath and holding it inches from her face. 'What I said was, *I'm* not going to kill you ...'

'What do you mean?'

Jack turns towards the stairs, looking up at the door that leads to the kitchen, the door he left ajar when he came in a short time ago. He raises his voice to a shout. 'You can come down now.'

'What?' Bella is more confused than ever. 'Jack, what are you ...?'

Jack turns back to her, smiling. 'What I said, Bella, was that *I'm* not going to kill you, but ...' He holds out one arm, like a show host introducing the next act. 'I can tell you for certain that someone else is.'

Bella looks up as the door at the top of the stairs creaks open, a heavy footstep hitting the wood. She screws up her eyes, trying to focus, to get her brain to concentrate on what's happening. See the scene before her through the blur of tears.

As she realises what she's seeing, all of her breath leaves her body in a whoosh, her stomach feeling as if she's been punched, her throat constricting as if someone is strangling her.

Bella gasps, open-mouthed, as she realises who is standing at the top of the stairs looking down at her.

Bella now

Lawrence Knox, the man who imprisoned her for five days nineteen years ago, stares directly at her. He alternates between a smile and a frown, as if he's not sure about what he's seeing. As if he thinks he might have been involved in some kind of game. 'Bella, why are you …?'

Bella can barely speak. It's as if her life has suddenly become one of the many surreal dreams she's had over the years, a nightmare.

Here she is, sitting in the basement where she's been held against her will. Twice. With the two men responsible. Her stalker and her husband.

Her words leave her mouth as if she's spitting out stones. 'You … What? What are you doing here?'

Lawrence walks slowly down the stairs, looking at his feet as if he's frightened he'll fall. When he reaches the bottom, he glances at Jack before looking back at her. 'Your husband invited me. He said you wanted to see me.' He looks at Jack again, frowning. 'What's going on, Jack? Why is she …?'

Bella is baffled; she has no idea what's going on either. Didn't Jack tell her Lawrence wasn't involved? She too looks at her husband. 'Why is *he* here?'

'Like he said, I invited him.' Jack is smiling, as if he's simply organised a social get-together. Like he's about to head upstairs to the kitchen and prepare afternoon tea for the three of them.

She looks at Lawrence Knox, the subject of her nightmares for so long. Now, as she peers at him more closely, she sees that he's different from how she remembers him. He's thinner and shorter somehow, as if he's a shrunken version of the person who caused her such turmoil, one leg seeming slightly shorter than the other. Although he's aged, streaks of grey decorating the thin hair he now wears in a ponytail beneath his trademark baseball cap, he still looks like the boy she remembers first meeting in the students' union that fateful night, the boy she'd actually quite liked. Most certainly not the fit and athletic person she'd chased through town, the one who escaped from her so quickly. How could she not have seen it at the time?

She turns back to her husband. '*Why*, Jack?'

Jack looks disappointed again. He sidles up behind Lawrence, as if he's a tailor, measuring him for size. 'There you go again, Bella. Not using your brain. What did I say to you just before our guest here arrived? Is your so-called infection so bad, that you've forgotten already?'

Bella gasps, remembering Jack's words of a few minutes ago. She shakes her head. 'No …'

'I'm afraid so, beautiful Bella. It seems that poor Lawrence here can't bear to be without you. Even after all these years. Can't bear for you to be happy with someone else.'

'No, Jack …' Bella sees the confusion on Lawrence's face. He genuinely doesn't know why he's here. What Jack is planning. 'Please …'

'Too late, Bella.'

Jack stabs the needle into Lawrence's neck, watching as the smaller man collapses to the floor at his feet.

He smiles at her. 'Have you worked it out yet, Bella?'

She nods her head slowly, shocked at the words coming out of her own mouth. 'Yes. Lawrence Knox is here to kill me and then he's going to kill himself.'

Jack now

He doesn't want to be too long. Leaving Bella and Lawrence in the basement together is a risk, even with Lawrence strapped to a chair and out like a light. Jack can only hope his second hostage stays under the influence of the drug until he can get back. What he has to do next needs to be done at a quiet time, under the cover of darkness. In just a few hours, the whole thing will be over. He'll be able to get on with his life. The life he's always dreamed of.

He looks up at the sky as he jogs down the lane, keeping to the shadows beneath the trees as he did during his daylight visits yesterday, one of Freddy's old caps pulled low over his face to hide it. He'll put it in his pocket when he gets to where he's going. At least it will be dark before long, he thinks, his arranged dinner with Jazz giving him something to do while he waits for the opportunity to return to the house and deal with what he needs to deal with. It's important that no one sees him sneaking back, especially now, when he's going to bring his plan to an end. Not to mention the fact that his social meeting with his PA is perfect for keeping his alibi strong. Showing his face in the outside world.

He'll eat with her before saying goodnight and, once he's back at the hotel, will make an impossible-to-ignore comment to the receptionist about being shattered and retiring for the night, before sneaking out of the nearest fire exit. Jazz couldn't have offered to meet up with him at a better time. It was as if she were handing his alibi to him on a plate.

As much as it seems so at times, his plan hasn't been an easy one to pull off. Convincing Bella's family and Jazz that his wife hasn't wanted to see him, that she needs some space, has taken some thinking about, but he thinks he's got it right, his brain more than a little fried after everything he's had to do over the past few weeks. There have been times when he's thought it might go wrong, when his plot to get rid of Bella and take over the house of his dreams has gone more than a little awry. Like when she crashed the car. What he said to Bella in the basement was true: that was certainly never supposed to happen. At least not with Freddy inside. Jack feels a twinge of guilt as he follows the quiet back roads into town. He's just glad his son is okay. That he'll get over it in time, with the support of his father.

He texts Jazz to tell her he's on his way, calculating that his brisk walk into town will take about forty minutes if he's not going to arrive looking bedraggled and breathless, as if he's run the whole way. Moving back and forth between town and the house has taken up a lot of his time since yesterday but he hasn't always wanted to risk bringing the car, sometimes driving it part of the way and parking it in a remote wooded area, where it's unlikely to be seen. Staying hidden as he's gone in and out of his own home has been one of the most difficult parts of this whole scheme. Jack is grateful that his parents-in-law picked such a remote location to live in; the lane is usually deserted aside from the odd distracted dog walker or jogger with headphones that have been easy enough to avoid, the neighbours too far away to see anything for sure. No CCTV anywhere. He smiles. His plan has been almost too easy at some stages.

He hopes the CCTV at the hotel is reliable. That, if needed, it will be able to prove that his car will be in the on-site car park throughout tonight and into tomorrow, the time when he most needs his alibi to be secure. As far as the outside world is concerned, he will be sleeping soundly as his wife is murdered, as the man who has stalked her all this time takes his own life, in desperation at the callous act he's just committed. It's crucial that no one suspects Jack is involved. Which they won't – he's sure of that. He's covered every eventuality. The case will be open and shut, as they say.

He can see the headline now: *Stalker released from prison kills his victim before committing suicide.* Why wouldn't anyone believe it? And Jack will have his game face ready, his high school drama skills coming in handy when he most needs them.

I had no idea. I was convinced Bella was simply imagining things. And, to think, Lawrence Knox was stalking her again, all this time. How could I have let this happen? Not believed her? Abandoned her when she needed me most? I completely let her down …

He has it all planned.

He thinks about Jazz, how she questioned him this afternoon, saying she herself might have found it difficult to leave Bella alone under such circumstances. He's sure she doesn't suspect anything. That she's simply being her usual concerned self. Worrying about others, even those she doesn't know especially well. Jack has worked with Jazz for years. He has no doubt he'll be able to convince her that he's just been trying to do the right thing for his wife. Keep up the façade of being the perfect husband she's believed him to be all this time.

If only she knew.

Jack quickens his pace. He's suddenly very hungry.

Bella now

'Lawrence, Lawrence ...' Bella can hardly believe what's happening. That she's sitting here, still strapped to a chair in her own basement, attempting to revive the man who put her in this situation in the first place, her words almost incoherent around the scarf Jack always makes sure he puts back in place before he leaves.

Lawrence stirs, drool wetting his own gag as he tries to bring himself to consciousness. He mumbles quietly.

'Lawrence!' She tries to raise her voice, shout as loud as she can, wondering if Lawrence can understand what she's saying. If he can even hear her. How long had it taken for the drug to ease out of her own system? Thirty minutes? An hour? She wasn't sure. Didn't even know what it was Jack had used. If the two dosages were the same. 'Wake up!'

Lawrence Knox opens his eyes, staring at her for a few seconds, as if he can't quite believe who is sitting here in front of him. Perhaps he thinks it's a dream. He makes a muffled, startled sound.

Bella takes a deep breath. She's felt so weak the past few hours. Weaker, she thinks, than she's ever felt in her life. She isn't well. Yet, deep in her heart, she knows that now is the time for her to find the strength she's sure she still has. She has to take action, her frustration that Jack has answered only some of her questions – told her it was him who she followed in town, who caused her to crash the car – almost unbearable. She has to see the bigger picture. And only Lawrence Knox can help her do that.

She begins to shuffle her feet, bouncing her body against the wood of the chair beneath her, every muscle aching, burning to the point she feels as if she might go up in flames. Slowly, the chair starts to move across the floor, Bella's progress agonisingly slow. It takes her ten minutes or more until she's close enough to Lawrence to lean into him.

Closing her eyes tightly, she rubs her face against his, trying not to retch, the musty smell of him, the feeling of his rough skin against hers, repulsing her, the irony of them being as intimate as two lovers not lost on her. Bella gasps as the scarf slips down her face, her cheek and mouth sore from the repetitive movement. Leaning in again, she uses her teeth to pull Lawrence's gag down. She can almost taste his stale breath.

When he speaks, Lawrence's words are slurred. 'Bella … What …? What happened?'

She tries to calm herself, panting heavily after the exertion. 'Jack injected you with something. You've been unconscious. Don't close your eyes again!' She needs him to stay awake.

Lawrence's eyelids droop before he forces them open again. He looks around the room. 'Where are we?'

'We're in the basement beneath my house. You know, the one you kept me in for five days? When you yourself drugged *me* and imprisoned *me*?'

'I …' Lawrence shakes his head. 'Shit.'

'And now you're imprisoned as well. In exactly the same way.' Bella looks at the tape strapped around Lawrence's body, holding him to another kitchen chair Jack carried down after forcing the needle into Lawrence's neck. She'd been unable to do anything but watch in disbelief as her husband strapped her stalker up before leaving the two of them alone. 'If that isn't karma, I don't know what is.'

'I'm sorry, Bella. I really am.'

'Sorry?'

'I can't tell you how much. For everything I put you through.' Lawrence swallows heavily, trying to sit up straighter in the chair, pushing his spindly muscles against the tape to no avail. The patterned scarf Jack used around his mouth, one of hers again, now hangs loosely at his neck.

'You think saying sorry makes up for everything you did?' Bella bites her lip. She wants to scream at this poor excuse of a man. Scream right into his ear, so he'd have no choice but to hear her. 'You ruined my life, Lawrence. You broke me so badly that I'll never be the same. Never be the person I was before I met you.'

'I know.'

'Do you? Have you any idea what it's like to be looking over your shoulder for the rest of your life? To be frightened every single time you step out the door? To think that everyone you meet might be someone who wants to do you harm?' She tries not to think about her husband, the one person she thought was the exception.

Lawrence shakes his head again. 'I know it's not enough to say it, but I'm sorry I did that to you. You've no idea how much.'

'You could say sorry for the rest of your life and it still wouldn't be enough.'

'I know.' A tear rolls down Lawrence's cheek. His face is pale, as if he too is in shock at what has happened to him.

Good, Bella thinks. *Let him be upset forever. Let him have some idea of what it's like.* 'I need you to answer some questions for me, Lawrence. If you're truly sorry, that's the least you can do. Give me some idea of what the hell's been going on.'

Lawrence's eyelids droop again. He's obviously still very much under the influence of the drug. He licks his lips. 'I'll try, but I really don't …'

'Stay awake! Tell me what's happened since you got out of prison.'

'I don't know what you …'

'Have you tried to make contact with me again? In any way?'

Lawrence's eyes widen. 'Absolutely not. I swear, Bella. I admit, I thought about writing to you, both when I was inside and after I was released. I wanted to apologise for everything that happened. I learnt a lot about myself in prison and I wanted to let you know how much I'd grown.'

Bella scoffs.

'My probation officer told me straight it wasn't a good idea. Part of my release conditions were that I was to leave you alone, not contact you in any way. And I haven't, Bella, I promise.'

'Did you contact me on Facebook? Send me a friend request? Using the name *Larry*?'

Lawrence looks completely confused. 'No. I don't even have a Facebook account. And no one ever calls me Larry.'

Bella thinks for a few seconds. So it must have been Jack. Did he set up an account in Lawrence's name, *Larry's* name, deleting it, and the friend request, before she had chance to show it to anyone? He must have known how terrified she'd be when she saw it. How frightened she would have been at her stalker entering her life once again.

'And the bouquet? Did you send flowers to my office?'

Another shake of the head. 'I wouldn't do that, Bella. I don't even know where you work. When I considered writing to you, at the beginning, I did think about sending a gift or a card instead, to your home, but it seemed too much like I was stalking you again, like when I sent the flowers before ...' His cheeks flush. 'I wouldn't want to do that to you again.'

Bella thinks back to the huge bouquet that ended up in the wheelie bin behind the office. Her husband again? Did he ask someone else to send it on his behalf? She remembers what the florist told her about it being a woman who ordered the flowers. Did Jack ask Jazz to order for him, his PA having no idea of the motive behind the gift? It's a definite possibility.

She sits, staring at the room around her, her whole system still feeling in shock at everything that's happened. Everything she's learnt about her family, her life, in just a few hours. She knows now that her husband has been behind it all, that Lawrence Knox has been doing exactly what everyone – Jack, her sister, the authorities – told her he was. Abiding by the strict rules of his release. Yet she still feels the need to ask, despite already knowing the answer. She looks at the man sitting next to her. 'I'm only going to ask you this once, Lawrence, but I need you to tell me the truth. Have you been in my house? Been anywhere near it? Since the last time, I mean. Since you've been out of prison.'

Lawrence blinks slowly, as if he's still trying to wake up and take in his surroundings. 'This is the first time, I swear. And it's a weird experience ...'

'Tell me about it.' So, Jack even drank the milk? Or threw it away, so she'd think she was losing her mind? Start to suspect someone might have been in without her knowing? Was that the beginning of his campaign to make her feel like her life had been upended all over again? 'And you haven't accessed my phone? My email account?'

'Of course not! How would I even ...?'

'I don't know.' Bella frowns, thinking. The estate agent turning up at her house, the email sent to Luke Rushfield later asking him to go ahead. Even the mix-up with the restaurant booking. Was Jack behind all those too? She can only guess he must have been. She looks at Lawrence. 'So, why now?'

'Huh?'

'Why are you here now? If you've been doing what you say you have – checking in with the authorities when you're supposed to, staying away from me – why are you here now? Surely you know that coming to my home town, coming *here*, is breaking the rules?'

'Like I told you before, your husband asked me to come. A few days ago ...'

'How did he even find you? Jack couldn't have got in touch with you through the authorities. They would have immediately wanted to know why. Would have wanted to talk to me about it. And you already said you're not on Facebook, so ...?'

'I have a website where I sell my art. Well, try to. There isn't much business at the minute, but Jack found me through that.'

'I see.' Bella remembers what she found when she googled Lawrence's name, after she'd found the Facebook friend request. Jack must have found the same thing. 'And you didn't think that was strange? That he wanted to get in touch with you?'

Lawrence shrugs. 'What he said seemed to make perfect sense. He said you and he had been reading about criminals who had made amends with their victims, gone on to build relationships with them, and you were interested in meeting up. To see how we could move forward. I had no reason not to trust him.'

Bella grimaces. Neither had she. She takes a breath. 'Lawrence, we need to get out of here.'

'What? But, how?'

'We'll find a way.' She knows he's still groggy, but she needs to get him to listen to her. They're running out of time. 'If we don't, Jack is going to come back and kill us both. And I refuse to let my children spend the rest of their lives with a murderer.'

'But how can we ...?' Lawrence looks frightened, bewildered, much like she was both times she found herself trapped in the basement.

She tries to quell her anger, to see him as simply a human being. Someone who needs to escape this situation as much as she does.

'Listen to me and do exactly what I say.' She speaks as clearly and precisely as she can, in the same way she often talks to the kids. 'I have an idea ...'

Jack now

Jack is feeling optimistic, practically on top of the world. Just one more thing to do and his plan will be complete. All that hard work. All the lies he's had to tell, the secrets he's had to keep. They've taken their toll, made him wonder at his own strength sometimes. Admittedly, the next task, getting rid of Bella and Lawrence, will certainly be the most difficult of the lot. Jack isn't especially looking forward to it. He's never had to kill anyone before.

Not since his mother anyway.

And she didn't count, not really. She'd pretty much been half dead already.

He remembers the look on Mum's face when he approached her with the cushion. His visit to her had pretty much gone as they always did: him trying to convince his mum to pull herself together, make the most of the years she had left. Of course, she hadn't listened. His mother was the type of person who thought she had no control over her own destiny, fate having been unkind to her, dealt her an unlucky hand. *Why doesn't Bella ever come with you to visit?* she'd asked as he'd sipped on the insipid, grey dishwater tea he never wanted but always accepted.

Because it's enough that one of us has to tolerate your company, even for this short a time, he'd wanted to reply, but didn't.

He hadn't planned to kill her, the cushion over her face, cutting off her musty breath, before Jack even knew what he was doing. The idea of having to spend the next decade, more perhaps, making the dutiful, unbearable trips to the outskirts of Leeds to see her was simply more than he could stand. Mum hadn't fought, her daily doses of cheap vodka making her lethargic. Part of him wondered if she cared. If she might even have *asked* him to do it one day, if she ever had the sense to realise what a waste her life was. No one had suspected a thing. Jack had acted suitably distressed when his mother's neighbour called him a week or so later to tell him the police had had to break in, led by the smell. There was no one left in her life who would miss her.

Now Jack is facing killing again, taking not only the life of the woman he married, but that of an innocent man as well. Although Lawrence Knox isn't so innocent, he guesses. It was Lawrence who started all this in the first place.

He lets himself into the back door of the house, looking over his shoulder one more time to make sure there's no one around before he pulls the old cap off his head. Jazz looked a little disappointed when he declared he was going back to the hotel for an early night. He wonders if she had an idea they might spend some more time together. His PA has never made any secret of the fact that she's had relationships with both women and men in the past. After all, it wouldn't be the first time she's flirted with him, the memory of a forgotten drunken pass at one of the office Christmas parties suddenly resurfacing in his mind. Jack had made it clear to her he was flattered but very much married. He guesses that status is going to change very soon. Imagine it. Him, a widower.

He thinks back to how Jazz insisted over dinner on turning the conversation back to Bella. Was it some kind of romantic interest in him that caused her to reach out to him today? That's been behind her attempts to delve into his relationship with his wife? Is Jazz secretly hoping he might say his marriage is over? He remembers, this afternoon, how she questioned what she seemed to see as his *blasé* attitude at leaving Bella alone in the house. That must be it, he realises. Jazz is hoping he doesn't love Bella anymore. That she has a chance of a future with him herself. *Rugged good looks*, wasn't that what she said when she was talking about his scar? He chuckles to himself. Women have always found him attractive. He's had to restrain himself a few times over the years when innocent flirting has gone a little too far. *Mostly* restrain himself anyway.

He looks around the kitchen, the light left on the last time he was here, to give anyone outside the impression that Bella is home as she's supposed to be. He's filled with a sudden feeling of smugness at the idea that the next time he comes here, it will all be his. Not just his home, as Bella has always insisted it is. Not just where he lives, but his property. His bricks and mortar. His *investment*. And Lord knows, he's invested enough, both practically and emotionally, into making it his. His mother never owned a house, never had any money apart from the few quid she lived on from day to day, after she'd paid her rent to the council. He suspects his absent father never did either. Jack may not have gone to uni like Bella, but he'll be the first in his family to have made a success of himself. To have had his own money. Not what has been handed to him by the government or his parents. And once the kids get over their loss, they'll be able to see how proud they should be of their father. He's a good role model.

He looks around the kitchen, wondering how long it will take for him to wipe away all traces of his wife once she's gone: the apron, hanging on the door, that she puts over her clothes when she's cooking, the handbag that's always on the table, where she keeps her phone and keys, as well as the rest of her junk. The smell of her, sweet and milky, that seems to always hang in the air. Will he miss her, he wonders? Maybe a little, for a while. Perhaps he'll keep a few mementoes. It wouldn't be fair on Freddy and Paige to make them forget their mother altogether.

He tries to imagine telling his children, Bella's parents, the news that their mum, beloved daughter, has been killed. That her stalker, Lawrence Knox, has finally caught up with her and ended her life as well as his own. It will be hard – he knows that. Of course it will. He might even cry when he breaks the news to them. There'll have to be a funeral, an open display of grief. All Bella's friends and family saying how loved she was, how much she'll be missed, while at the same time feeling an intense guilt that they all abandoned her. Left her alone in her hour of need. Just like they did last time. But they'll be able to support each other, Jack knows. And, eventually, they'll move on with their lives. That will be when all the hard work will reap rewards.

He straps the knife belt around his waist, pulling the weapon from its sheath and holding it in front of him while he searches through his keys with the other hand. Perhaps they'll keep the basement door open from now on, he thinks, the kids free to go up and down whenever they feel like it, Freddy maybe using the space for his drum kit if he'd like to, no longer having to worry about his mother's anxiety. Bella's paranoia, her obsession with the past, has been wearing over the years. She really has no idea how difficult she's been to live with, both for him and the children. They'll have so much more freedom now. Freedom to live their own lives without having to constantly tiptoe around her. He can't wait.

He turns the key in the lock and pushes open the door, peering down into the space below as he takes a deep breath and readies himself for what he must do next.

He frowns, confused. The basement is in darkness. Did he turn the light off before he left this afternoon? Surely he wouldn't have been so cruel as to leave Bella and Lawrence in complete darkness?

He reaches out and flicks on the light. Nothing. Perhaps the bulb has blown. The space at the bottom of the stairs is pitch-black. Jack feels his heart beginning to thud in his chest. Something is very wrong.

'Bella?'

He listens for an answer. Nothing.

Jack lifts his chin, holding the knife out in front of him. He can't afford for his plan to go wrong now. Not after all the hard work he's put in. He takes a tentative step forward. What he also can't afford is to fall and break a leg.

He puts his keys back in his pocket and pulls out his phone, switching on the small torch that shines from the back of it. It's not very powerful, the weak blue-white light only reaching as far as a step or two in front. Why didn't he think to buy a decent torch? Jack begins to creep down the stairs, putting one foot out to feel the next step before standing on it, listening carefully for any noise. Silence. He stops for a second. Can he even hear Bella or Lawrence breathing? He's not sure. He walks down further, the third step from the bottom creaking loudly under his weight. He's never noticed the sound it makes before, his journey down to the basement always hurried, confident.

He reaches the bottom, screwing up his eyes to try and focus, wishing his phone's light were more powerful. Looking around the space beneath the house, the place where he plans to kill his wife, he gasps suddenly. In front of him are the two kitchen chairs he strapped Lawrence and Bella to. They're empty.

The air around him suddenly explodes, Jack's head feeling as if it's being attacked by a million sharp needles as a shrill piercing sound enters his ears, heading straight for his brain. He drops the knife as he lifts his hands to try and protect himself. Someone – Bella? – is blowing a whistle right next to his head.

Jack twirls around, his torch forming an arc of light as his phone flies through the air. His hands in front of him, he doesn't know which way is up or which is down, where the stairs are or which direction the door is in. He tries to run. Too late. Just like he himself did to Bella in the kitchen upstairs, someone has stopped him in his tracks.

He gasps for breath as something tightens around his throat. Something sharp and wiry. Something that is threatening to cut into his skin if he doesn't loosen it. Soon. As his vision closes in, Jack wonders at the strength of the shadowy figure at his shoulder. Someone who is obviously a lot stronger than he first appeared to be.

I guess I underestimated Lawrence Knox, he thinks as he reaches up his hands and tries to stop his wife's stalker from choking him to death.

Bella now

She slams the basement door behind her, her legs wobbling as she crosses the kitchen. She's not sure they're going to hold her up for very long, her muscles weak and shaky, her throat now feeling as if it's on fire. Sweat runs down her face as she grabs her bag from the table. She has no idea what Jack has done with her phone, but she's hoping that at least her keys are still inside.

She heads for the door that leads to the outside, glancing over her shoulder at the basement before she leaves. She feels a little guilty at leaving Lawrence. He has literally saved her, wrapping one of the broken steel wires from Paige's old guitar around Jack's neck, pulling it tight, while she ran up the stairs, trying not to fall in the dark. Jack is strong and fit; there's no doubt he'll try to fight back. Will Lawrence be okay? Does she even *care* after everything he put her through?

Getting free from the chairs was a struggle, Bella's limbs aching now even more than they were before. Lawrence took some time to wake up from the effects of the drug. Panic had tightened Bella's stomach at the thought that he might not be able to carry out his part in their escape before Jack returned. Using all the strength she had left, it had taken her well over five minutes to coordinate her body and hands enough so that she could begin to loosen the tape that was holding Lawrence down, another fifteen or twenty to unstrap him. When he was free enough, he'd done the same for her, the two of them then working on their own legs and ankles. The whole process had likely taken more than half an hour. Lawrence had only just had time to stand on his chair and pull out the old lightbulb above them before crouching with Bella in the dark space under the stairs. Within seconds, they'd heard the top door open, Jack breathing heavily as he realised the basement was in darkness. She'd never been so grateful for her whistle. Her husband wasn't the only one who could pull off a plan.

She runs outside, the heat of the summer seeming to be breaking in the sky above her, a storm rumbling somewhere in the distance. Her legs slide from beneath her, Bella almost toppling as she moves as quickly as she's able around the side of the house and down the drive. She reaches inside her bag, a surge of relief travelling through her as her hand touches her keys, as if she's starving and has found food. As she fumbles with the lock on the car door, she wonders if she's capable of driving, even as she clambers inside. She looks back at the house, screwing up her eyes as she examines the shadows. Is Jack lying dead inside? Has Lawrence killed him? She doesn't have time to examine how she feels about the idea. She has to get away.

She starts the car. The accelerator slips from under her foot as she backs out of the driveway, her ankles feeling as if they're made of soft springs. She's never had to think about driving before, always having done it automatically. Now, it's as if she's a learner all over again. She turns and heads down the lane, hoping there are no late-night dog walkers around, not expecting her to be hurtling along at an unsafe speed.

There's only one place she can go, she thinks, as she remembers the cross words she and her sister have exchanged over the past few weeks, how frustrating her own behaviour must have been to someone who's had no idea what has really been going on. What Jack has been planning behind all their backs. How he's tricked them. Rosie will believe her now, when Bella tells her everything that's happened since yesterday. She has to. And once Bella is in the safety of Rosie's house, she'll call the police, send them to her own house in the hope that they can at least save Lawrence. Not that he completely deserves it.

She drives quickly, the roads quiet apart from a few drunken revellers trying to cross in front of her when she heads through town. As she pulls up in front of her sister's small, terraced house, she sees there's a light on in the living room window. Perhaps Rosie is up with the twins. Or even struggling to settle herself as she worries about the fact that she's not spoken to Bella for a few days, feeling guilty. They'll get over their rift, Bella tells herself. Everything will be okay between them once the shock of tonight's events has worn off. Now that the truth is out.

She wishes she had her phone so she could warn her sister she's here. She doesn't want to risk waking the children, causing even more upset than she's going to already. Instead, she taps her knuckles on the window, saying Rosie's name in a harsh whisper. Her throat is so sore.

It seems like an age before the front door opens.

'Bella ... What the hell? What are you doing?'

Rosie's face is pale, the blood seeming to have drained from it. She is fully dressed, despite Bella expecting her to be in her usual Saturday night attire of pyjamas and dressing gown.

'Can I come in?'

'Of course, but ...'

Bella barges into the hallway, her legs almost giving way before she reaches the bottom of the stairs. She sinks down onto the first step, gasping for breath. She feels as if she's run a marathon. 'I didn't know where else to go.'

Rosie looks completely confused. 'What's happened? Where's Jack?'

Bella takes a breath. 'He's at the house. In the basement. With Lawrence Knox.'

'What?'

'It was all him, Rosie.'

'What do you mean?' Rosie stands in front of her, arms folded. 'What are you saying?'

'It was *Jack* all along. Behind everything that's happened over the past few weeks. He drugged me yesterday morning and strapped me to a chair in the basement.'

'You're not making any sense, Bella. Are you ill? Still affected by the accident you had?' Rosie shakes her head. 'If Jack strapped you to a chair in the basement, how are you here?'

'Because I *escaped*. With the help of Lawrence Knox.'

'Now, you're really not making sense …'

Bella tries to swallow her frustration. She won't be able to explain everything to Rosie so quickly. It will have to wait. 'Look, Rosie, I need to call the police. Can I use your phone?'

A sudden cry resonates down the stairs: Katie or Cameron awake and wailing for their mother.

'The police?' Rosie looks flustered. 'Are you sure? Maybe you should wait 'til morning? You might see things differently in the cold light of …'

'He kidnapped me, Rosie! I've been trapped in the basement since yesterday. Just like last time!'

The twins are both crying loudly now, one of them obviously having woken the other.

Rosie moves towards the stairs. 'Look, I'll have to go up and see to them. You take a breather, make yourself a drink. Then I'll find my phone. Lord knows why Martin thought it was a good idea to get rid of the landline when Cameron enjoys hiding the mobiles so much.' She slides past Bella and jogs up. 'If you still want to call the police when the twins are settled, that's fine, but I warn you, they won't listen if you're not talking coherently. You might be better off waiting 'til tomorrow.'

Bella sits on the bottom step, trying to get her breath as she stares at a portrait of her nephew and niece on the far wall. Is she not making sense? She knows she has an infection, is no doubt not far from complete collapse, but what she's saying is the truth. Her husband drugged her and held her against her will. He's been gaslighting her for weeks, making her think she was imagining what was going on. Creating a rift between her and the children she adores. Inviting the man who stalked her to her house. Encouraging him to go against the conditions of his release.

Planning to kill her.

She needs to get her sister to listen. She needs to talk to the police.

She jumps as she hears a sudden sound, a phone ringing close by. All her nerves are on edge, as if she has electricity running through her. Looking at her feet, she sees she's brought her bag in with her. She doesn't even remember picking it up when she left the car.

Reaching inside it, Bella pulls out her phone, surprised that it's there. That Jack put it back where she usually keeps it after using it to pretend she was sending texts to him, leaving him voicemail messages. She stares at the screen as it vibrates in her hand, the ringtone muffled by the twins' frantic cries. She doesn't recognise the number.

'Hello?'

'Oh … Mrs Anderson?'

'Speaking …' If this is someone trying to sell her car insurance or a funeral package, she thinks she will throw the phone across the hallway.

'This is Lizzie, from Bloomin' Wonderful florist? We spoke a few weeks ago? Huge apologies, I know it's really late, and Saturday to boot. I wasn't expecting you to answer, to be honest. Thought I'd be leaving a voicemail. I've been meaning to call you all day, but we were so busy at the shop, and then I got caught up with the usual domestic drudgery when I got home.'

'Okay …' Bella feels fear build in her chest. She could be responsible for her own husband's death. Now that she knows where her phone is, she really needs to speak to the police, no matter what her sister says. Not to *a florist*. 'Look, Lizzie, this really isn't a good ...'

'I know, of course, but if I could just tell you something quickly? It won't take a second, I promise.'

Bella sighs. She glances behind her up the stairs, hears Rosie singing quietly to her children. 'Okay, sure, long as it's ...'

'It's just that I suddenly remembered something. About the person who ordered that bouquet for you. Might not be of any help, but ...'

'Oh?' She sits up straighter, more alert now.

'Yes, it came to me when I was on the phone to another customer yesterday. She had to cut the call short because one of her children wasn't well.'

Bella frowns. If what this woman is telling her, now of all times, isn't going to be useful, then she really does need to get off the phone. After all, she knows now that it was Jack who was behind everything that's gone on, no doubt including the flowers. What more information does she need? 'Sorry, but what does that have to do with ...?'

'Well, the woman who ordered your bouquet, I remembered that she also had children. They were making a lot of noise in the background, and she kept having to tell them to be quiet while she was on the phone. I commented that she sounded like she had a lot on her plate, and she said it was all part of life with twins. Does that help at all?'

Bella's blood runs cold, her whole body suddenly seeming to be paralysed. Upstairs, Katie and Cameron are still crying, the sound reaching her ears like the rattle of a machine gun.

'Mrs Anderson? Are you still ...?'

'Thank you, Lizzie.' Bella ends the call. She wonders if she'll ever move again. Or if she'll stay here, at the bottom of her sister's staircase, forever.

Adrenaline suddenly floods her system. She stands up, grabbing her bag and dropping her phone inside it, movement seeming crucial, the only way to keep herself alive. As she turns, her heart thuds as she realises her sister is standing on the stairs behind her.

'Going somewhere, Bella?'

Bella gasps. 'It was you.'

'I'm surprised it's taken you so long to work it out.' Rosie's smirk doesn't suit her; it makes her normally pretty face look old and haggard.

'*You* and *Jack* ...'

'That house should have been mine, Bella; you know it should. Mum and Dad were very wrong to think they could fob me off with a bit of money. You were always the favourite. Mum's golden child, ever since you showed so much more prowess with the violin than I did. I was just a hanger-on.'

'But ... How could you?'

'How could I not? We're in love, Bella. Jack and I ...'

'In *love*?' Bella wonders how many more shocks she can take without breaking down completely. Jack and *her sister*? All those things Rosie had said to her when Bella frantically accused her of being involved in what's been happening. All the upset she thought she'd caused ... 'So it *was* you who arranged to put the house on the market? Used my phone to email Luke Rushfield when I was in the loo. After everything you said about me accusing you.'

'Well, I couldn't actually admit it, could I? There's been a few times when I thought you were onto us, to be honest. Especially when I sent Rushfield to you and the *For Sale* sign went up. I thought you'd know then that it was all about the house, that you'd cotton on you didn't deserve to have it. But no. Jack has always said you weren't clever enough to suspect anything. That you trusted him completely.'

'So ...' Bella can barely find the words. 'It was Jack who made me think I was seeing Lawrence, that he was following me, but the rest was *you*? The flowers, the email? The Facebook friend request? Were you behind that too?'

Rosie nods. 'Yep, all correct, Detective Bella. It wasn't exactly difficult to delete the account before I spoke to you and then make you think you'd been seeing things. Lucky for me you happened to log in to the app when you were feeling flustered, when you didn't have your reading glasses with you. Your WhatsApp message, telling me something had happened, something I'd *never believe*, left me in no doubt that you'd seen it.'

'But … How *could* you? How could you do this to me? To Martin?'

Rosie scoffs. 'I've never loved Martin. Do you really think I could have ever been happy with someone so boring? Someone who's never here, away all the time? Surely you know me better than that, Bella? Jack has always been the one for me. Right from the moment I met him.'

Bella thinks back to when she first brought Jack home. How Rosie used to want to spend time with them, always hanging around, giggling at Jack's silly jokes. She thinks about the amount of time Jack himself spends away from home: conferences, training courses. Surely not? 'How long …? How long has it been going on?'

'Long enough. He's in love with me, you know. Much more so than he ever was with you. And I want the life you've got, Bella. I *deserve* it after being on the sidelines for too long. And, before you say anything, don't worry about Mum and Dad, or Freddy and Paige. We know we'll have to be discreet for a little while. We've waited this long. A few more months won't make much difference.'

This long? Bella could hardly think straight, images of everything that's happened over the past thirty-something hours flitting through her mind as if on a reel: Jack attacking her in the kitchen, drugging her, drugging Lawrence … She looks at her sister, still standing above her on the stairs. 'You gave him the drugs. To knock us out. They're from the vets' surgery.'

'Of course I did. Where else would he get a tranquiliser strong enough to do the job? I've put enough animals to sleep in my time to be able to tell him exactly how to use it, what dose to use, to just incapacitate you enough without the drug showing up in your system later if we needed to cover our tracks.'

Bella feels a tear run down her cheek. 'But, Rosie, *why*? Why would you do this?'

'Because I love him.'

'But think of the twins …' As she says the words, a thought occurs to Bella. She turns, looking again at the photograph of Katie and Cameron that hangs just inside the hallway: their smooth olive skin, nut-brown eyes, flecked with green. She remembers her own daughter at the same age, pictures Paige holding Katie on her hip when they were in town a few weeks ago, the two cousins laughing together. Except they're not merely cousins, are they? 'Oh God …' She covers her mouth with her hand as she looks back at her sister.

'Ah, I see you've worked something else out. Come on, Bella. I tried for years to have kids with Martin. Did you think he suddenly became fertile overnight?'

'They're Jack's.'

'Of course they're Jack's. We deserve to be together, Bella. Me, Jack, the twins, Freddy and Paige. One big happy family.'

Bella isn't sure what to do, where to go. Should she run? Grab her bag and get herself outside as quickly as possible? Call the police? She's told Rosie she escaped the basement with Lawrence's help, but what she hasn't told her is that Jack could be dead. How will her sister react when she hears the news? Will she try to kill Bella herself? Feel that she has nothing left to lose?

She jumps as she hears a sound outside, the slam of a car door, perhaps the jolly farewell of a taxi driver as he drops someone off, the words not reciprocated. Bella looks at the front door, realising she doesn't remember her sister locking it after they came inside, Rosie not wearing her sleep attire as she would normally be at the weekend, perhaps waiting for someone.

Waiting for the person who has promised to kill her sister.

Bella tries to swallow as she realises something else, something terrifying.

Jack isn't dead. And he knows she's here.

She looks at Rosie. 'You told him.'

Her sister cocks her head to one side. 'You mustn't have heard me, on the phone upstairs. Understandable, with the kids crying ...'

Bella screams as the front door bursts open, Jack's eyes as wild as an animal's as he launches himself into the hallway and towards her. She grabs her bag, her muscles still wobbly as she tries to run to the back of the house, heading for the kitchen, the back door. An escape route. She falls, her whole body slamming against the floor, her breath knocked out of her, as Jack grabs one of her legs.

'No ...' Bella tries to crawl away, part of her aware that her sister has disappeared, perhaps gone upstairs to make sure her children are settled, that they're in no danger of witnessing the sudden violence going on in their home.

She looks back at her husband, barely taking in the angry red gash across his throat, the bruises that decorate his face. She doesn't have time to worry about what's happened to Lawrence. Who came out of the struggle in the basement worse off. She kicks out with her foot, trying to free herself from Jack's grip. She won't give in now. She won't. Not after all she's been through.

Jack clings on, gripping both of her legs now, his hands like vices, bruising her skin as he climbs his way up her body, like a mountaineer desperate to reach the peak. As he pins her down, his teeth are gritted tightly. He spits words at her, the sound like the sharp cracks of a shotgun.

'You are *not* going to get away from me, Bella. Not. This. Time. You are *not* going to stop me from getting the life I deserve.'

Bella can feel her strength dissolving, as if it's leaking from every pore of her body. In another minute or two, her chances of escape will be down to zero. Jack will kill her. Probably strangle her once his hands reach as far as her neck. Somehow, he'll explain what has happened to the police. Make up some story they'll no doubt believe. Somehow still blame Lawrence, even though it now seems impossible. She pictures her children, enjoying themselves, oblivious to what's going on at home. To the true, evil nature of the man who is supposed to love them, protect them. Their father. The man who will bring them up in her absence.

Bella's bag is on the floor in front of her face, having dropped from her hand when she fell. With her last ounce of strength, she reaches into it, barely able to breathe now beneath Jack's weight. Scrabbling frantically, she pulls something out. Something that glints in the light of the hallway. Something that she kicked with her foot on the basement floor as she escaped, as Lawrence Knox fought with her husband. Picked up without thinking and dropped into her bag as she fled through the back door. Just in case.

Reaching behind her, she stabs the knife into Jack's face. The serrated blade slashes at the skin that is already scarred, the tip finding the soft flesh of her husband's right eye on the second jab, sinking in.

Jack screams.

Bella stumbles to her feet, not looking back as she grabs her bag again and runs through the house, praying her legs won't let her down. Not now. Not when she's almost there. Her hands shaking, she twists the key Rosie always leaves in the back door, slanted rain wetting her face as she opens it and runs through the garden, out of the gate and down the narrow passage that leads to the front of the house. Reaching the car, she thinks she hears her sister scream, her heart tearing in two at the sound. She can't go back. She just can't.

Climbing inside, she fumbles with her keys and starts the engine, having no idea where she can go, who will help her. Even where the nearest police station is.

As Bella pulls the car away from the kerb, she suddenly remembers a person who was once kind to her. Who offered to help her if she ever needed it. With one hand, she roots in the bag she's thrown on the passenger seat, hoping the flimsy restaurant menu is still where she left it that night that now seems so long ago. Finding it, she pulls it out.

Lightning splits the sky above her as she quickly types Jazz's number into her phone.

Eighteen months later

Bella enters the coffee shop, trying not to look around at the other customers. It's a difficult habit to break, looking over her shoulder, attempting to perceive any threats of danger, but she's trying. The kids think it's time she took the whistle from around her neck, but she's not sure she's ready for that yet. She still wears it every day, in the same way she might wear a treasured necklace.

Jazz is sitting in a far corner, looking as glamorous as always in a black polo neck and stylish accessories, her hair recently coloured a trendy silver-grey. She stands up and waves.

Bella heads over. 'Hi.' Leaning across the table, she kisses her friend's cheek before sitting in the opposite chair. 'The last time I came here was to meet Rosie, the week Lawrence was released. How is it a year and a half already?'

'Oh ...' Jazz's cheeks colour. 'We can go somewhere else, if you'd like? I'd never have suggested it if I'd known it held bad memories.'

'It's fine, honestly. My therapist says I need to start revisiting the places I used to go to with both Jack and Rosie. Instead of being tempted to hide away.' Bella shakes her head, pushing away the sudden memory of the night she'd stood at the top of the stairs, listening to Jack talking to her sister on the phone. *We just need to keep on at her* ... *It won't be easy, but we have to keep trying* … Not concern for her at all, as she'd thought, but the two of them plotting *against* her. In many ways, Rosie's betrayal has been the most difficult thing to deal with.

'Have you seen her at all? Spoken to her?'

'Only once, very briefly …' Bella swallows down the feelings of sadness and anger that still threaten to overwhelm her at times. She's trying to focus on the positives: Freddy and Paige, her new role at work since she's been promoted. Helping Martin out with the twins. 'She called me after Jack was sentenced, tried to apologise, but I hung up on her. I just couldn't do it. Martin says she's desperate to make amends, but I'm honestly not sure I can ever imagine a time when either of us are ready to forgive her.'

'Must be very difficult for Martin on his own, especially since he found out …'

'He's a superstar. The best dad Katie and Cameron could wish for, and since his name is on the birth certificates, and neither Rosie nor Jack now want to explore the possibility of anyone else making a claim to be their father, let's hope it stays that way.'

'That certainly seems best for the children.'

Bella nods. 'Part of me can't help feeling sorry for my sister though. I know I shouldn't, after everything, but she adores those kids; no one can deny that. And, since the divorce, she only gets to see them every other weekend, with Martin supervising.'

Jazz raises an eyebrow. 'She isn't a victim, Bella. She made choices. She knew exactly what she was doing and what the consequences would be if she got caught. You could have died. You were *supposed* to.'

'I know.' Bella shivers.

'Not to mention how lucky she was that Jack refused to point the finger at her when he was arrested. Denied that she was involved. And that you didn't press charges.'

'I couldn't. She's my sister. In a way she was as much manipulated by Jack as I was. Plus, I had to think about my parents, Freddy and Paige, the twins. We'd all been through enough.

Anyway—' she waves a hand '—we've been over this so many times. Let's not go there again.'

Jazz smiles. 'I'll get our drinks. Latte?'

'Please.'

Bella watches Jazz approach the counter, thinking about the day when she was here with her sister, the two of them sitting just a couple of tables away from where she is now. Lawrence had only just been released from prison and Rosie had expressed concern at how Bella was coping with the news. If only she'd known then what she knows now. Things might have turned out very differently. The kids might never have had to know what their father was planning. Might never have learnt how he'd lost the sight one eye because their mother had stabbed him, trying to escape, in fear for her life. It's going to take them a long time to come to terms with it. If they ever do.

She supposes she should be grateful Jack had the decency to plead guilty to all the charges, saving them all the horror of having to go through a trial.

She smiles as Jazz puts her coffee in front of her. 'Thanks. Shame Lana couldn't make it today. How's she doing?'

Jazz grimaces. 'Morning sickness is the pits. If I've held her hair back once, I've done it a thousand times over the past couple of months.'

'Don't fancy carrying the next one yourself then?'

'No, thanks.' Jazz laughs. 'Maybe I'll change my mind later, but I doubt it. Especially after we've been through the trauma of the birth.'

Bella points a finger. 'Don't think I haven't noticed how happy you are lately. You're going to make great parents. Lana's lucky to have you at her side.'

'She might not say that when I'm grumbling about night feeds and nappies.'

Bella sips her coffee, looking at Jazz over the rim of her cup. She's so glad they've become friends. Jack's former PA always

261

seems to be at the end of the phone when she's feeling down, when she needs to rant or sob, Freddy and Paige always out of earshot so she doesn't add to their trauma. 'I'm lucky to have you too. If you hadn't been there that night, I don't know where I'd have gone.'

'You'd have gone to the police.'

'I wasn't thinking straight. I just needed to see a friendly face. Someone I could trust before I could get myself together enough to tell the police what had happened. And I somehow just knew I could trust you. If I hadn't had your number in my bag, I might have driven myself straight into the nearest tree.'

'I was glad to be there. I just wish ...'

'What?' Bella raises an eyebrow, even though she knows what Jazz is going to say. They've had this conversation before.

'I know I've said it already, but I just wish I'd done something before it got to that stage. I knew something wasn't right. Just knew it. I even said it to Lana before I met Jack for coffee that Saturday morning. Something seemed really *off*. I asked him so many questions about you, about your marriage, I think he thought I fancied him.' She chuckles before looking serious again. 'What I should have done was insist that Jack take me to see you, to prove to me that you were okay. Or even just gone to the police myself.'

'It probably wouldn't have made any difference. Jack fooled all of us. He was a very good liar. Had everyone convinced, including me until he strapped me to that chair. I doubt the police would have listened at that stage.'

'Maybe ...'

'I didn't even know he was with you. I presumed he was in the house all along, upstairs, listening to me suffer. It never occurred to me that when he wasn't with me, he was out and about setting up his alibi.' Bella puts her cup down. 'You know, I've never asked you. What was it that made you suspect something wasn't right in the first place? That made you find an excuse to meet him that day in the hope you might find out what was going on?'

Jazz hesitates for a few seconds before speaking. 'I actually believed him at first, when he told me you'd sent him that voicemail asking for some time alone. It seemed to make sense, after everything you'd both been through, and I thought he was doing the right thing, respecting your wishes.'

'What made you change your mind?'

'Well, quite quickly after that conversation, I began to think about what had happened when I saw you at the restaurant and, the more it played on my mind, the more something didn't seem quite right. I hadn't really thought about it at the time, but I remembered you saying he'd asked to meet you at eight, but I was sure Jack himself had organised the meeting he was in. I checked his diary, but it didn't really tell me anything so, in the end, after I'd booked him into the hotel, I checked his phone, on that Friday when he went out for lunch. I know I shouldn't have, not very professional of me.'

'Except he wasn't at lunch, he was at the house. Visiting me in the basement. So, he left his phone behind? You knew his passcode?'

'Well, that's the thing. After Jack and I had had the conversation about you needing space and he'd played me the voicemail you'd sent, he went into his office to get his jacket and, a minute or two later, I followed him in without knocking. I'd forgotten to tell him about an appointment that had been cancelled, and, when I walked in, I happened to notice he had another phone, a different one from the one he'd played the message on. He was fiddling with it and, when he realised I was there, he quickly slipped it into his desk, probably hoping I hadn't noticed, but I remembered the pass pattern he'd used.' She sighs. 'So, when he went out, claiming to be going for lunch, I looked for the phone in his desk and when I opened it, I checked back through his call history and saw that he'd called the restaurant himself, that evening he was supposed to be meeting you. I recognised the number from my own booking. I saw the name Rosie on there too, numerous times, but obviously I didn't know who she was then, and I didn't have the time, or the courage, to look for anything else. But you'd told me that it was you who booked the table yourself so, that was when alarm bells started ringing.'

'Oh, yes, the *burner* phone. I thought people only used them in movies. He must have called the restaurant after I'd booked and said our plans had changed. Given them different guests' names.' So obvious now she knows the truth. 'I wish I'd noticed that he had another phone. Then I might have known a lot sooner what was going on.'

'You trusted him. You saw no need to think …'

'He tried to convince me later that I'd simply given the wrong names when I booked the table. Because Lawrence was on my mind.'

'He told me that was likely what had happened too. Said you'd probably had a drink or three before you even rang the restaurant.'

Bella shakes her head. 'He had me so muddled, I even called *him* Lawrence by mistake, which completely proved his point. He must have been delighted.'

'I guess that was the plan. Make it look as if you were losing your marbles, obsessing over Lawrence, pushing Jack away, creating a rift between you, then he had a legitimate excuse to leave you on your own when you supposedly asked him for some space. Otherwise, everyone would have wondered why he was so keen to be away from home, if you'd appeared to be in actual danger, which, according to him, you weren't.'

'I must have been a mug not to see what was happening. My husband and my sister. How could I not have known? Not to mention what they're now saying he might have done to his own mother. That neighbour of hers coming forward with his suspicions. How could I have missed that? Lived with him all those years after …?'

Jazz reaches a hand across the table, gently resting it on Bella's. 'Don't be so hard on yourself. I don't think any of us would have guessed, if we'd been in the same position. Not about your sister, *or* his mum. You've been so brave, Bella. What you went through before was bad enough. Let alone …'

'Going through it twice?' Bella scoffs. 'It sounds ridiculous, doesn't it? Poor Lawrence. I guess even he didn't know how much his life was going to change when he made the decision to kidnap me that night. If he'd known what it would lead to, maybe he wouldn't have done it. Can you imagine how different my life might be now?'

Jazz glances over Bella's shoulder. 'Speak of the devil. Here's the third member of our regular coffee trio.'

Bella turns, remembering how much she used to dread this exact moment. Sitting in a coffee shop and seeing Lawrence Knox walking through the door. She fingers the whistle at her neck briefly before letting it rest. How things have changed. 'Hi, Lawrence.'

'Morning, ladies. Anyone want another coffee while I grab my own?'

Bella shakes her head. 'We're good, thanks.'

She watches as he heads for the queue, his gait even more lopsided and clumsy now than it was when he came to the base-ment. Jack had beaten him so badly he's practically had to learn to walk again. Bella remembers the first time she plucked up the courage to go and visit him in the hospital, Lawrence having been there for a month or two before he was even well enough for visitors. The man who had changed her life so many years ago was like a different person: repentant, humble. So much more mature than he'd been before. It had taken a lot of red tape, a lot of emails and phone calls from Bella about restorative justice, to drop the conditions of the restraining order. Change the terms of his release so they could meet up every so often, with the help of a mediator at first.

She looks at Jazz. 'Who'd have thought I'd ever be having coffee with Lawrence Knox and feeling okay about it?'

'You're more forgiving than I might have been; that's for sure.'

Bella shrugs. 'It's not been easy, believe me. There have been times when I've thought I must be as mad as Jack tried to say I was. But it's better than the alternative: looking over my shoulder for the rest of my life. Not for one person, but for two.'

Jazz nods. 'Let's hope you never have to look for Jack. He deserves to be in prison for a very long time.'

Bella picks up her drink. She hopes Jazz is right. She can't bear the thought of what might happen if Jack is released from prison early. If he somehow manages to convince the authorities he's a changed man. Comes looking for her and his children, wanting to pick up where he left off.

She takes a gulp of milky coffee.

She's not sure she has the strength to go through it a third time.

A Letter from Jacqueline

Thank you so much for choosing to read *The Weekend Alone*. I hope you enjoyed it! If you did and you would like to hear more about my books and new releases, you can follow me on Facebook, Twitter, Instagram and through my website below.

The Weekend Alone is my first psychological thriller. It began life as an experiment, a way of getting back into the joy of writing after experiencing a bit of a wane in my enthusiasm (as all writers do now and then!). Little did I know then how much I would enjoy writing it and that the book would eventually find a home with a publishing house that I'd always thought of as my dream publisher!

If you have time to leave a short review on Amazon, Goodreads or your social media channels, I would be ever grateful. Reviews are crucial to authors in spreading the word, as well as making our future books stronger! Also, if you enjoyed the book, I would really appreciate it if you could recommend it to your friends and family. The more readers the better!

Thanks,

Jacqueline xxx

Facebook: www.facebook.com/jacquelinegrimawriter
Twitter: https://twitter.com/GrimaJgrima
Instagram: https://www.instagram.com/jacquelinegrimawriter
Website: https://jacquelinegrima.co.uk/

Acknowledgements

Firstly, I would like to thank Lisa Milton and the whole team at HQ Digital for taking a chance on the book that, when I first began to write it, seemed like it would only ever be 'a bit of fun to get my writing mojo back'. When I started working on *The Weekend Alone*, I was almost ready to take a long break from my writing and submitting journey, so I'm extra delighted the book eventually found its perfect home with HQ. Thank you all for welcoming me so warmly to the team.

Particular thanks must go to my editor, Abigail Fenton. Abi has been a complete joy to work with, making the dreaded editing process so much more bearable and insisting I 'don't panic' on more than one occasion. Without Abi and her never-ending enthusiasm, *The Weekend Alone* wouldn't be the book it is today. Her ideas and input throughout every step of our journey have been invaluable. Thanks, Abi. I look forward to working with you on the next book!

Thanks also to all the friends, on Facebook, Twitter, Instagram, WhatsApp and in real life, who have supported me while I write, as well as to all my writing 'buddies'. In 2015, I began to study for an MA in Creative Writing at Manchester Metropolitan University (Manchester Writing School) and the staff, tutors and fellow students I met along the way changed my writing journey forever.

Without them – especially Georgia, Lucie and Rianne – I'm sure I would have given up. Extra special thanks also go to my writing friend and avid beta-reader, Catherine 'Kitty' Murphy. Without our almost daily chats, I know for definite I would have stopped writing a long time ago. I'm so glad we got to experience this often stressful and sometimes surreal experience together.

Thanks, as always, to my boys, Dan, Mike and Andrew, for their support and (sometimes) their patience. To Krista for all the salads and noodles, as well as keeping me company during the endless edits. And to my dad, for cutting the grass.

And, last but, by no means, least, thanks to you, the reader, for choosing my book. I'm very grateful for your support. Without you, there would be no writers and no stories.

Dear Reader,

We hope you enjoyed reading this book. If you did, we'd be so appreciative if you left a review. It really helps us and the author to bring more books like this to you.

Here at HQ Digital we are dedicated to publishing fiction that will keep you turning the pages into the early hours. Don't want to miss a thing? To find out more about our books, promotions, discover exclusive content and enter competitions you can keep in touch in the following ways:

JOIN OUR COMMUNITY:

Sign up to our new email newsletter:
http://smarturl.it/SignUpHQ

Read our new blog www.hqstories.co.uk

 https://twitter.com/HQStories

www.facebook.com/HQStories

BUDDING WRITER?

We're also looking for authors to join the HQ Digital family!
Find out more here:

https://www.hqstories.co.uk/want-to-write-for-us/

Thanks for reading, from the HQ Digital team